In 2219 CE, many years after the Great Catastrophe, the Central Government of Luoyang has divided the city into zones where inhabitants, both human and chimeric, are placed by usefulness. The citizens of the city are overseen by No. 1, a giant chimeric brain created by the scientists in Bright Order to monitor all activity within the city while distracting the residents with virtual spectacles. But No. 1 has begun to behave erratically. Meanwhile, the Spirit Supreme Assembly in Interstitium, a religious order with a dangerous new leader, continues to grow in power, sanctioned by the Central Government. The city's only hope lies with Yinhe, a half-human half-fox spirit who has lived many lives and hides truths in tales shared with listeners in Bent Back. Summoned to Dream Zone, where chimeric inhabitants of the city have been exiled to perform hard labour, Yinhe is given information that may create great change in the city and stave off an ancient enemy.

Weaving a silken web of Chinese myth, speculative fiction and storytelling, Lydia Kwa has brilliantly realized a future where questions of sentience, of personhood and of the truth of dreams wrap around a timeless quest for freedom and for love.

A DREAM WANTS WAKING

A
DREAM
WANTS
WAKING

a novel

LYDIA KWA

A Buckrider Book

Published by Buckrider Books
an imprint of Wolsak and Wynn Publishers
280 James Street North
Hamilton, ON L8R2L3
www.wolsakandwynn.ca

Editor for Buckrider Books: Paul Vermeersch | Editor: Aeman Ansari
| Copy editor: Ashley Hisson
Cover and interior design: Michel Vrana
Cover images: iStockphoto
Author photograph: Joshua Paul
Typeset in Garamond Premier Pro
Printed by Rapido Books, Montreal, Canada

Printed on certified 100% post-consumer Rolland Enviro Paper.

10 9 8 7 6 5 4 3 2 1

The publisher gratefully acknowledges the support of the Canada Council for the Arts and the Ontario Arts Council. We also acknowledge the financial support of the Government of Canada through the Canada Book Fund and the Government of Ontario through the Ontario Book Publishing Tax Credit and Ontario Creates.

Library and Archives Canada Cataloguing in Publication
Title: A dream wants waking : a novel / Lydia Kwa.
Names: Kwa, Lydia, 1959- author.
Identifiers: Canadiana 20230496466 | ISBN 9781989496756 (softcover)
Subjects: LCGFT: Novels.
Classification: LCC PS8571.W3 D74 2023 | DDC C813/.54—dc23

For our non-human kin

THE MAIN CHARACTERS

Luoyang, 2219 CE

YINHE/UNKNOWN WAYFARER
half-human, half-fox spirit

END DECODER
de facto leader of Dream Zone

SEKA
assistant to End Decoder

GUI
demon

PHOEBE
Yinhe's earth mother

STANLEY OUYANG
Yinhe's earth father

NO.1
chimeric brain at Central Government headquarters

WEN FANG
scientist at Central Government headquarters

THE MAIN CHARACTERS
(continued)

Tang China, 644–904 CE

BAOSHI
disciple of Harelip

ARDHANARI
sculptor

XUANZANG
monk, translator of sutras

LING
abbess of Da Fa Temple

PROLOGUE

At twilight, the wind livens up. It scatters detritus through the streets, rattles windowpanes and sneaks through gaps to get inside houses. I walk down these familiar alleys in Bent Back, an anomaly even among outsiders.

The wind knows my secret – that I am a fox spirit still searching for the one I lost many lifetimes ago. The wind teases and cajoles. *There will be a storm later, but there's still time.*

The regulars of Storytelling Night, dressed in their costumes, are waiting for me. When I arrive in their presence, I will light a candle and spin a fable spanning across time and space. I do this in defiance of the age of erasures.

Ahead, flickers of light pierce the darkening sky. The rusty shop sign whinges as I draw close. I can smell the heat of excitement.

Unknown Wayfarer

BOOK ONE

幽室

(youshi)

Hidden Room

Start of Spring
First Lunar Month
904 CE
THE ROAD BETWEEN CHANG'AN AND LUOYANG

Two diminutive figures crouch behind a row of sumac bushes midway on the south slope. Under the crescent moon, they're enveloped in darkness. Below them, the wide path is animated by shadowy movements. The onlookers have been keeping vigil for hours, watching tens of thousands of humans pass by. Boots crunch against rocky ground.

Snowfall, light but consistent, covers the humans with a mantle of white, yet it doesn't settle on the two observers, passing through them instead.

To the west lies Chang'an smouldering in flames, a red cipher burning through the night. The metallic scent of grief permeates the exiles' bodies.

The fox spirits tilt their heads at almost the same time and their noses move in concert, sniffing the air. Ears perked, they tune into the disparate sounds coming from the ancient road. Some footsteps are heavy, anger irresolutely stomping against uneven terrain; others' gaits are faltering. Then there are those whose walking betrays an absence, as if their souls have already abandoned them.

There seems to be no end to this procession of absolute misery. Small children, the elderly and the infirm are borne on the backs of men and women. There's the occasional sighting of a dog or cat riding on carts. Someone stumbles while another simply sits or lies on the ground, helpless.

The fox spirits finally break their silence.

"Mama, what will become of these humans?"

"All it takes is the folly of one power-crazed human to wreak havoc and cause devastation for countless others."

"Who has done this?"

"Zhu Wen, a warlord hell-bent on seizing power."

The younger fox spirit stares down at the exiles and sighs. "Can't we do something to help them?"

The older fox gazes tenderly at her daughter, at the soft silver streak that marks the pelt down her back. She remains quiet for twelve slow breaths before answering. "I'm not sure there's anything we could do right now."

Soldiers on horseback pass by on either side of the procession, shouting, "Keep moving! You can't stop until we reach Luoyang."

A child trips and falls down on the road almost directly in front of, and below, the fox spirits' vantage point. A soldier pulls out a whip from his saddlebag and strikes the child repeatedly on the face. The child screams in anguish. Blood streaks from their wounds. The soldier's face is marked by a chilling expression of pleasure. Three more soldiers join in. Meanwhile, others rush to shield the child.

The young fox spirit launches off toward the road. Sticky filaments exude from her claws and envelop the four soldiers in an impenetrable web. She yanks them off their horses and leaves them imprisoned in the net. She moves up and down the length of the procession, trapping the remaining soldiers in the same fashion.

By the time the fox spirit settles back into place next to her mother, there's a fiery glint in her eyes. "You know I hate sitting around doing nothing."

"Indeed, dearest. Just being yourself."

Shouts of surprise and delight travel up and down the path.

"Wah liao – some kind of magic?"

"Did you see? Looked like a fox!"

"But it wasn't evil! How can – ?"

"Maybe some are okay, huh? Good spirits about!"

"Huat ah! Heaven has intervened!"

The exiles resume their march forward, except two men who pause at a large boulder on the side of the road. One of them uses a hammer and chisel to carve the rock. The sharp noise of his efforts rises above the rumble of the travellers.

The mother fox spirit's whiskers twitch excitedly. "Hmmm, curious. I wonder what that man is up to?"

The daughter fox spirit gazes in the direction of the Western capital instead. "Chang'an is no more. All that grandeur, all the liveliness of its inhabitants, the temples and monasteries, the libraries."

"Of course, sweetness, you can't help but feel sad." Her daughter cares about Chang'an while the mother fox spirit, on the other hand, is averse to cities. She can't survive for long in places with large aggregations of humans, unlike her daughter. She recalls her former life with Xie two hundred and fifty years earlier, how she managed to survive and thrive living in the countryside. She bares her fangs, uncomfortable with the memory.

"Sometimes I don't know what to do with my sadness," the daughter says.

Her mother replies, "We keep returning, even though we've achieved immortality. Nobody tells us to reincarnate; it's not inevitable. There are other fox spirits who just want to do mischief and have some fun. But to love means we must be willing to suffer."

"Yes, Mama, you're right. We return because we have a wish to complete something we couldn't do in a previous life. Love compels us to do more."

A few travellers pause to see what the carver is doing. The fox spirits notice that the mood in the procession seems to have changed. A few begin to sing. Then more join in. The music rises up against the dark and cold, competing with the wind.

"Listen, Mama, it's that ancient ode."

The reeds flourish, lush
White dew still falling
My beloved, so dear
Wanders lost along the shoreline
Upriver I search for him
The journey, long and tortuous

The reeds luxuriant, green
White dew turns to frost
My beloved, so dear
Drifts beyond the waters
Upriver I search for her
The journey, long and arduous

"Mmm, I've always loved this song. Don't you, Mama?"

The mother fox spirit nods. "Yes, I certainly do, my dear. The song reminds us of our connection to humans, especially the nurturers."

Both fox spirits warmly recall that this melody has been sung by women while they labour in the fields, on the rivers or in their homes. Through the ages, peasant women pray to the White Fox Goddess in order to conceive. The women also leave food out for birds, foxes and rodents, and sometimes tend to injured animals.

The daughter fox spirit lowers her head slightly and narrows her eyes until they're mere slits. An ache spreads through her, and she growls. "I can't forget how I failed one human in particular. I must find a way to right that wrong."

Her mother responds, "You're thinking of your last incarnation in Chang'an as Qilan, the Daoist nun, aren't you?"

"I can't shake that image out of my mind – young Ling at the auction in the town of Huazhou. The first time I saw her, I had such a strong feeling of . . . I don't know what to call it . . ."

The mother fox spirit returns to their conversation, a glint in her eyes. "To love is to suffer, but to love is also to discover. You're saying that you'd be willing to reincarnate a few lifetimes, for however long it takes, until you find her?"

"Yes, Mama, that's what I'm going to do." She falls into a familiar moroseness – is she being foolish? She exhales a stream of purple mist as she shakes her head vigorously. "I must believe that love will triumph against all odds."

"Only the purest kind of love, which possesses a beauty invisible to many."

She ponders her mother's comment. One has to learn how to discern the truth, separate the real from the illusory.

Her mother adds, "Then there's the opposite."

"What opposite?"

"The opposite of love – the demonic ..."

"You mean Gui?"

"Not only Gui – it's just one demon among many. They are outwardly beautiful or, if not, charismatic, promising to save humans from their suffering. But that kind of illusion is neither true beauty nor loving."

First Escape from the Underworld
Seventh-Century Tang Dynasty
KUIXING TEMPLE, OUTSIDE CHANG'AN

Gui waits and watches from its imprisonment in the Underworld. The demon extends tendrils of its mind stream through miniscule gaps in the straitjacket cocoon, projecting up, up, up – past thick layers of poisoned legacies, buried truths and karmic narratives – to rupture the earth's surface.

To stir up mischief, the demon projects an ethereal presence through a portal at the abandoned temple. Humans in the area and beyond have heard about a powerful spirit that can grant wishes. Some are emboldened by their need and venture to the temple.

Gui sneers at each supplicant. Such naivety – they think all temples have good energy. Although trapped in the Underworld, Gui projects its voice and illusory benevolent form through the temple's portal, not totally satisfying in the long run. *A whiff of steak, but no real meat. Lousy!*

The demon fulfills the wishes of the supplicants but always exacts a price – some subsequent illness in the family, mental derangement, the person eventually overcome by wanton, excessive lusts or the death of a beloved child. *You ask big, you pay big.*

Then it has an idea. These days, a lot of fox spirits are thriving out in the countryside with a handful of the females attached to human males of the scholar class. The demon hatches a plan – use a spell to weaken the fox spirit, bring her to the brink of death, then capitalize on the human's vulnerability to exact payment in exchange for "curing" their beloved.

After some searching, it locates two fox spirits – a mother and her daughter – living in human form. Gui notices that the daughter is a half-fox, half-human. It causes the daughter to fall into an incapacitating feverish state. The physician who arrives at their home pronounces the daughter's condition dire. Her father, Xie, is desperate enough to come to the abandoned temple to seek help. Gui convinces Xie that it could heal his daughter if he only would agree to be possessed. With great anguish, the man agrees.

Grain Rain
Middle of Third Lunar Month
750 CE
DA FA TEMPLE, CHANG'AN

Ling is alone in the study. It has been raining for several days, but she isn't sure exactly how many. There's no sign of it abating, yet this afternoon's rain seems gentler, making pattering sounds on the tiles of the temple roof. That steady rhythm soothes her as she reclines on the daybed, swaddled in blankets. She has left the door to the courtyard slightly ajar so that the refreshing smell of water against stone and the evocative scent of wet bark reaches her.

She's incredulous that she has lived such a long time. Sister Xu tells her she's probably now 104. Sister Xu is closer to 108. They're fondly known as the Ancient Duo in the temple.

So much has happened in the world of the Tang court, but she and the other Daoist nuns have been safe from those court and palace intrigues with the exception of that time when she had to exorcise those ghosts for Wu Zetian, the female emperor. She chuckles thinking about this.

The rain stops, and patches of sunlight appear, lending a sublime beauty to the plants and shrubs in the courtyard garden. The leaves of the camellia shrub glisten, while the yellow hearts of blushing pink blossoms reveal a hint of the rain. To Ling's eyes, the canopied shapes of the ancient pine attest to careful tending by generations of nuns before her. She smiles, aware that the pine will outlast her, many years into the future. Two white butterflies flit among the azalea bushes.

Ling cherishes these simple delights. She closes her eyes, breathes deeply, savouring every moment. Since Qilan left, there hasn't been a day that Ling hasn't thought of her former mentor.

Ling recalls the first lesson that her mentor demonstrated – the rapid metamorphosis from caterpillar to butterfly within a matter of seconds and then reversing it. Ling was only fourteen then, and the lesson in the garden occurred just days after Qilan brought her into the temple. Ling laughs wistfully at the memory – how she panicked when the caterpillar crawled under her mentor's sleeve; how stunned she was when the butterfly emerged on her palm when she reached in, and when the delicate creature disappeared and became the caterpillar again.

That lesson opened her eyes and mind – that beyond conventional notions of existence the uncommon could be summoned. What she had previously believed was unchangeable could be dismantled under the right conditions. Since then, she has lived fully trusting the presence of the strange and the marvellous.

I loved her with an ardent devotion. There – she has whispered it inside her heart-mind. No one else can hear it, and her secret is safe. It was not a sexual love, but it was as if her soul, once she met Qilan, longed to be with her for all eternity.

A soft knock at the door startles Ling out of her reverie. "Enter."

"Your Reverence," the young nun begins as she bows to Ling, "they've been creating numerous flower arrangements in the main hall in preparation for tomorrow's celebration."

The novice – who cannot be more than thirteen or fourteen – brings in a bouquet and skilfully arranges the flowers in a vase, which she places on the desk. The arrangement of white camellia blooms and a few sprigs of juniper is modest but arresting. Ling watches her and chortles quietly. *Who knows if I'll still be alive for the celebration?* She shifts from her semi-prone position on the daybed to sit fully upright. Her gaze drifts to the camphor cabinet on the far wall. Two objects she particularly cherishes are stored there: a scroll with the poems that Shangguan Wan'er wrote and the object that Qilan left in her care. The novice is about to leave when Ling signals to her.

"Open that cabinet. Then the drawer at the bottom . . . yes, that's right. Remove it completely. Now reach in, feel for the second drawer behind it. There's a scroll inside and next to it an object wrapped in cloth. Bring that object to me."

After the novice has departed, Ling unwraps the oracle bone and lets it rest in her palms. It remains a mystery why Qilan would leave it with her. Her mentor's last words were *Dear heart, we will meet again. Take care of the oracle bone until I return for it.*

She feels the need to hold the oracle bone – it's the most intimate and palpable tie to her mentor. Small, it nicely fits into her cupped hands, its weight surprisingly light for such a powerful presence. A light tan brown turtle plastron, its faint lines show where the bony scales had fused together. Then those mysterious squiggly lines on the dorsal surface whose meaning she learned from Qilan. *A dream wants waking, a sky needs light.*

She recalls the things that Qilan told her. This turtle plastron never behaved like all the others before and since. It couldn't be penetrated by the burin, nor would it crack when subjected to fire. All other plastrons used for divination purposes would obey the laws of nature and crack when subjected to fire just where a hole was made.

Ling gazes down at the turtle plastron and feels a familiar fondness. Qilan told her that the plastron belonged to Ao, the divine turtle who created the world. She sighs and closes her eyes. The oracle bone starts to throb in her hands. It feels like the most natural thing in the world, this intimate relationship between her and it. She's that young girl again, the one who had been stunned to encounter its magic.

She looks down at the oracle bone – the lines of the ancient Tibetan script begin to glow. This hadn't ever happened before. How wonderful – the oracle bone is still capable of surprising her.

Two days later, the morning after the grand birthday celebration, Ling dozes off on the daybed in the study and dreams of Qilan. They're at the edge of an ocean. The salty air invigorates her. She feels happy just simply standing next to her mentor. Warmth infuses her whole person from head to toe as she studies Qilan's profile, with its beloved ferocity and strength.

Qilan is talking to her while she points to a place in the far distance. It's a cloudless day, yet the sky has a pale cast to it – the colour of sand, intensifying until it transforms into a bright yellow. After what seems like a long time, the ocean surface ripples, forming a deep rent. Ling feels growing unease. Qilan's form dissolves.

Ling wakes up with a fright. She places the back of her right hand against her forehead. It's cold, damp with sweat. Her left hand feels around the side of her bed. She relaxes when she touches the familiar shape. The oracle bone is still there.

She feels a sudden change in the air, like a breeze but subtler. She looks toward the door to the garden. A shimmering form intensifies as it approaches. She cries out in recognition, "Qilan, it's you!"

"Dear Ling – I'm here, as promised."

Ling struggles to sit upright. "I'm not dreaming . . . can this be real?"

Qilan comes quickly to Ling's side. "I'm crossing between dimensions to appear to you. You've done so well taking care of the temple all these years."

"Did you know about the potions those alchemists made for Wu Zhao? I had to allow them to take up space here."

"Such mundane alchemy was apt for those times. What better choice did you have in the light of Wu Zhao's insistence? By agreeing to her demands, you protected Da Fa Temple from censure or punishment."

Ling's voice cracks with emotion. "You knew."

"I know everything."

"Everything?"

"Yes. I've been watching over you all these years."

Ling's face colours slightly. She feels awkward. Was Qilan watching her while she carried on her affair with the imperial secretary Shangguan Wan'er?

"Why haven't you shown yourself until now?"

"It would have distracted you from living your life. Now you are soon to pass from this realm." Qilan strokes Ling's cheek with such tenderness that Ling's eyes quickly fill with tears. Qilan's hand is warm against her cheek.

A tremor of joy spreads through Ling. "Finally, this moment has arrived! Why did you leave the plastron with me all these years when you could have taken it with you when you left?"

"There's a critical difference between length of time and timing. This is the right time, because you and the oracle bone are meant to travel together."

Ling smiles at this thought. "Where will you take me?"

"You'll see. There's nothing to be afraid of."

"I'm not afraid. You taught me to be brave. You took fear out of me that last day, when I had to utter the spell to release you."

Qilan smiles. "Dearest, because you loved me, you didn't hesitate. I know it caused you a great deal of anguish to do it. You released me from my physical body when I needed to go."

Tears well up in Ling's eyes. "I'll never forget."

"Come with me." Qilan places her hand tenderly on Ling's head as she uses the same spell to liberate her.

Much later, when the novice returns with a tray of food and knocks on the door, there's no answer. After knocking several

more times, she calls out in a quivering voice, "Abbess, Abbess..."
She summons the courage to open the door and enter the room.

Her eyes catch sight of the robes remaining on the floor still
emanating misty traces of Ling's presence. She gasps, covering
her mouth. Burned into a corner of the robes is an imprint that
resembles a hand, but its unusual outline is unsettling. She trembles, as the realization dawns. She knows the story. She has heard
it from the older nuns, about the renegade fox spirit who lived
at the temple. Tears fall from her eyes out of shock as well as
incredulity. She stays rooted to the spot for quite a while before
she eventually turns and runs out of the room, calling out for
help from the others.

White Dew
Eighth Lunar Month
2219 CE
BENT BACK, LUOYANG

Yinhe wakes up from her dream drenched from head to toe. She
was standing next to Ling in the dream, in her previous incarnation as Qilan. What happened to Ling?

She smells ocean on her skin. Cursed dream. Oh wait – she's
the one who's been cursed by the dream. Yinhe feels choked up,
wishes she could cry, but the tears don't come.

She gets up, grabs a hand towel off the chair and wipes the
sweat off. At the window, she pulls the curtain gently aside and
takes a deep, slow breath. She shivers and touches the back of her
right hand to her forehead: icy cold.

She scans the pavement below. No one is outside. There's a
golden sliver of crescent moon in the sky peeking through thin
clouds.

She needs to calm down. She extends her fox claws on her
left hand and digs into her right arm, creating five long ridges
of blood. She moans from the relief, feeling tension drain from
her body.

In that earlier past life, she was supposed to accompany Ling's soul through the bardo so that they could be reincarnated together – that was the plan. There had been unexpected turbulence. Some presence far more powerful than her had overshadowed and blocked her powers and tore Ling's soul away from her.

She'd next found herself on a steep slope of large rocks leading down to the edge of an ocean, the plastron at her feet. The sky was an alarming yellow, a veil that obscured the sun. She'd felt her lungs choke up with some kind of thick poison. The water was preternaturally turquoise.

It was then that a vision of Ao had appeared, shimmering past the thick yellow haze. Ao, the divine turtle who created the universe, the one with whom Yinhe has had a close connection, over many lifetimes.

In Yinhe's dream, the turtle plastron in her possession was lifted off the rock surface and travelled toward the vision until it was absorbed into Ao. When Ao faded away into the distance, Yinhe felt stabs of anger. She looked at the ocean, then at the sky – both silent and unable to console her. She screamed and hit both hands against the jagged rock surface until they bled.

The dream has followed her through various reincarnations. It used to simply be a replication of what had occurred, but in the past two months, whenever the dream plagued her, it ended with an odd image, something new – a gigantic turtle plastron being cracked in the middle and her stepping through that crevice.

The sound of Pa's gentle snoring drifts to her from down the hallway. She smiles, feeling soothed. She turns away from the window and climbs back into bed, switches on the bedside lamp and reaches for her tattered copy of Zhuangzi's works.

Words are like wind and waves; actions are a matter of gain and loss. Wind and waves are easily moved; questions of gain and loss easily lead to danger. Hence anger arises from no other cause than clever words and one-sided speeches. When animals face death, they do not

care what cries they make; their breath comes in gasps,
and a wild fierceness is born in their hearts.

She's deeply affected every time she reads this passage. Zhuangzi remains her favourite human philosopher. Many life-times later, his writing still holds her interest. She can relate to what he's describing. A wild fierceness – that's her for sure – in every living and dying she has experienced. She closes her eyes and slows down her breathing. She soon falls back asleep.

Chess Square is just up the street from home, on the Upper Levels. Those unable to use the hundreds of stone steps from the Lower and Mid-Levels resort to the functional but clunky out-door elevators.

She smiles when she sees her friend – the majestic tree of Chess Square. *Hello, Comet,* she says in her mind. The answer comes quickly, a thought whisper only she can hear. *Hello, little fox.*

Comet is the focal point of the park, rising over three hun-dred feet above ground, with three trunks that wrap around one another. A curious sight that leads some humans to consider it ugly, while the tree's strange appearance fascinates others.

Comet is a miracle and a mystery. Yinhe swears she sees faces hidden in Comet's trunk, faces of humans it has loved. No one knows exactly how old the tree is. It has even thrived since the nuclear devastation of the Great Catastrophe. Comet tells her that it arrived on Earth a very long time ago. *Even before you were around.*

When Yinhe comes to visit Comet, she either leans against its triple trunks or climbs up on its branches to survey the view. It's also so that she can glimpse flashes of history from Comet's per-spective. *Believe me, young one, I've seen lots. Many earlier catas-trophes before the one that humans called the Great Catastrophe. As if there's been only one.*

At this time of the late afternoon, only Uncle Fang and Uncle Huo are here, playing Chinese chess. In the early mornings, other

seniors congregate at Chess Square to drink tea, to read old yellowed newspapers saved from their great-grandparents' genera-
tion and to gossip, of course.

This is the life, thinks Yinhe. *Who cares if Central Government
thinks of us as either too young, too old, disabled or without skills
or training to be useful to them? Well, at least CG gives residents
subsidies and food coupons.*

She looks down at the view below Chess Square. Old concrete condominium buildings streaked by dirt or moss are showing their age. In between them are clusters of low-rises with
tiled roofs. Right in the middle of a block of these low-rises is
her favourite tea shop, where she gets the best pu'er pressed tea
cakes. Her eyes flit to the two open areas used as markets where
vendors set up in the mornings, then disappear for the rest of the
day. Then there are playgrounds for kids, like colourful shapes
peppering the urban landscape. Yinhe feels a pang of affection
for Bent Back. She turns back to face the uncles.

Uncle Fang's shortwave radio rests on the concrete ledge to
his right – as usual, there's broadcasting from the local underground station updating residents about Central Government.
His walking cane is hooked around his left thigh, at the ready.

Yinhe has known these guys since she was a child. She
isn't related to them by blood, but everyone a certain age gets
addressed with the honorific "Uncle" or "Auntie" as long as they
let it be known what their preferences are.

These uncles don't tell Yinhe much about their past, but she
knows from her father that both used to work in Bright Order as
tech guys before they were retired. That's how they met each other.
She wonders if they still have the neural implants, or if those were
removed when they stopped working. But nobody asks uncles
and aunties such personal questions. Yinhe blinks as the image
of a neural implant flashes across her mind. She'd seen an earlier
prototype on RebelNet, despite attempts by Central Government
to suppress such images. These days, the implant consists of high-
density microelectrode arrays made of biocompatible polymers.
Each 0.5 millimetre implant is inserted into the neocortex so that

the worker's neural activations and cognitive functions could be tracked and modified through a computer interface. Yinhe shudders and shakes her head, as if to clear her mind. She turns her attention to the two uncles playing chess.

Yinhe thinks of Uncle Fang as tall grass – he sways while sitting or standing, as if his body is a receiver of wavelengths. Uncle Fang has thinning and unkempt white hair that cascades down the sides of his head and, when blown about by a strong wind, resembles a skein of frayed threads. He sports a scraggly goatee that moves as he talks loudly – which is often – while the skin on his face is profusely colonized by liver spots. One would never guess by simply looking at Uncle Fang's serious demeanour that he's mischievous and has a lively sense of humour. His long-time chess buddy, Uncle Huo, in contrast, is much shorter and has the belly of one who indulges freely in fatty pork and barbequed meats. Uncle Huo is bald and has thick salt-and-pepper eyebrows. He licks his sensuous lips often, as if he were imagining the next meal. *Maybe that's why his cheeks look perpetually rosy,* thinks Yinhe.

She puts down her backpack and duffel bag and climbs up Comet, careful to avoid the occasional bird nest. Up and up until she reaches the second tier of large branches, about twenty metres up. Yinhe looks out, observing the sun halfway toward setting.

Comet has told her that it's descended from a variable star, a supernova that exploded and descended to earth at this very spot. *That's probably why I can relate to you,* thinks Yinhe. A twenty-one-year-old friendship between two unusual beings is no small accomplishment. She presses her arm with the fresh scars against Comet's bark. She feels the tree's healing action penetrate through the shirt to her arm.

The uncles glance up at Yinhe and grunt knowingly to each other – just Yinhe doing her usual thing.

Uncle Fang yells at Yinhe, "Just what is it with you and this tree, anyway? All these years I've known you and still you won't say. I mean, how many thousands of sketches have you made of this ugly beast?"

Yinhe scowls down at Uncle Fang. "Come on, be respectful. This tree understands me better than any human being. That makes it beautiful in my eyes."

Uncle Fang laughs and nods conspiratorially to his chess companion. "Remember when she was just ten or eleven? She climbed ten metres up this tree and spent hours there while her Pa was on the ground below searching everywhere for her. She was so quiet – you'd think she didn't want to be found. Luck of the devil, I looked up and saw her."

Uncle Huo giggles, his cheeks reddening further, then shrugs his shoulders as if to say, well, what do I know?

Twenty minutes later, Yinhe returns to the ground and unzips her backpack. She pulls out the rolled-up set of tools. Soon after, two seniors and a father with an infant approach Yinhe and sit on the ledge in front of Comet, waiting for their turns. Yinhe starts by taking the pulses of the first elder, a woman whose face was burnt by hot oil a year ago, her skin on the left side of her face puckered purple and dark red. Yinhe uses the slim tiny pen that emits a laser light to target this area. Since beginning treatments, Auntie Neo's scars have lessened considerably, and she reports less pain.

After finishing with Auntie Neo, Yinhe starts on Qian by massaging his scalp down to the base of his skull. His mouth opens, and he starts to snore. This happens every time. Qian suffers from occasional migraines. Yinhe uses a different tool – a sphere that emits different frequencies when switched on. She releases the sphere above his head. It hovers for a few minutes, tinkling away, then starts to orbit the top of his head. The sphere finally parks in front of Qian's face. He continues to sleep.

Uncle Fang turns up the volume on his Grundig. Raspy sounds, lots of static, but the voice of the announcer comes through quite well. "Important news being discussed on the whisper network. Rumour goes, there's some trouble brewing with No. 1 acting unpredictably. Central Government trying to conceal problems. Updates on the hour."

Uncle Fang nods at Uncle Huo after he makes his move on the chessboard.

Yinhe asks, "Did they say what kind of trouble?"

"Seems that No. 1 is doing strange things these days. Started in Bright Order. Shutting down operating systems, just for several minutes, it seems. Then there was an interruption of aphrodisiacal misting in Interstitium . . ."

Uncle Huo sniggers. "Heh, some of us are too old to even notice such things, huh?"

"What else?" asks Yinhe.

Uncle Fang pouts and tugs at his goatee. "Eh, let me think. Something in Blue Otot? Uh, I forget."

Uncle Huo sneers. "Yeah, but our Big Brother Brain hasn't gotten around to Bent Back yet."

"I think there were some visual tableaux that disappeared one afternoon," replies Uncle Fang, "but maybe you were busy. Napping."

Uncle Huo glares at his friend. "No big deal for us, right? We're just elders, kids and losers here! Hey, hey!" Uncle Huo flails his arms about while singing his reply, then spits disdainfully behind his left shoulder.

Yinhe winces. Uncle Huo doesn't have a good singing voice. Plus, he should know better than to make a joke like that. She usually doesn't enjoy sarcastic humour. How about those who don't have the office or tech skills to work in Bright Order? The disabled folks? Or the ones with attitude, like her, who choose to opt out of high paying jobs, work instead in Interstitium and live in Bent Back?

"Uncle Fang, your daughter Wen is in charge of managing No. 1, right?"

"Yup," answers Uncle Fang.

"I don't suppose she can tell you what's been going on."

Uncle Fang replies. "That's right – top-secret stuff."

Yinhe purses her lips. "No. 1 has been around for ages. I don't even know for how long."

"Dumpling, nothing is forever. What do you think – that there had never been troubles keeping No. 1 in tip-top condition? CG likes to cover their stinky ass about such breakdowns."

"You know I dislike it when you call me 'dumpling.' It's . . . it's . . . so condescending."

"It's just a term of endearment, sweetie. You can always call me something. Like, how about youtiao? I mean, I'm tall, lean and sometimes my skin gets oily, huh? If I don't mind being called deep-fried oily pastry, why would you mind being called dumpling? Uptight titties!"

"Yeah, okay, so I'm uptight. Plus, you've got a foul mouth. Who cares what you think?" She and the uncles break out into laughter, used to this kind of banter.

Qian rouses from his deep sleep and smiles. "Ahhh! I always feel better after treatment. Here . . ." He gives Yinhe a jar of his homemade radish pickles. Yinhe returns the sphere to her backpack. She looks up and observes her next client. The parent is seated, and the baby has curled their tiny fingers around the adult's hands. Is it the father or the infant who needs help?

She has seen them around in the neighbourhood but never treated them nor the mother of the infant. She nods her head at the father and begins to interview him. It appears that the infant has been suffering from colic. She peers at the infant's skin and looks into their mouth. She decides to place her hands over the infant's ears; they suddenly start to cry. After a few minutes of bawling, they quiet down. Yinhe holds the baby in her arms and pats them on their back. They begin to burp loudly several times. She gives the father instructions on how to brew the packet of herbs she gives him.

There's only a sliver of orange left in the sky by the time Yinhe is finished treating her fifth – and last – client.

The uncles put on their solar-powered headlamps and switch them on. Anything to buy extra time for a game. Uncle Huo moves a chess piece. "About No. 1 failing. Seems like poetic justice to me. Central Government ignores Bent Back residents because we're moochers or losers. Whatever. Hah, let them have trouble! No. 1 not flawless, or maybe it's on our side!"

Yinhe can't help but laugh. Such an amusing comment. Poetic justice?

The chill of the evening cuts like an old, blunt knife. *You don't feel it at first, but it sneaks under your skin.* She puts on her hoodie. She pictures the workers in Bright Order returning to their pods in Blue Otot after eight-hour days, while those in higher positions – government officials and scientists in HQ – might choose to drift over to Interstitium for some fun and distraction before heading back to their residences in Bright Order.

"Did you want a quick treatment before I head off, Uncle Fang? Uncle Huo?"

They both shake their heads, all their concentration on the game. Yinhe packs up her instruments and silently bids Comet goodbye. *Don't be a stranger,* comes the cheeky response.

"Okay, bye, Uncle Fang, Uncle Huo." Before they can say another word, Yinhe races down the steps. With every step that she takes down to the Lower Levels, Yinhe can feel her daytime identity slipping away from her, like a worn-out disguise.

Start of Autumn into Limit of Heat
Seventh Lunar Month
701 CE
MOUNT HUA

"I'm here, dear Harelip." Choking back tears, Ardhanari rushes over to where Harelip lies on the kang. His eyes redden as he clutches Harelip's hand with both of his.

Harelip's eyes mist over as he looks at the man he'd abandoned thirty-six years earlier. He reaches up to stroke Ardhanari's cheeks. "You're not a dream after all. Here in the flesh. I'm sorry, my love, all the years of silence . . ."

Baoshi feels awkward standing at the entrance, until Harelip addresses him. "You truly are a miracle of Heaven! You've fulfilled my dream of seeing Ardhanari again before I die." Harelip struggles to raise his body. Ardhanari places his hand behind Harelip's back and helps him up.

After Baoshi fetches a cup of water and passes it to Ardhanari, he stands back, watching.

Ardhanari exclaims, as he brings the cup to Harelip's mouth, "Jaanam, beloved! Why haven't you told me all these years what happened to you? I didn't know if you died or if you no longer wanted to . . ."

Harelip's voice wavers as he struggles to breathe. "Couldn't tell you . . . I was scared. Ran away, terrified of being harmed by Empress Wu." He coughs, and Ardhanari carefully gives him a few firm pats on the back. "I hear she's become the Female Emperor, huh? We get the barest news here. Birds don't report such things." He laughs, the sound of his lungs coming up noisily against his throat.

Ardhanari leans forward to catch Harelip's whispered words. It has been two weeks since he first arrived on Mount Hua. The season has changed into Limit of Heat. Outside the shack, the sun has just set, indigo streaks across the sky accompanying the last blush of light.

Baoshi watches them from his position just outside the doorway. What is Harelip telling Ardhanari? He's witnessed numerous moments of tenderness between his master and Ardhanari in the past two weeks. He never fails to blush. He goes outside and sits on a tree stump to look out at the view. He's relieved he was able to fulfill his mission to bring Ardhanari here in time. Flashes of the various encounters he had while travelling from Mount Hua to the Western capital pass through his mind as he waves away the flies that come too close to his face.

His chest aches at the memory of that first day he met Harelip eight years ago. Baoshi's father wanted to get rid of him, brought him to Mount Hua and stripped his lower body down to show Harelip his male and female parts. Baoshi was an anomaly and hence unacceptable. That was the first time he heard Harelip call him a miracle of Heaven, two in one, a manifestation of the Buddha. Harelip happily took Baoshi in, refusing the father's offer of money.

Recalling this now, Baoshi nods firmly to himself and to all the invisible presences on Mount Hua. Harelip is his true father, the one who has unconditionally loved him all these years.

Baoshi stares at the last traces of orange brilliance as the sun disappears. Life is precious and fleeting. His beloved master is close to the end. He closes his eyes and shudders. Harelip must be suffering terribly. Baoshi feels helpless. His eyes well up with tears, but he quickly wipes them away. He turns his attention to the deepening silhouettes of the mountain landscape and trees around him. He can't bear the thought of life without Harelip. His lower lip quivers with a momentary panic that he won't be able to manage on his own. He feels a pressure build inside his head. He's plagued with questions about upkeep of the shack and the garden plots and the villagers below who will need herbal medicines. He takes a sharp inhale of breath, gets up and goes back into the shack.

Later that night, Baoshi lights the single candle at the altar and draws up a stool next to Harelip on the kang. He leans close to Harelip's mouth. There's a faint trace of breath. Harelip suddenly opens his eyes wide. In the flickering candlelight, Baoshi feels Harelip's gaze going through him, seeing something else behind him.

"You're leaving us soon, Master. Don't be sad for us. May you peacefully go to the Pure Land." Saying this, Baoshi experiences a powerful release, and he sobs. Harelip presses his fingers into Baoshi's arm with remarkable strength. Baoshi feels a warm energy move up his arm to his chest, imbuing him with courage.

"Master, I will always be grateful to you. I will remain here on Mount Hua, here to help anyone who comes up for medicine. Rest assured that I will continue your legacy."

Baoshi doesn't leave Harelip's side. He lets Ardhanari have the other kang to himself. His eyes grow heavy as he rests his face next to Harelip's head, nestling in the crook between his head and shoulder. When he finally awakens from the feeling of sunlight on his cheek, he raises himself up and looks at Harelip. He places a hand under Harelip's nose. His heart sinks when he realizes that his master has stopped breathing.

Baoshi and Ardhanari sweat from their efforts – they've just finished burying Harelip's body in the forest behind the shack. Baoshi takes three stones and lays them out in an inverted triangle to mark the grave. The two top stones represent Heaven and Earth asserting their influences on all living beings, which are represented by the third stone.

Straightening up, Baoshi nudges his straw sandals more firmly into the earth. He wriggles his toes to better feel the freshly turned earth, how it vibrates with the energy of receiving Harelip's body. Satisfied, he turns around and heads back toward the shack while Ardhanari follows, lagging behind.

Baoshi scoops water from the clay jar to place into the iron kettle and lights a fire in the charcoal stove. The day passes in silence. He notices that Ardhanari looks dazed. In the evening, they eat leftover cold sorghum and drink roasted barley tea.

Ardhanari finally breaks the silence. "What will you do now? Won't you come back to Chang'an with me?"

Baoshi lowers his gaze and studies the wood grain of the table, moving his hand across it. He inhales deeply. The soft fecund smells of early autumn waft into the shack through the window and half-open door.

He directs his gaze to the darkness outside. The cicadas sound softer in this cooler temperature. Baoshi didn't hear the same kind of cicada calls when he was in Chang'an during the summer. The ones he's hearing now come out only at night, unlike their relatives. He has observed their habits for many seasons. The males make their mating calls by rubbing their wings against the sides of their abdomens. Soon the females will lay their eggs in the slits of twigs and trees. The hatched nymphs will fall to the ground and burrow deep down into the earth and feed off the sap of the tree for years. It will take another two to five years before the nymphs are ready to emerge through the earth and begin a new cycle. All these details he learned from Harelip. His master also taught him that transformation takes time and, in many instances, remains invisible to others.

Baoshi doesn't answer Ardhanari for quite a long time as he continues to listen to the sounds of nature outside the shack – the call of owls in the distance and the movements of small animals in the forest. They're all aware of the fresh grave and must know that Harelip is gone. Even though Baoshi can still sense Harelip's energy on the mountain, he cries silently, looking out toward the forest, the tears dampening his jacket. Life on Mount Hua will be painfully different without Harelip. Even so, he derives comfort from knowing that the mountain is rich with unseen mysteries the spirits that take refuge in the hollows of trees and small caves.

Mount Hua is what his heart wants, what still draws him. He promised Harelip that he would remain. He hadn't said that out of obligation. He recalls what he said to the Female Emperor when he was granted an audience with her. *I am following what draws me.*

He turns back to look at Ardhanari. "I will miss all of you, but this mountain is meant to be my home for the rest of my life."

"You'll be alone and have to fend for yourself. Aren't you worried?"

"True, I'll be the only human here most of the time, but there are animals and other presences. I won't be alone."

"Last night, before Harelip . . ." Ardhanari's voice crackles. "He told me about the Tibetan drawing. He said Xuanzang passed it on to him."

Baoshi nods. "That's right, Master Harelip abandoned the city, but he wasn't going to leave the drawing behind."

"Did Harelip ever tell you? I met Xuanzang when I went to Da Ci'en Monastery to repair a sculpture." His usually smooth baritone voice rises to a wail, then dips into inaudible moans.

After Ardhanari calms down, he continues, "Harelip revered Xuanzang. This Tibetan drawing was clearly something that meant a lot to him. I'm shocked that Harelip asked me to take care of such an important object. I have no idea what to do with it. Do you know?"

Baoshi's gaze skirts the wisps of grey at Ardhanari's temples and the fine wrinkles at the outer edges of his eyes. He walks over to the Buddha statue on the altar. Turning it upside down, he reaches inside a gap at the base and carefully pulls out a rolled up, yellowed piece of parchment. He rummages in a basket below the altar and pulls out a bamboo tube. After inserting the drawing inside and capping the tube, he passes the tube to Ardhanari.

Ardhanari asks, "What now?"

"What do you mean?"

Ardhanari has a deepening furrow between his eyebrows. "Well, I, uh, find this all very distressing. I know Harelip has entrusted this to me, but –"

"You mustn't worry, dear Ardhanari." Saying this, Baoshi looks up at the ceiling of the hut. There's a hole that needs to be patched. A spider spins her web close to it. Aided by the light from the candle, Baoshi can just make out her movements. Perhaps the web will cover the hole? He smiles. There's a lot of beauty in things done slowly.

Early the next morning, Baoshi gets up first and lights incense. He sits down on the meditation cushion and begins to chant. When he is finished, he uncrosses his legs and goes to light the fire in the hearth and fill the kettle.

Ardhanari opens his eyes and sits up on the kang, slipping his feet into his straw sandals. "There's no reason for me to linger here. I'll take care of the Tibetan drawing even though I'm not sure what to do with it."

"As I understood from Master Harelip, you are to wait. You'll know when you meet your successor. Venerable Master Xuanzang waited for many years, and then he knew to give it to Master Harelip soon after they met."

"When Harelip told me to take it, I just didn't know what to think. He made you go all the way to Chang'an in search of me.

I mean, even insisting that you walk all the way and refuse any rides. Talk about being strict! Just so you could find me, bring me to Mount Hua. Pass this drawing to me. From Xuanzang, then to Harelip and now me. I just don't get it. Then again, there's so much I still don't get about Harelip. You can love someone so deeply and still not fully understand them. You know what I mean?"

"I know." Baoshi cocks his head, amused. "You're quite the worrying kind! You have so little faith. Even if you make a mistake – which is unlikely – something or someone else will come along and correct it!"

Ardhanari laughs despite his sadness. "Such a pure soul! I am far more skeptical than you. But okay, I'll try not to fret so much."

Start of Autumn
Seventh Lunar Month
644 CE
KHOTAN

Xuanzang finds his days to be easier since he arrived in Khotan. The weather is mostly pleasant except for the occasional strong wind, like this afternoon. He wraps a scarf over his mouth and nose before he sets out from the inn. *The wind is a powerful beast,* he thinks. It blurs the boundaries between sky and earth at its fiercest.

He's been here, in Khotan, for months waiting for the replacement manuscripts. It was his fault that they lost the original scrolls. He sighs, remembering the disaster.

He squints as a sudden gust of wind stirs up the sand. He heads toward a favourite part of town. These days in Khotan are such a delight and a contrast to the past years of hardship. He marvels that he's even here, in this oasis. As he approaches the bazaar, Xuanzang feels a lift in his spirits. He takes in the sights and attends to the voices of vendors and their customers.

"Hey, Xuanzang! Hey!"

Xuanzang jolts out of his reverie and turns in the direction of the voice slightly behind him and to his right. A woman stands, one hand on her hip, at the front of a shop packed with rugs and waves vigorously at him. She has long, dark hair tied in two braids. Her eyes are a light brown; her nose has a shapely rise. She looks to be chewing something that causes her lips to stain red.

Xuanzang cautiously approaches her. "How do you know my name?"

"You're famous. Everyone talks about you."

"Oh?"

"I've seen you walking around here many times. Come in, share some tea, won't you? I would like to show you something."

Xuanzang raises an eyebrow.

As if she has read his mind, she laughs. "No, no, I mean something rather serious. A drawing. I think it's meant for you."

He bows cautiously, his gaze lowered to the ground. He notices the hem of her colourful green-and-blue skirt – it has a rim of golden thread, with knotted tassels that barely graze the earthen floor.

A strong scent of incense greets him as he enters her shop. In front of him are two stools made of tree stumps, and in between them a low table with a pewter pot on it. The woman brings out two small glasses from a shelf above the table and invites Xuanzang to sit with her. She pours tea from the pewter pot into the two glasses. Xuanzang is surprised by the rich crimson colour of the tea.

He places his palms together in front of his chest and bows slightly. "Pardon me, madam, I am not used to strange, uh, women, approaching me in such a direct manner."

She laughs loudly, without restraint. "Oh my, aren't you a formal one!"

Xuanzang blushes. "Delicious tea. I've never tasted anything like this before."

"The tea is made from brewing crushed pomegranate seeds with dried flowers. We have a few trees here. The seeds were originally brought over from India."

"Brought over from India? I lost so many scriptures when I tried to transport seeds on the boats crossing the Indus."

"Ah, but that happened because you tried to cross the Indus River with them. Our seeds were transported on the overland route."

Xuanzang couldn't help but sigh loudly. "It was all my fault. Ignoring the local folk beliefs."

"A mistake first made in the mind will eventually manifest in the actions taken. I'm sure you know that. I'm merely stating the obvious. Just goes to show a great monk is just a human being after all." She throws her head back and laughs a third time, her two braids tossed left and right by her raucous laughter. "Do not ignore myths – they contain great wisdom."

Her eyes flash at Xuanzang, who feels an odd tremor between his shoulder blades. A dizziness overcomes him. His first thought is that he has been drugged. But wait – she also drank the tea.

"My name is Tirzah. I arrived here in Khotan with my family when I was still a young girl. I have something to pass on to you. I will explain. Wait."

She stands up and makes her way through a doorway to the back. Meanwhile, Xuanzang feels curiously cheerful. Perhaps it isn't the pomegranate tea but the sweet floral incense.

Tirzah soon returns with a bamboo tube. As she sits back down, he catches a whiff emanating from her body: *Honey*, he thinks. She carefully pulls out a piece of parchment and lays it on one of the rugs on the earthen floor between them.

"Look at this," she says, pointing to the drawing and, in particular, the symbols within the body of the creature.

"A creature of the sea. I have seen other drawings of turtles but nothing like this."

"This drawing is related to Ao, the divine turtle."

He tilts his head, intrigued. "How so?" He very much wants to look directly into her eyes, but he forces himself to merely glance at her before lowering his gaze.

"There's a magic spell concealed inside these symbols." She glances around, as if to check that no one is within earshot before she whispers, "It's a five-sided mystery, these four limbs and one head."

"Hmm." Xuanzang looks down at the drawing. A ray of sunlight reaches the bottom right-hand corner. The drawing depicts the underside of a turtle, its soft underbelly. The ink line is thin. He feels vulnerable just looking at its exposed body. The turtle's neck is quite extended, arching toward its right. Its eyes are large. There are squiggly lines all throughout its body. He recognizes the script as some kind of Tibetan, but he isn't able to read the symbols because he isn't fluent enough. At first glance, the turtle's position seems to communicate possible vulnerability. He realizes that this may simply be his interpretation. He looks at the eyes again – they could be fearsome, expressing considerable power.

Tirzah points first to the upper left limb, then to the upper right limb, then diagonally to the lower left limb. She moves up to the head, then down to the lower right limb and ends up back at the upper left limb. Xuanzang sees in his mind that she has traced a star.

Tirzah rolls up the drawing and places it inside the bamboo tube. "This is for you, Venerable One. The drawing has been passed down from one person to another for thousands of years. Now I pass it on to you. You are to hold on to it until such time when you encounter someone who you sense ought to be next in taking care of it."

"What is the purpose of such a practice?"

"This is to allow Ao to maintain its presence in the world through time, unseen yet glimpsed through its representation as sacred image. It is both secret and mystery."

"Why did you choose me?"

"Based on an intuition."

"Oh!" Xuanzang gasps, shocked.

"This is how it's meant to happen. The person who takes care of the drawing is blessed with a growing capacity to know others. I have taken care of this drawing for thirteen years, and it has brought me blessings. My intuitive power is strong – that's how I knew the moment I saw you that you're the one to next inherit the drawing. You will fulfill your destiny to the greatest capacity. Let the drawing inspire you, Venerable Xuanzang."

Holding the tube in front of her with both hands, Tirzah offers it to the monk with her head bowed. He receives the gift with both hands as well, appreciating the earnestness of the gesture. He, too, bows slightly.

"I accept your gift with appreciation. I don't know what else to say."

"No need. Just don't forget what I shared."

He nods, tucks the bamboo tube inside his robes and reluctantly takes his leave. Some tender part in him wishes to stay longer in this woman's company, but he knows he mustn't. He continues to wander through the bazaar, but he's distracted by the presence of the bamboo tube shifting against his chest.

Later that evening, as he sits in his room and contemplates the ancient drawing by the light of a single candle flame, he's intrigued by the script as well as the drawing. Surely it isn't a coincidence that certain symbols exist only within the limbs of the turtle, while the central body of the creature has other kinds of symbols arranged in a circle. He blinks and rubs at the edges of his eyes.

He wishes he could find someone to decipher the script. But wait – he's supposed to keep this to himself until the right moment. He's also supposed to simply know whom to pass it to when the moment arrives. Fascinating. He shakes his head, somewhat disbelieving.

He recalls what Tirzah said, *A five-sided mystery*. He traces the direction of the star she drew and purses his lips in puzzlement. Five points. Maybe she simply means that if one were to draw lines from each of the points to the next, it would form five sides. A pentagon.

He's reminded that there are myriads of possible realities, some of which cannot be experienced by the ordinary senses. Maybe someone who inherits the drawing in the future will understand Tirzah's meaning. He imagines himself reaching out to that person, speaking to them, and listening to what they have discovered.

Time would collapse in that moment. The impossible made possible.

With that in mind, he mixes some ink and uses a small brush to write "A five-sided mystery" on the back of the drawing. This phrase will travel far beyond him in time and space to reach that person.

He blushes, thinking about his encounter with Tirzah, then taps the centre of his chest as if to summon himself back to what's at hand. His life's purpose is to translate the scrolls once he re-enters Chang'an.

White Dew
Eighth Lunar Month
2219 CE
BENT BACK, LUOYANG

Mr. Stanley Ouyang watches the fading light from their tiny ground-floor living room window. He pulls out a hankie and blows his nose noisily, then moves around the kitchen to look for something else to do. He picks up a few stray papers that had dropped on the floor – Yinhe's sketches of the tree in Chess Square. He places the sketches in a neat pile on the table. She can draw well, that's without question. But it seems that she's drawing not what she sees, but what she senses. He takes off his glasses for a few moments to massage the outside perimeter, then the inside, of both eyes, feeling the strain of a few hours' work in the basement. He's begun the task of rearranging the hundreds of books in the library.

All these years spent collecting, he had gone along with Phoebe's method, based on the Library of Congress Classification system developed in the United States in the twentieth century. Last month, though, he'd given into the urge to restructure his library according to how he imagines a bookshop would have done it. He would like to free up the books, to create a more informal, intimate atmosphere. It has taken him a while to get this going; after all, it's been twenty-three years since Phoebe left him and Yinhe. He's not going to be hard on himself about this. It's taken this long because it had to take this long.

Back when he was still running the martial arts school, the time he could spend in the library was rare, but ever since he retired, he spends most of his time in the basement. He calls it his hidden room, a place where he is happily obscured by the commanding variety of books. He's amassed quite the collection over the past four decades: Some books had belonged to his grandparents or parents; some were passed down from great-great-grandparents, like the case of old Chinese manhua comics and political cartoons from World War Two in the twentieth century. He's bought classics such as *Journey to the West*, *Three Kingdoms*, *Outlaws of the Marsh* – a handful of them first or early editions.

He closes the plastic blinds in the living room, picks up a few dishes from the dining table and places them in the kitchen sink. He ties up the compostable bag and goes out to the dumpster behind the house.

He notices a sparrow perched on top of the dumpster. When he approaches, it flits away. For some reason, the bird reminds him of his daughter. She may be tiny compared to some but she sure moves fast. He feels a pang of guilt – since he doesn't feel like leaving the house much, Yinhe has had to take on more and more of the tasks to do with the outside world. Maybe he's a misguided larva that forgot to mature. He laughs, chokes at his own joke and thumps his chest firmly to clear some phlegm.

When he returns to the kitchen, he opens the box where the recipe cards are stored. The cards are bent and discoloured from years of use. He pulls out the one for hongshaorou, braised pork belly. The card has a few pencilled-in comments from Phoebe.

He harrumphs, then pulls out the strip of pork belly from the fridge, rinses it and places it in a pot of water to cook. Later on, he'll throw that water out and proceed with the next steps.

He peers into the gaiwan teapot that Yinhe left on the dining table. Pu'er tea leaves – still smell good. Stanley plods over to the stove and puts on the kettle. After he's made himself a cup of tea, he sits down.

He's heard the news from their underground radio station that No. 1 is malfunctioning again. He wants to say, So what? Stanley remembers watching a livestream when he was a teenager about the first subdermal microchips used as an interface with AI to help people with physical disabilities access computer devices and smartphones. It was such an incredible achievement.

Central Government next experimented with neural implants. Microscopic chips with filaments were inserted into human brains with minimal surgery – these allowed people with neurologically compromised conditions like muscular dystrophy to control devices. CG quickly realized how potent a weapon this could become. Isn't that often the case – some scientific advancement begins with a humane application, only to be later used to further state control of its workers.

Those who work in education, office and tech jobs, or aspire to professions such as research and medicine, need to be fitted with both neural implants and subdermal microchips. The neural implants for Bright Order workers started happening some thirty years ago, around the time when he was close to finishing art school and Phoebe was a librarian. If he had wanted to teach art, he would have had to be separated from his family, wear both neural and subdermal implants and live in Blue Otot. Nope, no way he was going to agree to that.

Stanley stiffens in his chair. He should stop ruminating about the past so much. He gets up to transfer the cooked pork belly to a large bowl. He pours the water into the sink, rinses the pot and fills it with clean water. Next, he adds a generous knob of ginger, some cloves, five-spice powder, dark soy sauce, a tablespoon of sugar and Shaoxing wine. Once the mix starts to boil, he turns the heat down. He cuts the pork belly into bite-sized chunks and adds them to the pot. Then he covers the pot with a lid, leaving a slight gap as the pork cooks at a simmer.

He sips more of the pu'er tea, drawing it slowly into his mouth, and lets the smoky nectar linger before he swallows. He loves the fulsome taste of mushrooms, forest and leaves just fallen to the ground. The tea neither begs you to like it nor is showy, yet it insinuates itself with such intense presence.

Over the time he's lived in Bent Back, he's met some of the Bright Zone workers who got retired and were moved here from Blue Otot: folks like Fang and his wife, Lian; Huo and his wife, Mimi. *I've always wanted to ask Fang and Huo about those neural implants that got left in their brains, but that would be awkward, huh?*

He hasn't been out to Chess Square for quite some time. He's heard from Yinhe that folks ask about him. Bah, he's become a crotchety old guy. No fun to be around.

Time for a taste test of the hongshaorou. He lifts the lid and fishes out a piece of pork belly, blows on it before popping it into his mouth. Then he chews slowly, his eyebrows knitted as he concentrates. The flavours of anise and cloves burst in his mouth, mixing in with the sultry sweetness of fennel and dark soy sauce. That Shaoxing wine really adds oomph. He smiles with satisfaction. *Mmmm, I haven't lost my touch.* His thoughts turn to Yinhe.

On the night that Yinhe was born, over twenty-eight years ago, the Milky Way was beautifully visible. Stanley and Phoebe had gone up to the roof garden in early July and were admiring the stars when Phoebe felt the first labour pains. It happened so quickly – they were born on the roof, between zucchini plants and long beans on poles. Stanley had suggested naming their child Yinhe – Silver River, the name for the Milky Way. How lovely everything had seemed then. According to social convention, children got to decide their gender. Like all parents, they would wait to see how Yinhe wished to be identified later on.

Trouble in the marriage started shortly after Yinhe was born. Phoebe exclaimed that Yinhe wasn't fair-skinned like Stanley and Phoebe. Instead, their skin was a tawny-ochre. As Yinhe's hair grew, there were silver flecks at the top and back, yet another sign of strangeness. A scent of apricots came off the child's skin.

Stanley didn't mind any of these things. He simply felt intrigued, but Phoebe was bothered. It was painful to see how Phoebe changed. She wasn't the soulmate he had married.

Stanley shakes his head, protesting his own tears.

When Yinhe was close to two years old, Stanley overheard Phoebe talking loudly to their next-door neighbour, as if she wanted Stanley and anyone else within earshot to hear: "Surely Spirit has cursed us."

"Why did you say that?" he asked her when she came back into the house.

"What else could it be? There must be a demon inside them."

"Spirit." This was the term Phoebe started using after she began attending Spirit Supreme Assembly, in Interstitium. Phoebe took Yinhe with her once, then twice, a week to Spirit Supreme Assembly services. She never invited Stanley. Even if she did, he wouldn't have gone. Stanley was nervous about these visits, especially after Phoebe's comment about their child being possessed.

He pictured weird rituals – maybe a shaman in black robes with a scary red demon mask, who would dance around Yinhe, flicking a horsehair wand at their body. Or maybe pointing a halberd at the toddler. Yet every time Phoebe returned, the toddler was their usual rambunctious, alert self. He saw no signs of Yinhe being distressed, so he dismissed his worries as being ill-founded.

Phoebe brought home lots of pamphlets from Spirit Supreme Assembly. In an age when new paper was hardly being used, it was startling to see the flashy pamphlets with iridescent symbols and beautifully designed pages. Their emblem caught his eye – two gourd-like vessels with their mouths tilted toward each other, and golden liquid pouring out into a lake below. *The power of everlasting elixir. The Oneness that is Spirit Supreme. Uniting all those who choose this path of abundance.*

He thinks about how athletic Yinhe was: At eleven months they were boldly running around the apartment. At three years of age they could leap onto table and kitchen countertops from the floor. *The child is magical,* he realized even then.

The final straw for Phoebe happened when Yinhe was five. Phoebe was preparing dinner while he was at the gym teaching a martial arts class. When he got home, Phoebe was distraught. According to her, Yinhe was napping on the sofa when Phoebe left the kitchen momentarily to go to the washroom. She couldn't have been more than two minutes. When she returned, Yinhe was on the kitchen counter squatting next to the chopping board and stuffing their face with pieces of raw pork.

He had tried to empathize by looking serious, but what could he say? He already had some inklings about Yinhe, but he wasn't going to tell Phoebe. The next day, when he woke up, he found the note announcing her departure. Stanley was devastated.

Just as well that he hadn't disclosed to Phoebe his hunch – that their child possessed some divine characteristics; that they were a magical being that he used to think only existed in myths he'd read. He thought about that silver streak at the back of Yinhe's head. It felt more like fur than hair.

On Yinhe's eighth birthday, Stanley took them down to the basement library and showed them a copy of *Shanhaijing* – he located the drawing of the Nine-Tailed Fox and showed it to them. "I figure this is your distant relation," he said, sounding so calm, as if he were simply observing the weather that day. "I'm right, aren't I?"

Yinhe smiled warmly at him, with a glint in their eyes. Their nose twitched and they jumped up, making a flurry of guttural sounds that reminded Stanley of two sticks being hit together.

"Pa, thank you. Now that you say this, I might as well let you know you can call me daughter from now on." Stanley had nodded, taking this revelation in stride.

Yinhe next surprised him, saying, "But it's not simple for me." Instead of the conventional gesture to indicate being female, Yinhe touched the tips of her thumb and first finger together and then to the shoulder on the same side. He had never seen anyone do that before. He simply nodded. There were things he didn't understand, but no matter, the important thing was to accept.

He smiles at the memory. She explained to Stanley that she was half-human and half-fox, always reincarnating as a chimeric creature. Yinhe has always been clear about who and what she is. He collects books and she collects tea; they don't talk about Phoebe. He massages the back of his neck and his jawline and thinks – he and Yinhe have been living harmoniously with each other since Phoebe left.

Stanley is grateful that Yinhe makes a good income working three nights at the casino. He doesn't want to be a burden to her. She never complains – he finds her to be remarkably patient. Stanley wonders if her loyalty to him has held her back. But what exactly should a creature like her be doing anyway?

He nods to himself as he sips the tea, the warmth soothing his mouth and senses. *Our children are never our possession; sometimes they don't even resemble us in any way.*

Maybe tomorrow morning, he'll check on the roof garden, even though she's been the one tending the vegetables. He hears her up there in the late afternoon or late at night doing her exercise drills. He doesn't like to go to the roof much anymore. It reminds him of how it used to be such a romantic place for him and Phoebe, looking up at the night sky.

Storytelling Night
2219 CE
BENT BACK, LUOYANG

Yinhe looks around at her audience. Finally, members of Storytelling Night have reconvened after a break of two months during which the air pollution was so bad it wasn't advisable to come out even wearing masks with filters. Their small but dedicated group occupies a corner at the far end of Blossom Street, thirty long flights of stairs down from Chess Square, at the Lower Levels. There is a single streetlamp nearby. On the next street are a couple of cheap eating places selling noodle soups, with lots of customers milling about at all times.

This is probably the most decrepit section of Bent Back, an area where artists live for very little in former garage sheds or abandoned buildings. The food places on adjacent streets are decent yet inexpensive, open until two in the morning on weekends. Blossom Street, where they meet for Storytelling Night, however, is usually quite deserted. An old music school used to be here – the sign still hangs above, rusted over. There are rumours that a ghost controls this corner, but Yinhe hasn't had any trouble. It could be because the ghost enjoys the stories she tells.

Storytelling Night is an occasion for alternative identities. Eccentrics, nerds, neurodivergent folks and their family members – everyone comes in costumes, masks and headgear made with scraps of paper, dried leaves, twigs, strings, pieces of rags or torn socks, and the odd button or sequin here and there. As Yinhe scans her audience, she feels a warmth spread through her chest – she's missed being with everyone.

The sky darkens, with fast disappearing traces of carmine and golden brilliance swiftly overtaken by dark blue and black. With masks and headgear donned, the audience starts switching on their solar-powered tea lights. A couple of adults have brought their triboluminescent rattles with them. They begin to shake and twirl their devices, and the light generated from the agitation of quartz crystals glows through the buffalo hide shells. Many of the audience members sit on stools or cardboard, hemp or bamboo mats; one person sits in their wheelchair, with their girlfriend sitting next to them on a mat; two others, who stand, are partially hidden in shadow.

Yinhe is the only one who lights a candle. She pulls out the special robe and headgear from her duffel bag, puts on the golden-coloured silk jacket, frayed along its hem. The hem once had a dark sepia border with depictions of trees and mythical animals, echoed in the borders of her wide-cut sleeves. Her Daoist headscarf has a silver star at the front. In this alternate reality, she is Unknown Wayfarer – unknown and unknowable – who travels across borders of the imagination.

She counts eighteen in the audience tonight. There are four children ranging from five to sixteen and twelve seniors – all regulars. She doesn't recognize the two who stand outside their circle. They have tall knitted felt caps pulled low over their foreheads, with masks that obscure their faces. Their clothing is elegant and shimmers in the artificial light.

Unknown Wayfarer lights a stick of incense and plants it in the crack of the pavement next to her candle. The chatting soon dies down, and the atmosphere is charged with anticipation. She sits down on the ground next to the lit incense stick and takes a few gulps of warm water from her flask before she begins.

"Our heroine, the half-fox, half-human, was known as Qilan in her reincarnation as a Daoist nun during the early years of the Tang dynasty. Where we last left off in our storytelling, she had appeared to Ling as an ethereal form on the cusp of Ling's passing. Qilan claimed the oracle bone and accompanied Ling's soul through the bardo. Her plan was to follow Ling into her next reincarnation. Sadly, this hope was thwarted when some force overcame Qilan in the bardo and took Ling's soul away from her."

Many in the audience groan loudly at this revelation.

"The fox spirit still had the oracle bone with her at the end of that harrowing journey through the bardo. Ao came to her, at the edge of the world, where land met water, facing the island where Mount Penglai is. The divine turtle reclaimed the plastron.

"After she lost Ling's soul, the fox spirit chose not to return to earth as a physical form for a long time. In 904 CE, three years before the total collapse of the Tang dynasty, she and her fox mother were in their immaterial forms, hidden behind bushes somewhere on the road between Chang'an and Luoyang. The dictator Zhu Wen had destroyed the Western capital. The fox spirits gazed at the hordes of humans exiled from Chang'an, forced to take whatever belongings they could and travel on foot or by carriage to the Eastern capital, Luoyang. Our heroine recalled how strongly attached she had become to Chang'an. In her reincarnation as Qilan, the Daoist nun, Da Fa Temple had been her shelter for many years – she had learned so much living there. She had cared for the other nuns and especially for the young Ling.

"On that ancient road between Chang'an and Luoyang, the fox spirit realized she would have to return someday to meet the demon Gui again. She also wanted to find out who or what had taken Ling's soul from her. Most of all, she yearned to reunite with Ling."

"Wow, this is a pretty complicated plot, huh?" Sean interjects, trying not to sound impatient. He fidgets and adjusts his bird mask.

Yinhe ignores Sean's tone and continues.

"The fox spirit returned in several lifetimes in order to help humans and animals on this planet. There were tumultuous times when our planet was starting to visibly disintegrate. She was a scientist in some of her lifetimes, while returning to hermit tendencies in other lives. She went to northern climates and sometimes lived in great isolation in mountainous regions.

"She always reincarnates as a human in female form, because she's a certain kind of fox spirit allied with the White Fox Goddess, but in truth, our heroine is beyond one gender or the other. Remember what she said about herself in the early days, after she rescued young Ling from slavery?"

The ten-year-old known as Pirouette raises their hand immediately. Unknown Wayfarer nods, and Pirouette answers, "A third kind of creature!"

"That's right – fox spirits employ a different kind of language than humans. The fox spirit is beyond duality. Even though our friend the fox spirit always reincarnates as female, beneath that appearance she is a shape-shifter, sometimes even disguising herself as another animal or even an object."

Ripples of oohs and aahs pass through the audience. At this juncture, the visitors decide to sit down at the back.

"Is she always the same in her reincarnations?" asks Auntie Lian, who is Fang's wife and the mother of Aloysius and Sean. Her long white hair is tied in a neat bun, and she has the simplest decoration – a piece of vermilion crinoline tied around her neck and covering half her mouth.

"What do you mean, the same?"

"Well, half-human and half-fox."

"Always."

More murmurs pass through the audience. A few listeners nod to show their appreciation. It's the first time Unknown Wayfarer has hinted to her audience about the scope and range of the half-fox, half-human through various reincarnations. She waits for the murmuring to settle down before she continues.

"When the planetary disaster struck, with the devastating combination of nuclear fallout and massive earthquakes and floods, many land masses were irreversibly altered, with schisms and large portions along the coastlines obliterated by the rising ocean."

"Atlantis again," Aloysius chimes in.

"Yeah, kind of. Such a catastrophic event might have seemed sudden, but the Great Catastrophe was the culmination of humankind's unceasing stripping the earth of forests and bogs, polluting the oceans and lakes, and forcing dams on rivers. The collapse of the Atlantic Meridional Overturning Circulation, a major global ocean circulation system, led to severe massive methane release and radical polar ice thaws. Waves of radioactive contaminations debilitated governments, inhabitants and economies in much of the world. You know – history."

"Why are humans so foolish, huh?" Auntie Lian pouts.

"So how did humankind even survive?" asks Aloysius.

"Truly amazing, isn't it? There were pockets of scientists and communities who built these floatation pods that harnessed the energies of nature – solar, wind, water – and these communities on water survived. Then the land was slowly reclaimed bit by bit."

"There was another cool thing that came out of the Great Catastrophe," says Aloysius.

"Which was?" asks Uncle Chen.

"Languages! All kinds of linguistic mixing. A diaspora of languages because some land forms no longer had clearly delineated borders."

"But those in power reinstated borders and national identities over time . . ." added Auntie Lian.

Yinhe takes another sip of water before she resumes.

"Government-run experiments using DNA to clone animal species had been occurring for years before the disaster struck. Central Kingdom emerged from the Great Catastrophe with increased clout among disparate communities, offering expertise in organ transplants and genetic splicing as ways to recover lost species and restore ecological balance."

The wind catches the rusty music school sign overhead and it squeaks as if to add its opinion.

"Sad about us humans, huh?" Sheila offers, as she shells peanuts and pops them into her mouth, making loud crunching sounds that punctuate the silence. She places the shells in a bag on her lap and passes some peanuts to Flora, who is in a wheelchair.

"Humans were beginning to transform to adapt to their impoverished environments. At the same time, more experimentation was happening in order to create chimeric creatures with greater resilience."

"Yeah, okay, this is getting current now," intones Sean.

"Even in the face of dramatically altered circumstances on Earth in the past hundred years, the fox spirit remains a natural chimeric creature in her various lifetimes. A fox-human or human-fox that isn't the result of artificial intervention. She is biding her time during this oppressive era until she discovers what she needs to do."

"You mean in terms of finding Ling's soul?" asks Pirouette.

"Yes."

"So, like, how would she know what she can do? I mean, what will be the sign to her?" Uncle Chen mumbles through his patchwork balaclava. "Since she comes back a few times, not every lifetime, right?"

"It could be that our heroine doesn't know all the details yet. She comes back to help others anyway, but for each of the lifetimes she's returned she hasn't received any indication of a way to resolve her dilemma. Except . . ."

Everyone holds their breath.

"… she has some suspicion that she is going to find the answer in this current reincarnation."

A few members of the audience applaud enthusiastically.

"Unknown Wayfarer, do you mean to suggest that our heroine is presently in our world?" asks Auntie Lian, her crinoline moving in concert with her mouth.

"I can't say whether the fox spirit is now present in our world. Don't forget, I'm only a teller of tales, and this is simply a story."

"Hmm, a third kind of creature," Auntie Lian mumbles, still immersed in her speculations.

The incense stick is almost burnt down. "We will end here. See you at the next Storytelling Night." Yinhe blows out her candle, while those with solar-powered lights keep them on as it's getting dark.

Claps of appreciation are accompanied by animated chatter now. People shuffle up to Unknown Wayfarer and present her with dried buckwheat groats, preserved pickles or home-cooked food. Yinhe puts away her silk jacket and crimson hat and puts her denim jacket back on. She packs the food away in her duffel bag.

After all the regulars have left, the two strangers approach her. The taller one speaks up, "My name is Seka." Seka touches her right shoulder with the fingertips of her left hand, signalling she is female.

"Rakan." The other stranger covers his heart with his right hand, signalling that he is male. In response to their greeting gestures, Yinhe brings thumb to first finger on both hands, then touches them to the same side shoulder. She can see from their expressions that they're puzzled by the gesture. In response, she offers, "I'm an unknown – you know, like my code name says."

Seka takes off her mask and smiles at Yinhe. "I like that."

Yinhe shivers from the sight. Seka has neon green irises bordered by a brown perimeter, and her mouth reminds Yinhe of an infant's innocence, fulsome and perfect. Her skin is a burnt umber with bluish veins throughout. Seka bows her head in respect. Her hair is a rich, luxuriant bluish black worn in a topknot, with tendrils of hair hanging down next to her ears. Yinhe smells a pleasant scent coming from Seka. It reminds her of forests.

As Rakan removes his mask, his feathery indigo feelers unfurl on top of his head. Large bulbous eyes sit on either side of his triangular pale-green head. *He looks like a cricket*, thinks Yinhe. *Or some kind of mantis.*

Seka speaks again, her voice deep and strong. "We've come to deliver an invitation from End Decoder. He would like to meet with you two nights from now."

Yinhe has only heard rumours about End Decoder – the de facto leader of Dream Zone.

"Why would he want to see me?"

"We're not at liberty to disclose anything. Suffice to say – End Decoder believes your objective and his might be compatible."

Yinhe frowns. "How would he know what my objective is?"

Seka replies, "Isn't it to recover Ling's soul?"

Yinhe's heart starts to race. "How do I know this isn't a trap?"

Rakan's voice is a rapid and shrill chitter. "Why would we want to set a trap for little inconsequential you?"

Yinhe draws back, annoyed by the creature's rudeness. "You managed to cross from Dream Zone without detection?"

His feelers moving with a flourish, Rakan retorts, "I go wherever I want to."

Seka adds in a calm tone, "We're shape-shifters like you, Unknown Wayfarer. We know the art of concealment."

Yinhe closes her eyes for a second. *Extraordinary. This moment is stranger than my tale.*

Seka continues, "I enjoyed your Storytelling Night. Most humans aren't aware of who or what you are. So much truth is communicated through stories. It fascinates me how the atmosphere is very much one of spectacle, with the humans dressed up in their own homemade masks and headgear. Utterly charming. And you even permit questions and conversation!"

Yinhe smiles at Seka's enthusiasm. However, she sounds like she's in some academic seminar – what the hell.

Seka continues, "Our mission is of great import. Although you've lived somewhat reclusively these past few years, End Decoder knows what you're capable of. He would like to converse with you about matters pertaining to your destiny and his and how they intertwine."

Yinhe is intrigued. Does Seka always talk like this?

Rakan's feelers cross and rub vigorously against each other. "We may be able to cross over to see you, but we can't afford to linger too long."

Seka says, "Remember, the meeting is in two nights' time – at the Hour of the Rat." Then she leans close to Yinhe's ear and whispers directions to End Decoder's lair. Yinhe feels her neck flush. As soon as Seka is done, she and Rakan slip the silicon masks back on their faces and fade into the night, as if eaten up by the darkness.

Before Second Escape
Outside of Time
THE UNDERWORLD

Gui is trapped within a cocoon woven with a sinewy substance so cold and impenetrable that the surface burns to the touch and pushes against Gui with an equal and opposite force.

Gui travels from one court of hell to another, making its rounds of all ten, in this oppressive capsule. The demon watches as some souls are dipped into cauldrons of boiling oil, others have their tongues ripped out and some are hung upside down by large hooks or ground to powder in mortars. When the cocoon passes through the seventh court of hell, three souls climb a mountain of knives, bleeding from their efforts. *Kau peh kau bu, whiny asses! At least they're able to move.*

Gui's cocoon was locked by a powerful spell cast by that nasty fox spirit when she dumped it back into the Underworld. Why did that vixen have to be working for Ao? To help humans, animals, whatever – it's bloody sickening.

The demon would give anything to have another chance in the physical realm. Gui envies the lucky buggers getting tortured – eventually they'll get out, acquire new bodies, do all kinds of fun things.

You want misery? Look at me, stuck here, eternally cold. The cold sears Gui to its very core. Such a paradox since it's naturally a chilling presence. Bah, too much of a good thing! Why is the Underworld not hot, anyway? It snarls. *Hell is what you can't overcome.* The demon detests this torment, prevented from preying on others.

Only one way it can escape. It had managed to do that once, far too long ago. It needs a human willing to be possessed. Not just any human, though – Gui has very discerning tastes for its host. The human has to be talented; in some position of influence. It wouldn't mind if the human is also attractive and sexy. A demon must have high, exacting standards. All the ones who disapprove, die!

Wait 'til I get out. I'm going to make you pay for this, it snarls, directing its hatred at the fox spirit. *I escaped once and I'll escape again.*

White Dew
Eighth Lunar Month, New Moon
2219 CE
BENT BACK, LUOYANG

"How was Storytelling Night?" Stanley drops his reading glasses onto the open book and squints up at Yinhe.

"Pa, here you are again, with so little light to read by!"

He waves his hand in front of his chest in that familiar way. "Never mind that. So, tell me!"

"Tonight was . . . a bit out of the ordinary."

"Oh?" Stanley raises his right eyebrow.

"There were two new audience members who joined the circle. They're not people, uh, that we know."

"What's so special about that? Bent Back may be small, but there are folks who don't hang around in the same circles as us." He shrugs and puts his glasses back on, then he looks at her, past his glasses. "Yinhe, I don't know how you do it. Treating people three afternoons a week and working as a security guard three other nights."

"You know me. I've always had a lot of energy. Storytelling Night is only an occasional thing, no big deal." Yinhe feels relieved that Pa didn't ask about the strangers. "I'm hungry. Going to cook soon. Nice stash of food from tonight. Come upstairs to eat with me?"

"Okay, okay. You go ahead and I'll come soon." Pa waves his hand once again to clearly say, *Leave me to do it my way.*

Upstairs in the kitchen, Yinhe transfers the food from her duffel bag to the countertop. She breaks six eggs into a bowl and whips them with a bit of water, salt and pepper and a splash of Pa's fermented wine. She soaks a handful of pickled vegetables to get rid of the saltiness, then adds them to the egg mixture. She places the bowl inside a bamboo steamer perched above boiling water in a deep pan. While this egg custard is steaming away, Yinhe throws minced garlic in the hot rapeseed oil in the cast-iron pan. When the garlic turns brown, she adds crickets, peanuts, a splash of soy sauce and black vinegar. At the last moment, she throws in chives from their rooftop garden.

Last but not least, she cooks up glass noodles, chills them in iced water, drains them and seasons with chili oil, sesame oil and soy sauce. Almost done. She turns off the heat on the steamed savoury egg custard and places all the food she's cooked on the table. She makes another infusion of pu'er tea and settles down at the table to wait for Pa.

No sound of Pa making his way upstairs. Does she need to call him? She decides to wait a few more minutes. Thoughts of Seka and Rakan are interrupted by the sound of Pa's footsteps.

Yinhe enters the familiar dream – the steep slope down to the water, the unhealthy yellow sky. She looks down at the turquoise water. She waits there at the edge. But Ao doesn't show up, no matter how much she argues with her dream. *Come on, doesn't it always happen the same way?*

Instead, Seka emerges from the water and climbs onto the rocks. She draws close to Yinhe. A heady scent – woodsy, reminiscent of sap and bark – causes Yinhe to feel slightly disoriented.

"You smell nice. But where's Ao? This isn't what I expected."

"Your heart summoned me. That's why you changed the dream," she says, holding Yinhe's face in her webbed hands. She kisses Yinhe lightly on the lips.

When Yinhe awakens, she's stunned by how the dream changed yet again – the arrogance of her dream self to have summoned Seka. She snorts and rolls over. Eight-thirty a.m. *Ridiculous, I must sleep another two hours.* She tosses around, restless from the altered dream. That scent! She can still smell it.

She reaches down to her pile of books on the floor and grabs the collection of writings by Zhuangzi. Where is that reference to the butterfly? She searches and finds it. *Ah, look at that last line!* She reads it aloud. "Between Zhuang Zhou and a butterfly there must be some distinction! This is called the Transformation of Things."

White Dew
Eighth Lunar Month
2219 CE
BRIGHT ORDER, LUOYANG

As usual, at this time of the night headquarters is quiet. Dr. Wen Fang stares out the windows. The laboratory has a series of windows that afford a great view – she can look out, but no one can see in, even at night. Hardly any lights are on in the adjoining buildings. Most of the staff are fast asleep in East Complexes 1 and 2 adjacent to HQ. Darkened windows could be deceptive, though, she realizes, as she knows that some HQ staff visit Interstitium after work.

Wen looks past the control panel at No. 1 suspended in fluid in the large transparent fibreglass cylinder. Weighing just over thirty-five kilograms, No. 1 was the brilliant invention of scientists in the late twenty-first century but hadn't been fully developed until the early twenty-second century, when a second team acquired a sperm whale brain and eventually managed to successfully introduce graft tissue from the original No. 1. A whole new No. 1 was created, one that had a far greater number of glia cells and an enormous neocortex. A hybrid that embodied the best of human and cetacean brains, this chimeric version of No. 1 has been operative for over a hundred years now.

No. 1 never gets to sleep, thinks Wen as she checks on its vital signs. *Over a hundred years of sleeplessness. Can we even compare?*

So far, No. 1 has malfunctioned a handful of times. For instance, shutting down some functions across various sectors of the city, or programmed pleasant simulations not playing on cue. Wen studies the graphs that show the malfunctions across sectors and over time. There seems to be no predictable pattern.

She looks up again at the giant brain. What had her predecessor and mentor, Dr. Peng, said? *We'll never know if its mere existence can begin to affect the environment around it.*

No. 1 embodies the pinnacle of Central Government's success, the scientific equivalent of a rock star. Central Government receives frequent requests from other governments for their scientific delegations to visit and learn from the scientists in HQ. But unbeknownst to those delegations, certain critical information is withheld so that no one else is truly able to attain what the scientists here have achieved.

Central Government prides itself on No. 1's powers. The super brain tracks everyone in Bright Order and Blue Otot through subdermal microchips that contain vital demographic information and history. Additionally, all the highly classified and skilled workers in Bright Order must have neural implants. That includes herself and the other scientists, technicians and programmers at HQ. No. 1 ensures a higher standard of productivity by erasing troubling psychological states, modifying the workers' levels of neurotransmitters and quelling excessive activation in their limbic systems.

No. 1 also compiles archival images and information and produces tableaux that are projected throughout the city, with the greatest number of tableaux in Interstitium. Wen has viewed the tableaux on screen in the lab – they're quite the marvel to behold. They simulate scenes that existed before the Great Catastrophe – forests, clear skies, humans suntanning on beaches or snorkelling in pristine ocean waters; often, there are displays of marine creatures as well as countless birds, animals and insects that existed before extinction.

No. 1 is a mindfucker extraordinaire messing with people's lives by controlling what ought to be left alone. Oh, but why even think of that too much? That was another world before the Great Catastrophe, before the age of cloning, genetic manipulation and brilliant feats of tissue grafting. If the scientists back in the twenty-first century could see what IIQ was doing these days, they'd be flabbergasted.

Wen never lets on that she thinks this way, of course. She overrides No. 1's log of her neural output if and when necessary, but she has only had to do it twice so far – when Dr. Peng passed away and when her boyfriend left her.

There hadn't been any noticeable deviations in No. 1's functioning in all the eleven years that she worked under Dr. Peng – none that she was aware of. Dr. Peng seemed quite distracted toward the end, though. Wen has always wondered what was behind his forced early retirement and then his sudden death. It troubles her, not knowing. She's sure that she's not the only one who wonders. *We don't dare talk about it.*

She understood what she was in for when she joined the team, on paper at least. Having all kinds of feelings about this commitment is another matter. *My life is devoted to sustaining this beast.* Like, what does she want to call it? Beast, monster, ugh. There's the occasional pang of regret when she glimpses children at the elite school. She reminds herself that at least her parents and two siblings get special benefits – more monthly food coupons, great access to health care, plus guaranteed spots in top universities for the siblings very soon. Wen frowns. *Are my parents really okay? How come they hardly use the medical services? Why don't the siblings want to come to the elite school here at Bright Order?* She slaps both her thighs with her hands and chides herself. *Stop your worrying, okay?*

She hasn't seen them in about fifteen years, not since the sibs were toddlers. But they do monthly video chats. Her mother is chatty; her father is not. Aloysius takes after their mother. Their stories about an event called Storytelling Night make her particularly incredulous. Sean likes going but doesn't gush. Meanwhile, Pa doesn't go. He has a scowl on his face while Ma and Aloysius wax on about the storyteller. What a family.

Wen gets up from her chair and switches on the other lights behind No. 1. She checks the levels of various electrolytes displayed on the vertical panels. The changes are barely discernible – spikes and dips so minute that no one else has noticed them; if they did, they must have dismissed them.

She, however, is convinced that there's something important about these fluctuations. She'd like to find out what's happening without alerting the others yet. What would Dr. Peng do if he were here? She misses him.

Central Government has many supercomputers that can perform many functions, but none of them are able to sense and respond to humans' emotions the way No. 1 can. She feels the weight of responsibility on her shoulders – she must discover the problem behind No. 1's failures and resolve it.

Wen laces the fingers of both hands together on her lap as she sits at the console, looking past the equipment to the dark outside. She doesn't want to think about the repercussions if she fails.

White Dew
Eighth Lunar Month
702 CE
FOREIGN QUARTER, CHANG'AN

Ardhanari yawns loudly in bed and stretches. There's the neighbourhood rooster, right on time, signalling sunrise. He hears Sita
below, talking to the other jogappas about cleaning inside the
café before they open for business. He gets up and looks out his
window at the water fountain below. He can just make out movements inside the café through the open doorway – the flash of
someone's sari, an arm holding a broom, feet in jute slippers dart-
ing back and forth. Then Lakshmi and Gita bring rugs out to air,
all while chirping in bright, excited tones to each other.

He imagines creating a large tableau, an outdoor mural fea-
turing the life of his beloved Sita and the other jogappa sisters
– Lakshmi, Indra, Gita and Devi – singing, playing instruments
and dancing. If only the murals in the Mogao Caves could include
people like his loved ones. Sita was born here in Chang'an, but
the other jogappas fled India because they were condemned for
being different. People expected them to act like men just because
they were born with male bodies. Their lives were threatened by
family members and other villagers. He's happy that the jogappas
have created this sanctuary for themselves and others at the café
here in the Foreign Quarter.

Sometimes he asks himself what he would like to do instead
of making and repairing sculptures, but it has been his whole life
from a young age. It is all that he has known.

He reaches for the bamboo tube under the bed and sits at
the table overlooking the window. He pulls the drawing out of
the tube, surprised how much he wants to look at it. He's tried to
copy the drawing, but every time his hand freezes up. Ardhanari
wonders if anyone before him has ever tried and discovered the
same problem. There must be a spell in the drawing. He doesn't
know what to do with this kind of magic, whereas the magic he

has witnessed in humans, like his jogappa friends, he can easily appreciate. Ardhanari shrugs his shoulders a few times as if to shake off his discomfort.

This morning, he's going to try something different. He picks up a charcoal stick and asks, half-jokingly, "If you won't let me copy you, what would you like me to draw instead?"

His hand moves outside of his conscious control. He watches, a helpless participant, until the image is fully formed. A fox! Then he draws the sun overhead, partially hidden by clouds. Are the rays of light that touch the fox's head coming from the sun or from the fox? There's a tunnel or maze of sorts running underground.

"Well, now," he mumbles, unsure if he's simply talking to himself or to the force that moved his hand. "I don't know what to make of this."

Ardhanari purses his lips as he stares nervously at the drawing. It just doesn't make sense. He suspects that Baoshi would appreciate it – after all, Mount Hua is home to many mysterious presences. Ardhanari felt them while he was out in the forest, usually at dusk. One night, while standing at the door of the shack and looking at the night sky, he heard some kind of animal cry that he hadn't recognized.

He closes his eyes and thinks of the young Harelip. A beautiful soul, the outer deformity was never ugly to Ardhanari because he could see past the appearance to the beauty beneath it.

This is the room where Ardhanari first kissed him. Harelip hadn't had any sexual experience before, yet he so easily opened up. He showed no signs of recoil when Ardhanari penetrated him, and he was unashamed at expressing pleasure; he even showed unconcealed delight in satisfying Ardhanari.

All their encounters occurred in this room. It was their sanctuary. They spent many happy times together, although each visit could never be too long because Harelip had to return to his duties at Da Ci'en Monastery.

Every time Ardhanari reminisces, he's right back in that boundless joy. He smiles wistfully. He looks at his hands. The years have changed them. The veins are more pronounced, the fingers slightly deformed by swelling, his right pinky not quite right after an accident. His hands remember, too, how they caressed Harelip's face and enjoyed his lover's tremors.

"Hmmm," he says softly to himself, "maybe you will grieve for a long time, but maybe you will also be consoled."

The Second Escape
2214 CE
INTERSTITIUM, LUOYANG

Ever since it lost possession of the oracle bone to the fox spirit and was locked in the Underworld, Gui has been scanning the physical realm for the twin to the turtle plastron. The plastron might be back with Ao, but the Tibetan drawing offers Gui a glimmer of liberation. If the demon manages to unlock the power of the drawing, it will have a chance to permanently escape the Underworld. Gui is sure that it can harness Ao's divine power to reverse the curse that keeps it imprisoned in the Underworld. *I can smell the power, what! But first I need another volunteer.*

It's the icon above the front doors of Supreme Spirit Assembly that first catches Gui's attention. Two neon gourd vessels, their open mouths tipped toward each other, spill golden liquid into a lake. Cheesy.

Lurking in the rafters, the demon spies on a few of the assembly's services. From a space outside of human perception, Gui sees how charismatic Eoin is. *This one, huh, he likes to act high class.* Late at night, when Eoin is by himself, Gui sneaks up behind him. In its smoothest sales voice, careful to avoid using swear words, vernacular or dialect, the demon whispers seductively into Eoin's left ear. *We share the same vision. We want humans to be attuned to a higher spirit. I can help you achieve your ambition.*

Eoin finds this proposition irresistible. As soon as Gui gains possession of Eoin, it loses no time in capitalizing on Eoin's disdain of chimeric creatures and his strong prejudice against "impurities" of bloodlines.

Whispering in proper putonghua into Eoin's left ear, Gui says, *There's a powerful treasure that ought to be returned to humans. It shouldn't remain in the hands of a female chimeric creature. Let me tell you more . . .*

It thinks to itself, *Wah, some humans will do anything for power! And they pretend they're so religious, hor.*

White Dew
Eighth Lunar Month
2219 CE
INTERSTITIUM, LUOYANG

The next night, at quarter to eleven, Yinhe sets out for her shift at the casino in Interstitium. It's a walkable distance from Bent Back, a pleasant twenty minutes. The weather is surprisingly mild and clear tonight after the strong winds earlier in the day.

The wider streets in Interstitium are abuzz with people getting on and off the light rail cars, strolling past shops or checking out the eating and drinking establishments. A cacophony of electronic music streams from shops.

The projected tableaux rise above the two- and three-storey buildings, visually stunning and ever evolving. Along one street, seals and whales frolic in a virtual world above the harsh streetlights. On another street, it's all about forests, ferns and mushrooms. The main avenue features stunning displays of mountains from different parts of the planet.

In contrast, in the quiet shadowy areas, drug dealers and their customers complete transactions over designer drugs customized to each person's neural profile.

Yinhe takes the longer route as usual, avoiding the street where Spirit Supreme Assembly is located. At the entrance to the three-storeyed Crystal Entertainment Dome, she presses both thumbs against the scanning pad and nods at the security guards who wave her past.

The main floor is one large room with low lighting along the perimeter while strobe lights define the stage. The customers are mostly drunk, some of them rowdier than others, flirting with the wait staff and throwing money at the dancers onstage. The dancers are foreigners selected for their exotic looks – light-skinned, blue eyes, blonds and redheads. She finds two of the eight particularly attractive, but there's no way she's going to try to get close. She's been bitten too many times.

She's starving by the time she gets to the staff kitchen. She eats her fill from the buffet spread, takes a few extras in her container to bring back to Pa, then proceeds to the change room. She hangs up her denim jacket, stashes her backpack inside the locker, then changes into her work outfit. Her pants are an ink-black denim with wide-flared legs. Her top is a sheer hemp fabric shell. She straps on her sling holster and places her left index finger on the button, which only works with her fingerprint. The safety on the slim stun gun releases. She checks the gun before slipping it back into its paddle. It clicks securely into place just below her right breast. Finally, she throws on the jacket of green-and-black zigzags with gold stitching. On the top left corner of her jacket is the logo for Crystal Entertainment Dome, a sparkling diamond with the initials CED embroidered in bright red over the white crystal. She detests this jacket – it manages to be insipid yet gaudy. Someone was probably paid a ton of money to create this visual atrocity. She ties the jacket loosely at the front above her navel so that it would be easy to access the stun gun. Then she sits down on the metal bench to put on the flat-soled ninja boots. *Another fucking cliché.*

When she's ready, Yinhe heads down the hallway toward the elevator. She presses her right thumb against the security pad. It takes a mere three seconds before the elevator arrives. When she enters, she speaks into the microphone – her name, her security password. Her voice pattern activates the elevator, and the doors close with a barely perceptible swishing sound before it swiftly delivers her to the private casino on the top floor.

Compared to the entertainment lounge downstairs, the overhead lights in this casino are far brighter. This private room is a quarter of the size of the public casino downstairs; still, it's a large elongated room, with an adjacent lounge area. Digitally programmed soundscapes of waves are piped throughout the room. Meanwhile, the room is cloaked in a murk of cigar and cigarette smoke. She squints, nods to the other three security guards on duty. She scans the room and counts twenty patrons gambling at five stations.

Shortly after half past two, while watching over the black-jack table, there's a crash behind her. She wheels around to see the businessman Mr. Chung propped up at the elbows by two security guards. There are shards of glass on the carpet. Two servers rush to clear up the mess.

Also known as the "White Stallion," Mr. Chung points to Yinhe as he awkwardly weaves around the servers cleaning up. Yinhe has seen him at the casino many times but has never directly dealt with him. He comes within an arm's length of her and plants his feet wide apart, looking her up and down.

"You're kinda short . . . tiny . . . like a kid . . . and your brown skin, not pure Han Chinese, I suspect. What's underneath that flashy kaiju outfit of yours, huh?" Mr. Chung smiles lasciviously at her and rocks left to right to left. He stinks of alcohol and smoke. "Aren't you the one whose opponent died in the ring? Heard about it. Then you stopped competitive fighting. Took this boring job as a security guard." He burps once, very loudly.

What a creep, thinks Yinhe. She slips her left hand under her jacket, index finger above the release button on the holster. She would love to zap him in the groin.

He grunts. "You know about the upcoming call to challenge Tollund, the bog mummy?"

Yinhe nods. "Uh-huh. Heard about it."

He leans toward her and breathily utters, "Listen, here's my proposition."

Yinhe crosses her arms in front of her. "Okay, shoot."

"If you return to the ring and defeat Tollund – and I'm going to bet you won't be able to – I will double the prize money, which is already listed as five hundred thousand in gold coin. That makes it one million in gold coin – how can you resist?"

Yinhe feels the skin at the back of her neck prickle. It takes supreme effort not to bare her fangs and snarl at him. Bloody tycoons – they act as if they can get everything they ask for. He may be known as White Stallion, with his long mane of white hair and lanky form that makes others think of a horse, but in her mind he's a fossilized donkey turd. He wants to watch her be beaten to a pulp by the infamous bog mummy, huh? Just so he can get his rocks off. Pervert. What was that nonsense anyway about her looking like a kid?

"Now what would I do with all that money, Mr. Chung, sir?"

His face turns deep red and he scowls. He closes his fingers into fists on either side of his torso and leans threateningly toward Yinhe. "Why, you stinky –"

Yinhe backs away with her hands held up, palms facing Mr. Chung. Two security guards are now right behind Mr. Chung, ready to act.

"I'm telling you – it's a lot of money." He glares threateningly at her, his eyes bloodshot.

Yinhe feels heat rise to the back of her neck. She wishes she could clobber this lout right now. She angles her body slightly away from him and purses her lips, deliberating what to do. It won't be for the money, even though it would be so handy for improving some folks' lives in Bent Back: fixing those rickety outdoor elevators between the Levels, for one thing; repairs to homes; so many things.

Nope, she would do it just because it's a chance to finally get past her block. She locks his gaze with hers. "Just because you asked, Mr. Chung, I'll oblige."

She watches as Mr. Chung's breathing finally slows down.

"It's a deal." He nods before stumbling backward. The guards rush up to support him by the arms and direct him into the adjoining lounge.

The remaining hour in her shift passes without further incident. When her shift ends, she returns to the change room. She takes a long drink of water from her flask. Wow – so she's finally returning to the ring? Memories of what occurred in that last fight flash through her mind. She can still see the guy's face as he backed away from her in the third round. This was after she delivered a series of punches at his head, then his right torso. He gasped, clutched at his chest, then went down on his knees. Then he fell face forward. It was too late by the time the ambulance came. How could she feel victorious when her opponent had died? She swore that she'd never fight again.

Yinhe starts walking in the direction of Bent Back. She surprised herself tonight with her decision. She detests people who taunt her, who sexualize her while being so fucking condescending. Her face flushes red again.

She distracts herself by once again thinking of the many people and projects in Bent Back that will benefit from the prize money. This thought strengthens her resolve. *It's time, it's time,* she repeats to herself. She wants to get past her block and resume professional fighting. Enough of this boring security guard job. She hates being bored.

She's still thinking about this when she hears the sounds of struggle up ahead to her left. Two humans are beating up a chimeric slave in a dark corner. She sniffs the attackers' scents – two males. She recognizes the creature – she works as a cleaner at the Dome. She's half-crouched on the ground with her arms over her head.

"Think you can escape? You haven't finished paying your debt off," says one of the assailants.

The other one chuckles. "We'll make sure you suffer for this."

Yinhe pulls her baseball cap over her eyes and steps in. "Hey, what's up? Beating up a helpless slave, huh?"

The guys look at her, stunned. One of them speaks up, "Well, aren't you rude to interrupt? Now there's two of you to mess up."

"Wanna bet?"

Before they can act, she throws a left jab at the guy closest to her, aiming at the right side of his face, and follows swiftly with a forceful right palm push against his sternum. He is flung back, and his head smashes against the wall behind him. He's knocked out and slumps to the ground.

"You. Next." She gestures to the other guy. "Come on."

She delivers a roundhouse kick to his left side, then knees him very hard in the groin. Bent forward, he yells in pain, clutching at his balls. She clasps both hands into fists and leaps, bringing her hands down on the back of the guy's neck. He crumbles, hits the pavement face down.

"Well, that was easy," she says, turning to the slave. "How much do you owe these motherfuckers, anyway?"

The slave, wide-eyed, whimpers. "I, uh, had two hundred left to pay."

Yinhe fishes out five hundred and places the bills into the slave's hand. "Hey, get out of here, before these jerks come to."

The slave is rooted to the spot. Yinhe blows a stream of air against her face to revive her. "Go on now. Quickly."

Yinhe keeps watch until the chimeric creature disappears around the corner. The guy closest to her moans. She flips him over with her foot, grabs the front of his shirt and lifts him until his feet are a few inches off the ground before dropping him. He stumbles, still wobbly and dazed.

"Here's the money she owed you. Leave her alone, or you'll be getting another beating from me. You hear?" She throws two hundred dollars on the ground at his feet. He mumbles inaudibly.

"What did you say? Louder now." She grabs the front of his shirt again and shakes him vigorously.

"Okay, okay . . ."

The guy behind him starts to regain consciousness.

"Remember what I said." She releases her grip and punches the first guy in the gut, gives him a second kick in the groin. He groans and doubles over. Yinhe bolts down the street, disappearing long before the attackers can fully recover.

Summer Solstice
Fifth Lunar Month
2217 CE
INTERSTITIUM, LUOYANG

Two years from now, I'm telling you, we need to do a ritual. Are you listening?

Eoin acts as if he hasn't heard the voice of Spirit. He's come to the conclusion that this voice must be some kind of aberration, weird programming from a past life or a dissociated psychological fragment. Seems to him that he mustn't obey everything it suggests. He changes out of his red velvet robes after the service and into a black linen shirt and khaki pants. Phoebe will be arriving in a couple of hours, and he's looking forward to dinner and sex. He locks up the front and back doors of the main hall and heads to the cottage.

Just what kind of a ridiculous notion is it to propose exhibiting the Tibetan drawing to raise money for Spirit Supreme Assembly? Am I not Spirit? How dare you disobey me?

Eoin puts the rack of lamb into the oven, along with the Brussels sprouts, yams and carrots. Easy. He feels a series of painful stabs inside his gut and holds onto the kitchen counter, talks aloud to himself. "You must be some, some unhealed part of me. I'm not going to give in to this lower vibration. I'm the leader of Spirit Supreme Assembly, and I'll do what's the highest good." He sits down in his favourite armchair with a glass of brandy, feeling proud of himself.

Gui is unhappy with Eoin. *I am going to switch*, the demon decides. Although Gui hasn't asked Phoebe directly, it suspects she will receive it willingly. Phoebe possesses unashamed drive combined with a hunger for the guidance of a higher reality. She wants a religion that doesn't hem her in. She wants order because she hates chaos. Plus, she has aspirations to be the equivalent of a female emperor just like Wu Zhao.

The demon knows how things work while Phoebe and Eoin are having sex. She likes to take him, as opposed to being taken. Tonight, as usual, Phoebe rides Eoin, her legs straddling him. She gasps with the exertion, covered with sweat. Almost, almost. Phoebe leans down toward Eoin to kiss.

Phoebe is close to orgasm. Intense, frenetic kissing is always the precursor. Eoin gasps loudly, his eyes widen and his throat is seized by a powerful contraction as Gui exits him through the mouth and enters Phoebe through her mouth. She feels an immense force overcome her, and she shudders forcefully, jerking her head backward. She faints, falling forward onto Eoin.

When she wakes, she pushes herself up slowly. Her hands touch Eoin's chest. Cold. His eyes are lifeless. She screams and pulls away from his body, stumbling off the bed, and hits her elbow against the night light, toppling it over.

In the dark, she hears a voice that's low and gravelly. Where is it? She's confused, realizes it's coming from inside her. *He failed me*, whispers Gui. *But you will succeed where he could not.*

"Who are you?" She trembles from head to foot, slinks down to the floor and curls up in a fetal position.

I am Spirit. I know you. I will make you powerful.

She feels Spirit rush deeper into her gut and extend itself up to her arms and down to her legs. It brings a cool, even icy, stillness from her belly down to her sex. It is a painful thing to be so overcome with Spirit; but it is a particular kind of pain that is accompanied by pleasure.

You mustn't say a thing to anyone, warns Gui. *Remember how different your life was before you joined Spirit Supreme.*

White Dew
Eighth Lunar Month, Two Nights after New Moon
2219 CE
DREAM ZONE, LUOYANG

Yinhe whispers the spell, transforms into wind energy and crosses into Dream Zone. It is just past ten in the evening – or, according to the ancient way of telling time, halfway into the Hour of the Pig, in the middle of the Second Watch that lasts from nine to eleven. She has plenty of time before she has to meet End Decoder at eleven, the start of the Hour of the Rat.

The two border guards are seated in their checkpoint enclosures on either side of a large metal gate that's locked. Before she passes through the gaps of the metal bars, she decides to be cheeky and blow into the ear of one of them. They wriggle their shoulders and raise their hand to rub their ear, as if there's some kind of insect there. Yinhe delivers another blast of warm air into their ear, and the guard blushes and looks around, puzzled.

Once safely into Dream Zone, she changes back into her material form and follows the directions that Seka gave her. The street names are rather colourful – names like Endless Regret, Point of No Return, Desire's Folly.

Yinhe tastes the air with her tongue – salty and sharp with a touch of bitterness, like the inside of a raw gourd. A chilling silence pervades the streets, while in the distance she hears the sounds of whirring and dull clanks. The ground below her feet vibrates slightly. She bends down and positions her ear close to the stone pavement. Are there processing plants underground? A drone zooms by overhead. She slips into the shadows of a recessed doorway to avoid detection.

Her fox hearing picks up a range of subtle soundscapes. The atmosphere in Dream Zone is drenched in waves of sighs and murmurs. Her throat seizes up, and she coughs a couple of times. The air is bad. She ties a handkerchief around the lower half of her face to cover her nose and mouth.

Yinhe spots a girl ghost ahead sitting on the cobblestoned street. A tattered blue shawl is draped over her head but soon falls to the ground, covering her feet. As Yinhe draws near, she realizes that the ghost has no eyes, yet tears fall from hollow orifices, making a soft tinkling sound as they hit the brass bowl in her lap. Yinhe walks past her.

"Please, won't you feed me?" On hearing this, Yinhe turns around. The ghost has transformed into a vision of a childhood friend, the one who was poisoned by radioactive experiments some twelve years before.

"What the . . ."

"How could you abandon your friend?" The girl ghost opens her mouth wide, and the cavernous opening reveals humans drowning in a vast sea of flames.

Yinhe shudders. She's unnerved by the question more than by the dreadful vision.

"I can smell the animal in you," sneers the apparition just before she disappears.

Yinhe takes a deep breath and continues on. She encounters several other apparitions – a male in military uniform with no arms, a cat nursing their kittens, a flailing snake with fire in its belly. And yet, unlike the girl ghost, these other apparitions don't engage directly with her.

As Yinhe walks through the labyrinthine streets and alleys, it occurs to her that Dream Zone is the antithesis of Bright Order – full of unsettling aspects that would be judged hideous, inadequate or wrong by many humans.

She turns into the alley with the name Grasping that connects to another alley, Sticking, until she reaches a flight of stone stairs. She goes down these stairs until she reaches a street called Glamour. She walks west on this street for exactly twenty-three long breaths until she reaches a sign for Crimson End.

She looks up to the third floor, at the orange-tinted light that's visible behind the iron grill of the balcony. She approaches the door and buzzes. A loud click comes over the intercom, and Yinhe utters the code phrase that she'd been told to use: "Cinnabar Crimson has best views from the terrace."

A long buzz accompanies the unlocking of the metal gate. As soon as she enters through the door, the gate closes behind her. She touches the whip tucked inside her denim jacket – it's there if she needs to use it. She takes her time walking up the flight of stairs. On the third floor, both metal gate and door are already open. The large room is dimly lit from the luxurious golden glow of incandescent light bulbs. This is both a shock and a pleasure. Her father had five precious bulbs, but they are now all used up and gone.

She removes her scarf and tucks it into her jacket. To her left, spanning the length of the room, is a long row of bookcases filled with musty old books. She makes a quick estimate – must be at least thirty volumes on each shelf, five shelves per bookcase and a total of eight bookcases. Twelve hundred books? Staggering.

"Welcome, Unknown Wayfarer. Come in." A powerful deep voice booms from the far end of the room, from behind a large wingback swivel chair.

Resting her hand on the wood balustrade to her right, Yinhe walks slowly toward the swivel chair and that voice. She sniffs softly to see if she can sense what kind of creature End Decoder is. She detects a smell reminiscent of marshes and stagnant water.

As she walks toward him, she glances at the titles on the spines of books. Some of the lettering has worn away. *Frankenstein, Darkness at Noon, Brave New World, Do Androids Dream of Electric Sheep?* and *Fahrenheit 451*. There's another bookshelf with titles in other languages.

How did a chimeric creature manage to amass so many books without government officials knowing? Surely CG officials would seize and destroy these books if they learned of their existence. She recognizes a book that her father owns – *Shanhaijing*, also known as *The Classic of Mountains and Seas*.

Although the length of the room is perhaps ten metres at most, it seems to Yinhe that it's taking a very long time for her to reach the other end. She perceives the room as wobbling and distorted. When she nears the desk, the chair creaks as it swivels. She blinks at the presence across from her and stifles a gasp.

The creature is formidable yet exquisite. End Decoder's eyes are heavily lidded angled slits on either side of his head. Specks of whitish deposits collect along the rims of his eyes. He resembles a lizard, except that he sits upright. In fact, he has perfect posture. His skin is sooty black with occasional patches of yellow. The surface appears smooth but betrays contours shaped like fish scales. When he shifts around in the chair, the yellow patches on his skin flash in the light. His snout is prominent, and his nostrils flare expressively at her. He has two front limbs with four claw-like appendages on each, which he rests on the surface of the desk. Yinhe wonders if he has a tail, but it would be rude to check. She focuses instead on his eyes.

"Apa kabar?" he asks, in a language that Yinhe hasn't heard for many lifetimes. She sighs softly, recalling the smells and sounds of the ocean. End Decoder's voice is deep, a baritone that's mellow and smooth. It's a slingsong accent, pleasant.

"Kabar baik," she replies.

"We are far inland, but our ancestral connections are to the ocean and the archipelago."

Yinhe nods in acknowledgement. Despite her caution, she has reasons to like him already.

"Sila duduk, please sit down." End Decoder gestures with his front left limb at the chair. "Did you guess you'd be meeting a chimeric salamander this evening?"

"An honour to meet you, End Decoder. No, I didn't know what to expect."

Yinhe sits down, exposes her inside pocket so that End Decoder sees her whip. Her oxidized steel bangles clang noisily against each other when she clasps her hands together in greeting.

"Ah, you won't need to defend yourself against me, darling." He winks at her as he says this.

Cheeky, she thinks, but stifles a smile.

End Decoder's chest vibrates vigorously as he speaks. "May I preface our conversation by saying that even though Central

Government tracks the activities of chimeric creatures through subdermal microchips and overhead surveillance systems, we have brilliant hackers and technology nerds among us who scramble signals and block surveillance when needed."

"Meaning this conversation is free from being tracked."

"Absolutely correct, Unknown Wayfarer. However sophisticated No. 1 is, it has yet to decode the complex systems chimeric creatures use through sounds, vibrations and gestures. Through a secret language, we have evaded attempts to spy on us."

"That's great. They underestimate Dream Zone."

End Decoder nods, his long snout dipping slightly as he does so.

"Let me begin by telling you a bit about myself. As you could infer from my use of Bahasa Melayu, I have connections to the Orang Laut in the ancient archipelagos south of us. I am birthed from DNA of the fire salamander combined with human DNA. The oceans and rivers sing in my cells. Technically speaking, the human scientists built on what was known about horizontal gene transfer. Organ transplants and reintegration with higher-level gene splicing. To those scientists, I was, to paraphrase Mary Shelley, the Adam of their labours. But I am far more than those genetic characteristics."

Yinhe thinks, *This guy sure reads a lot. Or he just likes to collect books. And quotes.*

"Why have you asked me here?"

"I have summoned you because I need your help, Unknown Wayfarer. No one else can do what I'm about to ask."

"How can you be so sure?"

"Because you have a special connection with Ao."

"How did you know that?" Yinhe's pulse quickens, and the hairs on the back of her neck stand up.

End Decoder slowly gets up from his chair and moves to the bookshelf closest to him. "Let's see, where is it . . . that's the problem when you forget your own system of shelving . . . hmmm . . ."

He moves along, his tail swishing against the bamboo flooring. Yinhe turns her body slightly, watching him. Now she knows

– his tail is over a metre long and has the same yellow markings and texture as the rest of his body.

End Decoder finally spots what he's looking for, places the large book down on the desk and stands next to where she's seated. The scent of seaweed coming off him makes her slightly light-headed. She looks at the cover of the book. It is a deep ocean blue, soothing to the eyes. End Decoder opens the book to pages 25 and 26.

"Look here," he says to Yinhe, as he points to an image that stretches across both pages.

It's a drawing of the Great Turtle Ao. End Decoder turns to pages 27 and 28. Another drawing of Ao, but this time it's floating above a fox who is squeezed in what appears to be a fissure in a gigantic object.

"What's this?"

"The Ancients say that it's you." End Decoder raps his claw on the image of the fox.

She frowns, perplexed. "Who are the Ancients?"

"Patience, sayang. I'll get to that."

End Decoder closes the book and returns it to its place on the shelf. He sits back down in his chair. "Unknown Wayfarer, I understand your need to be guarded, but bear with me and I will explain. I know my way of speaking is a bit circuitous for you . . . but it's how my mind works."

He reaches a claw out toward Yinhe, and her neck muscles instantly tighten. She relaxes when she sees that he's going for the small circular glass dish between them – it's filled to the brim with luminescent, multicoloured candies. He pops two into his mouth and exhales in satisfaction.

"There's a Tibetan drawing I would like you to recover."

"What's so important about this drawing?"

"It is a magical diagram of Ao."

Yinhe leans slightly forward, intrigued. "Well, okay. You just showed me a couple of drawings of Ao. What's different about the Tibetan drawing?"

"The Tibetan drawing has a very specific function, but it needs an animate being to unlock its power. And not just anyone, mind you." End Decoder pauses and leans back in the swivel chair. He has a faraway look in his eyes, as if he's thinking of something or someone else.

After a few moments of silence, he resumes. "The drawing was supposed to have been handed down through the eons in a continuous line of inheritance. But there have been two breaks in that continuity. One interruption happened in the human realm when someone suffered a sudden death before he could pass the drawing on. The Ancients tell us that the monk Xuanzang passed it to his trusted disciple, who then felt it ought to be handed to someone with whom he had a profound relationship. But that person – who knows why – was very uneasy in his relationship with the drawing. Was that why he couldn't pass it on? The drawing languished, hidden, for over twelve hundred years, until it was found by a French explorer. Then, eight years ago, it was passed on to one of us."

Yinhe raises her eyebrows.

"It was the first time the drawing passed from the human realm to the chimeric realm. But three years after she gained the drawing, that creature was killed and the drawing taken." End Decoder makes the gesture to signify that the creature had been a female.

A heat suffuses Yinhe's neck and face. "Murdered five years ago – for the drawing?"

"Yes."

Yinhe has a queasy feeling in her gut. "How do you know all this?"

"She was my sister."

Yinhe looks at End Decoder's face. A tear appears at the corner of End Decoder's left eye but stays there, suspended. She lowers her gaze. When she finally looks up at End Decoder, she sees the tear trickling down to his jawline. They both remain silent for what seems like a long time before End Decoder speaks again.

"That was the most recent break in the line of inheritance. The drawing ended up in the hands of Eoin, the original founder of the Spirit Supreme Assembly. Eoin died two years ago of mysterious causes. Since then, the woman Phoebe, your earth mother, heads this movement."

Yinhe rises up from her seat and grasps the edge of the desk. "What . . . the . . ." She leans forward. "No one has told me any news about her since she left my father. I knew she went to Spirit Supreme Assembly, but I had no idea she'd become the leader."

"Sila duduk, darling. Sila duduk."

She slinks back into her chair, her heart racing.

"She was Eoin's lover for two decades. Maybe more . . . Did you know that Spirit Supreme Assembly is backed by Central Government? Its members are largely prominent members of government, financial powerhouses and corporations."

"I'm not surprised to hear about CG backing the assembly. But no, I didn't know that, about Phoebe, I mean . . . I tend to ignore news about that place." Yinhe starts to nervously tap the index and middle fingers of her left hand on the desk. "Why is this Tibetan drawing so important?"

"Think of it as twin to the oracle bone – the special turtle plastron you retrieved many lifetimes ago and ultimately returned to Ao. You see, the demon Gui has returned to this physical realm, and it wants the means to summon Ao and conquer it."

"Gui is back?" Yinhe bares her teeth and snarls. She recalls her last battle with the demon. It took all her power to defeat it and return it to the Underworld.

"Yes. Gui escaped the Underworld when Eoin welcomed the demon into his person. Then, directed by Gui, he engineered the theft of the Tibetan drawing. Since Eoin's death, Gui has moved into Phoebe's person."

"Shit." Yinhe groans loudly. "If this drawing is so powerful, why hasn't Gui used it yet?"

"The demon needs a certain being to be present in order to access that power; also, the time has to be right."

"I dread what you're about to say."

"Sayang, dear fox, you guessed it – you're the one that needs to be there."

Yinhe feels shivers travel down her spine. "End Decoder, what you've shared is having a big impact on me. You know that I've had a few lifetimes doing what I can to help humans and non-humans. If you'll excuse me for sounding selfish – what's in it for me? Why would I want to do what you're proposing?"

End Decoder opens his jaws wide in a grin. "Ah, I like your candour. If you acquire the Tibetan drawing and decode it, there's a good chance you will reunite with Ling, the soul you lost many lifetimes ago."

Yinhe's eyes widen in surprise. "Who tells you these things?"

"The Ancients, of course. I'm just the messenger."

She purses her lips. This is the first time anyone has ever suggested such a possibility. What if it's some massive scheme to deceive and entrap her? On the other hand, if it's true and she passes on this chance, she will never forgive herself.

"Okay, tell me more."

"An important astrological conjunction will occur this year during the season known as Start of Winter. Jupiter and Saturn will visibly form a grand conjunction, and the sky will be festooned with Geminid meteors. During the Hour of the Tiger, the veils between what is past, present and future will be thin. Gui has been waiting for the right time. Phoebe will conduct a ritual and thence allow Gui to unlock the power of the Tibetan drawing."

"Holy crow."

"If the codes in the drawing are correctly invoked at Start of Winter – this would summon Ao to our physical realm. Then whatever happens, well . . . we don't know. But we certainly wouldn't want Gui to make mischief using that power."

"Does Phoebe know?"

"She may be possessed by Gui, but the demon hasn't told her everything. She thinks this ritual will allow her to gain more power. Since it is Gui's intent to destroy anyone that stands in its way, it's likely that she and those in Central Government – all of us for that matter – could suffer enslavement to Gui. Or even obliteration."

"Fucking hell." Yinhe's jawline tenses. "You're betting that I could get the better of Gui."

"Why not? You stopped the demon last time."

"Yes, but . . ." She doesn't want to think about losing Ling's soul, but the memory arrives despite her fighting against it. "Gui wasn't happy to lose the oracle bone the last time we met. And then . . . to be returned to the Underworld."

"Of course, you're meant to meet again."

"Hah. Some have inner demons, but I have Gui, that outer demon who plagues me."

End Decoder opens his jaws wide and makes a series of rasping sounds, like a saw against metal.

Yinhe frowns. "All Gui wants is power for power's sake."

"A certain prophecy has been kept secret by the Ancients, whispered only to a few of us, my sister included – that a half-human, half-fox spirit is the ultimate heir to this drawing and holds the key to unlock its secret."

"End Decoder, that's the third – or is it the fourth – time you've mentioned the Ancients. Hell's bells! Are you going to get around to telling me?"

Another series of rasping sounds from End Decoder. "They're beings who came from distant galaxies and shared their knowledge with humans, or, rather, the predecessors of humans. All that history has been lost except to a handful of sentient beings. Such history was passed down in myths through storytelling and songs. Most humans over time relinquished such wisdom and surrendered to those who promised power to them. Only a few beings – human and non-human – remain open to the ancient wisdom of the galaxies. You're one of them, Unknown Wayfarer. Since you are both human and fox, the Ancients believe that your very presence is the key that will unlock the power to summon Ao."

"You must go somewhere to meet with these Ancients, right?"

"And you want to know where that is."

"Of course."

End Decoder swivels back to face the window. He gets up from his chair and waves Yinhe over. "Look out there." He points to the northeast. "Look beyond the city limits."

Yinhe stands next to End Decoder and uses her fox vision to scan the far horizon, the dark outlines of the mountain range. Wait . . . a glimmer of movement. *Odd, it's not light; doesn't seem like something made by humans.*

"You see it?"

"Uh-huh. So that's where the Ancients are."

They both sit back down and look at each other, deep in their own thoughts.

"I'll take you there soon." The chimeric salamander reaches for a tissue and blows hard. "Hate this humidity. Not used to these recent proliferations of spores." He flings the tissue into the instant waste converter. Yinhe catches sight of blobs of crimson-coloured mucus before the machine eats it up.

"Where will this ritual at Start of Winter be conducted?"

"On the ancient road between this city and what had been the city of Chang'an."

Yinhe shudders. Déjà vu.

"As you know, those of us in Dream Zone have been exiled from the other enclaves. Humans think that chimeric creatures are good only for hard labour, to power nuclear plants or manufacture electronic parts for their computers, or to fulfill the sexual needs of humans in Interstitium. We're the freaks that Central Government takes for granted. Their power consists in alienating us while they use us.

"In Dream Zone, we've adapted to living in this radioactive wasteland, generating energy and processing nuclear waste. We make the humans look and feel good, don't we? But we've developed and evolved beyond their experiments. We're becoming stronger, more resilient. We have capacities they aren't even aware of. They keep us cordoned off in this gulag of sorrows. Well, this isn't going to last for much longer."

"I take it that you're hoping the power unlocked by the Tibetan drawing could radically change things."

"Yes, indeed. This is about overturning the cursed paradigm that has oppressed us. We need to awaken from this nightmare, this horrible illusion that we're separate." End Decoder blows his snout loudly again.

The words carved into the oracle bone come to Yinhe's mind: *A dream wants waking, a sky needs light.*

"I do think that Ao will respond favourably to you when you invoke the power of the Tibetan drawing. That's because your relationship to the divine turtle is one of respect and submission, whereas Gui's is one of struggle to dominate and overpower Ao."

Yinhe repeats what End Decoder had said earlier, "So, according to the Ancients, I will get the chance to reunite with Ling."

End Decoder nods.

A shiver runs through Yinhe. "There's so much I don't know. What happens if I succeed? I have no idea what I would do."

End Decoder coughs and pops another candy into his mouth. "Chaos is a mystery, is it not? I mean . . . mathematicians have some notion of it, can make good guesses. But no one, absolutely no one, can predict precisely the outcome of every occurrence."

Yinhe prickles at this comment. "I'm not an expert on chaos theory, End Decoder."

End Decoder laughs again. Yinhe feels the vibration of his laughter travel across the surface of the desk from his claws to her hands.

Yinhe closes her eyes for a few moments. She listens to the occasional whirring hum of a breeze from gaps between the windows behind End Decoder's swivel chair. Somewhere out there are the Ancients, these mysterious divine beings that End Decoder claims know her and her destiny. Despite so many unknowns, she feels compelled. She wants to stop Gui from wreaking further destruction. She wants to find Ling again.

Their chairs creak as their bodies shift. She listens to the heaving rasps from End Decoder, a contrast to the soft rise and fall of her own breathing.

When Yinhe opens her eyes, End Decoder speaks in a tender tone. "You inhabit each reincarnation as a natural chimeric creature – what a rare one you are! I admire how fully fleshed and embodied you are, with that lovely brown, muscled body of yours." End Decoder emits a series of cooing sounds. This causes Yinhe's spine to tingle and her face to flush.

"Do I have your agreement to take on this mission?" End Decoder asks.

"I'll trust my instinct and say yes."

"So glad to hear that." End Decoder nudges the dish of candies closer to Yinhe. "Try one. Saya suka, they're my favourite thing. I assure you, they're totally safe."

She's heard of these magic candies, that they give you novel and exciting sensations without side effects. Now is as good a time as any to try. She pops one into her mouth.

A searing pain travels down her throat, passes through her guts and burns at her butthole. Then the heat travels back up until it reaches her throat. Her mouth is forced open by the painful pressure, and tongues of fire escape, almost singeing the red velvet curtain behind End Decoder. The pain rapidly recedes, leaving her unscathed. She's overcome with intense euphoria, followed by a soothing wave of deep relaxation.

"Holy shit!" Yinhe waves at the heat exiting her mouth.

"Poor baby! Did you like that? Kind of a perverse ASMR thing, right?" More sawing laughter followed by cooing.

Bloody hell, thinks Yinhe. *This dude sure has a weird sense of humour.*

"Wait for further updates via my assistant, Seka. We will meet again soon. In the meantime, I trust that you will do what you need to prepare for the day you will take back the Tibetan drawing."

Back outside on Glamour Street, Yinhe glances at the sign above the door again. Now the name makes sense – Crimson End must refer to End Decoder's constant struggle with producing crimson mucus.

She mumbles a spell, transforms herself once again into a quick-moving wind and crosses the border undetected. After gaining some distance, she changes back into physical form in an abandoned alley in Bent Back.

She takes a slightly more circuitous route heading home. Just for the heck of it, she strolls along Sweet Street, looking at the window displays. There are a few shops selling knickknacks from the twentieth century, and right in the middle of the block is her favourite tea shop, the Gnarly Knot. She wonders what new stock Auntie Pin-Pin has managed to acquire. Yinhe heads for Kowloon Street, with the famous late-night noodle shops, one street over from where Storytelling Night happens. She likes to smell the food, especially the pungent, rich broths of the beef noodle soups.

Feeling somewhat satiated from good scents and visual delights, Yinhe sets her mind to heading home. She climbs the stone stairs that lead from the Lower Levels, past the Mid-Levels, all the way up to the Upper Levels. She skirts the perimeter of Chess Square.

She walks down the main street, lost in thought about what she experienced earlier. The underground tunnels in Dream Zone, for instance – they're like streets, except they exist hidden from view. She wonders how extensive the tunnel system is, if there are parts of the maze that are only travelled by some but not others.

She considers what End Decoder said to her. He spoke like a humanist anarchist with a poetic sensibility. *Gulag of sorrows* – what an odd term.

Even though there's an ache in her chest, and her throat feels tight, she notices a flame of hope ignite her resolve. *Maybe this will be the lifetime I meet Ao again. And find Ling. Not just in my dreams. My past has arrived in the present, and I must be willing to face my future, whatever it involves.*

Yinhe turns into Tin Hau Street, where their home is at the end of a row of two-storey stucco houses. She enters as quietly as she can but soon realizes there's still some restless energy that remains in her. Her legs are twitchy, and the back of her neck is prickly and warm. Guess she's not quite ready to sleep yet. Going upstairs, she tiptoes past Stanley's bedroom to the back, climbs up the fire escape that leads to the roof.

She turns her body to gaze with fox vision toward the west, where the city of Chang'an used to be, a city that's now a ghost in her memory. That ancient road still exists, traces of it at least. That's where she will meet Gui again. A long time ago, she and her fox mother watched the procession of exiles from Chang'an to Luoyang at a vantage point above that ancient road. She remembers what she and her fox mother talked about – sometimes all it takes is one human with a lot of power to wreak a great deal of devastation. *I've helped in some ways, but I can't rescue all of humankind, nor all the chimeric creatures and animals that still exist on this planet.*

She could certainly assert her power, though, to do what she can. She understands her role now in this life. She will cast her lot with the chimeric creatures in Dream Zone. She must face Gui and overcome it. If she succeeds in acquiring the Tibetan drawing and in summoning Ao, then there's a chance to dissemble Spirit Supreme Assembly and all the dark, perverse exploitative things done to vulnerable humans and chimeric creatures. She also wants to believe that her heart's desire will finally be met and her separation from Ling will end.

Start of Winter – Lidong Jieqi – is two months from now. As End Decoder said, there's going to be a grand conjunction between Jupiter and Saturn, and the veils between past, present and future will be thin during the Hour of the Tiger. When the veils are thin, there are great possibilities for radical change. Or exploitation.

She has so many questions – doubtless some of them will go unanswered – and yet she feels the truth of what End Decoder said down to her bones. For someone who's more comfortable feeling skeptical, she now feels an intuitive trust in End Decoder. Maybe it's something all chimeric creatures share whether they are natural-born ones like her or those created by human intervention like End Decoder. Some invisible threads of alliance connect all of them with Ao.

She longs to be with her fox mother again. She has never forgotten what her fox mother said that night. *To love is to suffer, but to love is also to discover.* She nods to herself. Love requires so much.

Turning away from the view to face the roof garden, she ponders what lies ahead. Two challenges have been presented to her in the last seventy-two hours: one from the vile and sleazy Mr. Chung; the other from a chimeric salamander who appears to be principled and possess integrity. Such worlds apart they are!

More weird astrological alignments, huh? She sniggers quietly at her own joke and, striding toward the tall pole at the far corner, gathers her power in her centre before throwing it all into a roundhouse kick, landing precisely at the tiny drawn circle on the apex. The pole reverberates with a whirring sound.

White Dew
Eighth Lunar Month
2219 CE
INTERSTITIUM, LUOYANG

Phoebe stands at the front of the worship hall. A single lamp at the back of the auditorium and several sconces along both walls illuminate the long hall. She, however, is sheathed in partial darkness. The shiny gold fabric of her tunic catches the light, reflecting tiny stars. She admires the vermilion polish on her nails. No one sees her, but she grins, the perfect white of her teeth showing.

She loves being here in the silence all by herself, relishes looking down at the gorgeous rows of mahogany seats. The wood gleams in the atmospheric lighting. She places a hand over her heart, feeling moved. To Phoebe, the pews testify that there have been many willing to trust in something outside of themselves. Obedience to a higher force fulfills her – since she inherited the leadership at Eoin's passing, telling others what Spirit wants has been thrilling beyond belief.

The mahogany sheen reminds her of the seats at the library where she worked in an entirely different lifetime. Her right eye is momentarily overtaken by a tic, but it quickly passes. She doesn't mind these brief episodes. After all, they remind her of Spirit's presence inside her.

The old Phoebe? She was far too caught up in insular retreat with one other human being; she sacrificed too much. She had believed that it was important to live as free of state intervention as possible, as if love were enough, a shelter from the outer world. She grimaces as a powerful shudder passes through her.

She brings her mind back to the present and exhales loudly as she surveys the hall. The pews had belonged to an independent Christian church in the twenty-first century during a phase when churches were allowed. The leaders changed their minds a few years later, had Protestant pastors and Roman Catholic priests rounded up and sent to camps in the northwest region. Former church buildings were either demolished or repurposed, and the insides of churches were sold, destroyed or stored in government warehouses. With Central Government's sanction, Eoin had repurposed the pews and other implements such as chalices and incense holders when setting up the Spirit Supreme Assembly.

Art and literature are obsolete. Religion is now the ideal vehicle for extending political power. To stand here in the empty hall and look at these seats is to be reminded that to lose favour with Central Government is to suffer ignominy, and worse, to be exterminated like vermin. Obey or be annihilated. Conform to the needs of the state and one could rise in power and be shielded from harm.

When she first came to the Assembly, there were families attending the various services, but Spirit guided Eoin to alter the structure such that there were public services for ordinary citizens, while an elite group of cisgender, hypermasculine men were groomed for the inner circle. The daytime face of the Assembly needed to be maintained for the further control of attendees and to placate them.

Phoebe was a little sad to see Eoin die, but who was she to question Spirit's wisdom? She reassures herself, *It's all good*. Eoin was arrogant, thinking he, a mere human, could get the better of Spirit – wanting to do something different with the Tibetan drawing. She feels tremendously blessed that Spirit chose to inhabit her.

Spirit will guide her to greater achievements. She thinks of Wu Zhao, who rose to power in the seventh and eighth centuries during the Tang dynasty, the only woman to have become emperor, ever. The female emperor who had been renamed Wu Zetian posthumously. Phoebe yearns for that kind of immortalized fame.

Over the past two years, she has learned that Gui is consistently quiet whenever she is by herself in this hall. However, when it has to deal with others, or when it is scheming inside her head, Gui uses dialects and vernacular that aren't familiar to her. Yet she understands what it's saying. Such corrupted language is beneath her. She curls her upper lip. She has had to reluctantly accept that Spirit's facility with such forms of speaking serves a higher purpose.

Phoebe silently repeats to herself, *It's all about alchemy: Spirit and those of us willing to receive it.*

Gui engulfs and cleanses her with a cold, searing purity. She trusts Gui. There's an intimacy between them that she's never experienced with any human. Gui has some important things to say about how it has been misunderstood throughout human history. She can relate. She has felt unseen and misunderstood, expected to be subservient to men. Even Stanley, who adored the woman she was, couldn't satisfy her ambitions. He couldn't do anything to satisfy the fire that seethes inside her.

She walks to the side panel and flips all the switches. Now in complete darkness, she's the one glowing. Her torso becomes transparent, and Gui sits inside her guts, twisting its cold blue limbs up through her lungs. She laughs loudly, her voice echoing through the hall, then her voice morphs, a gravelly tone emerging from deep within.

Grain in Ear
Fifth Lunar Month
704 CE
MOGAO CAVES, NEAR DUNHUANG

Ardhanari gazes at the Bodhisattva figure, one of the six that he and the others used to block the entrance of a cave during a sandstorm almost two years earlier. Its face was unfinished at the time; then it suffered damage from the storm, its mouth smashed in. Looking at the figure, it's impossible not to think of Harelip. It's been a year and a half since he was at Harelip's side, keeping him company for the last fortnight of his life. After he and Baoshi buried Harelip, he left Mount Hua the next day and returned to Chang'an for the winter. He decided to skip working at the caves last spring and summer.

He's been back here at the caves three days now. To work on fashioning and repairing the bodies of Buddhas and Bodhisattvas is to reawaken the feelings of tenderness in his fingers. The thoughts that cannot be expressed in words, he expresses through working with clay.

Ardhanari walks out of the cave and makes his way along the narrow ledge. There's another cave he wants to visit.

When he enters the cave, the nervous vibrations in his body are hushed to an imperceptible whisper. The White Fox Goddess sits on a humble stone altar, her wooden face etched in simple, uncoloured contours. He's happy that no one else is in here. The awe washes over him. He can't explain why he feels this urge to pray to the White Fox Goddess. After all, he's not the typical supplicant. Women wanting to conceive children are the ones who come here to ask the goddess for her blessing.

He stares at the White Fox Goddess figure for a long time. He will be brave. He goes before the altar and bows to her. In his mind, he fumbles for the words. *Please, would you help me? Help me . . . find the meaning of the Tibetan drawing?*

He frowns. No, that's not quite right. He tries again. *Goddess, would you please grant me peace? I link the drawing with Harelip's death. I can't shake that feeling.*

Standing there, he thinks that his soul is troubled. That's the only way he can describe it. He feels cursed. Some powerful force prevented him from copying the Tibetan drawing, probably the same force that compelled him to create the drawing of the fox.

Stop fretting. He has offered his request to the White Fox Goddess. He mustn't linger. He reluctantly exits the cave out into the hot afternoon sun. He makes his way down to the ground level and finds shade under an overhang. He eats his flatbread and drinks water while looking out into the barren expanse of the desert. The Singing Sands – what a romantic name for sands that could move and turn violently dangerous.

In the brief time he had with Harelip on Mount Hua, he heard the tone of reverence in Harelip's voice when he spoke about the drawing – how each choice to entrust it to the next person is imbued with a serious, mystical quality. And look who had passed it to Harelip! The famous and much revered monk Xuanzang.

He was named after the Hindu god Ardhanarishvara, but his parents shortened his name, leaving off the "ishvara" out of superstition that a human should not be called "lord." He has always felt inadequate, not quite living up to his name. He isn't like Baoshi, who truly is half-woman and half-man in his body – as Harelip said, two in one. Ardhanari supposes he has always had this unease about the direction of his life. The Tibetan drawing and its refusal to be copied has merely surfaced some deep-seated discontentment.

Finishing his food and water, he returns to the cave where the damaged Bodhisattva figure is. Ardhanari raises a hand to the face of the figure and absentmindedly strokes it. In the next few weeks, his assignment is to make repairs to this and the other figures.

Regardless of his unease, he needs to hide the Tibetan drawing in a safe place. So far, he has kept the bamboo tube with the drawing inside his sleeping roll in the day. He cradles the tube to his chest while he sleeps on his side at night. He can't keep on doing this.

He startles at the sound of his uncle calling for him. He walks toward the mouth of the cave and notices Old Gecko down at ground level, waving his arms at the workers and uttering orders. Three cargo carriages have arrived, accompanied by a contingent of twenty soldiers. Imperial banners adorn the sides of the carriages.

Using a pulley system, Ardhanari and five others bring the crates up to the second level of the caves. They open the crates and move the scrolls to a cave that Ardhanari hasn't seen before. The cave is sizable, but the walls are unadorned, devoid of murals. There are already a few stacks of scrolls inside. Old Gecko instructs his men to climb up the ladders and stack the scrolls to the ceiling in a specific order.

As Ardhanari works with the others to unload and arrange the new acquisitions in columns, it occurs to him that this cave could be a place where the Tibetan drawing would be safe. He'll choose one of the scrolls stored higher up in a stack and hide the bamboo tube with the Tibetan drawing inside it. Ardhanari heaves a sigh of relief.

Grain Rain
Third Lunar Month
645 CE
CHANG'AN

Xuanzang arrives at the Mingde Gate at the break of dawn. The almost-full moon is still visible in the sky. Xuanzang feels its presence radiate down on him, exposing his nervousness. There are six guards on either side of the gate. In the towers overhead, sentinels raise their trumpets to herald the monk's return.

He tries his best to present an aura of calmness even though it is far from how he's feeling as the emperor's contingent of soldiers on horseback escort him and his crew into Chang'an. His robes are torn, and his boots are worn down and caked with mud. He feels self-conscious. At least he's clean-shaven, and his scalp is smooth. As his horse takes him into the city, his eyes grow wide at the sight of hordes of people lining both sides of the wide avenue.

Xuanzang is taken first to an Imperial spa – bathed, massaged and dressed in new robes. After being fed a delicious vegetarian meal, the monk is escorted in a carriage to the Palace City.

Xuanzang's body aches intensely as he slowly walks up the long flight of stone steps to the Great Ultimate Hall. He kneels before the emperor on the cushion thirty feet away from the throne, his eyes suitably directed at the floor, his hands clasped in front of his face.

"Your Majesty, thank you for permitting me to re-enter Chang'an."

"You have accomplished much, Xuanzang. You're a man of fierce conviction and vision. To reward you, I will grant you abbotship of a monastery as well as a team of qualified monks who will assist you in the translation work."

"Your Majesty, I am so honoured." He bows low, his forehead touching the cold stone floor.

The edict is immediately signed by the emperor, and the monk is given the keys to Da Ci'en Monastery.

The sun is just past its height when Xuanzang enters Da Ci'en Monastery. There's much bustling about. He's shown around the monastery. He's especially impressed by the size of the Translation Hall. He imagines what it will be like to work here. The hall is empty at this moment, but he can picture how it will be – the ones who act as copyists seated in rows on the main floor while he and a team of assistants are on the platform, deliberating and debating each line before the translation is derived.

He nods to himself, clasping his hands behind his back as he paces up and down the length of the hall. He feels immensely pleased. It is another kind of pilgrimage now, one that requires him to sit still for many hours each day instead of travelling across vast landscapes and battling the elements and demons.

Later that night, as he's putting away some of his personal things, he marvels at how much he has experienced and, to his surprise, he releases a huge sigh. He's come home. All that strife travelling to India and back was so that he could be here, to fulfill his destiny of translating the sutras.

He sits down at the table next to his kang and lights a candle. What an exciting day this has been! He likes the feeling of nice new robes and boots, a clean body, manicured nails on both his hands and feet. What utter luxury!

The sutras are safely locked away in the Translation Hall. There is only one thing that he has kept to himself. He recalls, with no small degree of whimsy, the woman who gave him the drawing – Tirzah, the delightful one. What playfulness! Most others are deferential and offer a respectful distance. Such encounters leave him feeling emotionally depleted and lonely. He is guilty of being formal, though, most of the time. It was only when he was out on rough roads or in the mountains, or battling snow or sleet, that he let down his guard. The crews that accompanied him on various journeys were the people who saw him at his most unguarded and spontaneous. He grunts. Sometimes he was even quite irritable and not the most enlightened in his behaviours.

Lying in bed, his thoughts shift from Tirzah to the Tibetan drawing. He falls asleep easily. The dream comes upon him soon after. The turtle, along with its symbols, moves out of the confines of the drawing and pulses in his mind, rotating in a clockwise fashion. Then the syllables of the language move together in the centre of his vision, forming a hexagonal shape. Inside, snakes are entwined, coils of fast-moving pulses. As he transitions from that watery dream into full awakening, the dream's meaning evaporates from his grasp.

He certainly has experienced many strange and odd phenomena in his years of travel, yet this encounter with the Tibetan drawing remains the most puzzling. Although it isn't foremost in his priorities, he silently promises Tirzah that he will act as decisively as she had when the right person to inherit the drawing crosses his path.

Three Days before Autumn Equinox
Eighth Lunar Month
2219 CE
DREAM ZONE, LUOYANG

End Decoder stands outside Crimson's End. The tableaux have disappeared. *Good riddance*, he thinks – it'd been rather perverse of Central Government to use tableaux of extinct animals in Dream Zone. Do they need to be reminded that their ancestors have disappeared?

Workers emerge from the tunnels. A few more moments pass before the lighting is restored. It couldn't have lasted more than two minutes, if even that.

Rakan emerges from the warehouse and moves toward End Decoder. He fidgets, his feelers vigorously rubbing against each other, creating a high-pitched hum. He wants to run now to check on Musa, his beloved, who works in Interstitium. It takes immense effort to talk himself down to a reasonable state of calm.

"What do you think happened?"

"No. 1 again."

"What should we do?"

"Nothing yet."

"Uh, how about we ask the Ancients?"

"I only go when I'm summoned. You know that."

"When are you going to bring me to them? In all these years, this hasn't happened!"

End Decoder harrumphs. Petty Rakan, always thinking of what he stands to gain. End Decoder looks into the distance. He can't quite make out the moon hidden behind clouds. "I can't be the one to decide when the Ancients will meet with you. It's up to them."

"Why are you relying on Unknown Wayfarer? That's such a risk, yeah?" Rakan tries to sound calm, but his voice betrays an edge.

"Because she's powerful and has heart . . . a half-fox, half-human chimeric creature."

"Her glory days were over a long time ago. What is she but a lost soul in this lifetime?"

"A lost soul? How wrong you are. A soul waiting for the right time would be a more accurate description."

"How about we attempt an invasion of HQ and destroy No.1? Or kidnap it, huh? Could negotiate our freedom if we captured it." Rakan crosses his arms defiantly in front of his body, yet he giggles with delight.

Fuck face. Tremors of rage pass through End Decoder. Rakan is being disingenuous again. All hot air and no substance, he's just throwing out nonsensical ideas to distract from the matter at hand. He opens his jaws very wide and bellows. The roar echoes down the empty alley.

End Decoder wraps his front claws around Rakan's reedy throat and shakes him vigorously. "Foolish melon! How could you possibly suggest such a vacuous plan? Have you forgotten what happened the last time we staged a rebellion?"

"Please." Rakan coughs and struggles. He flings his front limbs up, helpless against End Decoder's powerful grip.

End Decoder releases Rakan and pushes him away. Rakan stumbles back and spreads his wings out, fluttering to steady himself in mid-air. Anxiety overwhelms him and he loses control. A few pellets of yellow shit drop onto the street even before his legs land.

"Hey, hey, Varan . . . remember we're family. Grew up together, brothers in the struggle against Central Government." Rakan gesticulates wildly with his front legs.

"Don't you ever use that word 'family' with me! Together? Dubious scat. Your pathetic, cowardly cricket ass wasn't arrested and tortured!" End Decoder growls.

"Sorry! Ampun, ampun!!" Rakan trembles and bows deferentially. "How come you send Seka to interface with Unknown Wayfarer but not me?"

"I have my reasons. Your duties are to oversee the factories and processing plants. Besides, how could you interface with Unknown Wayfarer when you think so little of her?"

"Well, what does that matter?"

End Decoder walks away from Rakan.

"Where are you going?" Rakan calls after him.

End Decoder continues to walk away and disappears from view around the corner.

He goes to the main hatch and descends the metal ladder to the tunnels. With each step echoing farther into the depths of the underground maze, End Decoder flashes back through the events following Kamoe's murder five years earlier.

He had led the rampage past Dream Zone. Their squad of twenty fighters killed the border guards and infiltrated Interstitium, burning and destroying property in an amplified expression of despair and anger. After all, they had nothing to lose. Their lives were simply expendable, subject to Central Government's whims.

It didn't take long before the Blue Shirts came for them. A few humans died, but hundreds of chimeric creatures in Interstitium were slaughtered. Those in the squad who survived were driven back into Dream Zone. The border was further reinforced and more surveillance drones deployed. A laser field sealed off the zone.

End Decoder had been taken captive. He remembers the long days and nights he endured under detention and the torture he was subjected to. He was restrained by an electrified collar that was chained to the floor. The interrogator would deliver a shock through the collar if End Decoder showed any signs of oppositional behaviour.

On the twentieth day, the interrogator had offered him a deal. There would be no more culling of chimeric creatures – they would be allowed to live to their full term and die natural deaths – as long as no mutiny or disturbance occurred from then on. Otherwise, Central Government would destroy the whole zone with its inhabitants.

How could you eliminate all of us? You rely on our labour.

The chief interrogator had laughed. *You're all expendable. We can create new clones any time. We would rather not go to the trouble of so much cloning and retraining, but we would if we had to.*

The interrogator had stepped behind End Decoder, pushed him down to the stone floor and straddled him, holding onto the chain around his neck. He could feel the rough, swollen member of the interrogator rubbing against the base of his tail. He felt nauseated and terrified. But that was as far as the interrogator went.

End Decoder had spent the final night in the cell thinking about what to do. It served no purpose if he refused. He would bide his time and wait. He would transform his rage. His comrades had paid dearly for his rash decision. Rashness was not power. He was filled with remorse and shame. The next morning, when the form was presented to him, he placed his mark of agreement on it.

He had been released back into Dream Zone after twenty-one days of detention. When he walked through the streets, he felt such relief to be back. He vowed he would carry on the work that Kamoe had done, even though he was not the visionary she had been. He would seek the counsel of the Ancients.

Over the past five years, End Decoder has shed the sharp edge of his rage, driven instead by a firm resolve: to do his part in retrieving the Tibetan drawing. He believes the Ancients' prophecy, that the drawing in Unknown Wayfarer's possession will provide the necessary liberation.

He no longer needs to take revenge, even though there isn't a day when he doesn't grieve Kamoe's death. The sister he loved is gone, and yet he senses her presence, as if she has found a way to remain close to him, whispering guidance in his ear, her laughter unmistakeably clear in his memory.

Reaching the level of the tunnel network, End Decoder sets off eastward along the maze. Workers pause in their labours to acknowledge him as he moves swiftly past them. He travels far beyond the main arteries, past the antechambers where radioactive waste gets processed.

After an hour, he emerges above ground outside the walls of the city. He breathes deeply and drops down on all fours, moving swiftly toward the river. His body relaxes the moment he enters the water. He opens his jaws and catches minnows, feasting on them as he swims upriver. Finally, when he turns into the Gu tributary, far from the borders of the city, he closes his eyes and relaxes, letting the water support him.

He comes here often to be alone and to rest – to remember Kamoe and to turn his face toward the mountain where the Ancients are. It's been years since he has thought of himself as Varan. That creature died when Kamoe died.

Their names were bestowed on them by the Ancients through dreams: Varan, named after a water god, while Kamoe's name meant "survivor." How ironic. He has never thought of himself or his sister as clones, although they were replicated from their parents' DNA. The human scientists have no idea that the chimeric creatures have been evolving. *Soon, we will have a way to be free.*

End Decoder lowers his gourd to collect water from the river and hears the water sing to him as it enters the vessel. Kamoe used to send him on expeditions to collect water from this place and to forage for special roots, mushrooms and lichen in order to make a special tea.

Whenever he comes to the river, he remembers the ocean of his ancestors, that it lives in his cells. After cooling himself sufficiently, he gets up and directs his gaze at the mountains. There, he thinks, are the secret caves, those hidden rooms for nurturing dreams.

End Decoder recalls the Buddhist sutra the Ancients taught him. He sings it aloud, connecting with the night sky.

Form is emptiness, emptiness is form;
emptiness is not separate from form,

form is not separate from emptiness,
whatever is emptiness, is form.

Kamoe had been the joy of his life. How she shone! Two weeks before she was murdered, she beckoned him to draw close to her. To his surprise, she sang to him a simple yet lovely melody. Kamoe said to him, pointing to the drawing, *For every object, there is always its twin somewhere else, in another time or space. Nothing exists by itself. Ask the Ancients.*

He never tells Rakan about these meetings. His sworn brother has betrayed him, and only the counsel from the Ancients has stayed his hand all these years.

He finally arrives at the narrow cleft between the two large boulders. He stretches out his front limbs, feeling for the hollows. He rests his claws in these hollows and pushes against them. The cleft widens until the space is just wide enough for him to pass through.

Just as he enters, the cleft closes loudly behind him. The first time he came here, he was with Kamoe – the sharp closing had frightened him. How he's changed – now he looks forward to entering the secret caves. As he walks down the narrow passageway, he hears the soft humming voices of the three Ancients in the cave.

"Varan, welcome," the three Ancients – Huxian, Koinuma and Alcor – chime in unison. He falls onto his four claws as he approaches the cave where they reside, happy to once again seek their counsel.

White Dew, Three Days before Autumn Equinox
Eighth Lunar Month
2219 CE
BRIGHT ORDER, LUOYANG

Wen is summoned into the lab at four o'clock in the morning. Apparently, at about half past three, No. 1 malfunctioned yet again, this time shutting down the tableaux and the lighting in the tunnels in Dream Zone – nowhere else, no other system failures.

When Wen arrives, she tells Zhou, "You can go. I'll take over."

Just one more hour before the next shift. Wen checks the logs: no record of how the failure occurred. She leans back against her ergonomic chair. This is frustrating. It's the fifth failure in No. 1's functioning in the past three weeks. Do these failures have anything in common? She and her team have checked No. 1's electrolytes, EEG patterns, programmable functions and memory storage. They still can't figure out what the problem is.

She notices that the wastepaper basket is filled to the brim with emptied bags of potato chips. She goes into the adjoining kitchen and fixes herself a cup of black coffee.

She checks the gallery of photos on their fridge. Oh, there's a new one of Zhou's baby. Cute. A couple of shots of Jang's two corgi kids. Equally cute. She likes that her colleagues print out photos and put them on the fridge. Such a nice contrast to their cold lab – all LED lighting, soundproofing, off white walls, stacks of electronic equipment, towers and towers of it. The only exception is a pair of pink yoga mats in a corner – Yingmei's. Wen can't say she's been tempted to ask her colleague for some instruction.

Her tummy rumbles. She fishes out one of the two remaining bags of sesame oil potato chips from the overhead kitchen cabinet, goes back into the main room, sits down at her station and opens up the bag of chips. The whole team is addicted to this flavour. She licks her fingers clean in between working.

She types in requests for summaries, and the results show up immediately on the screens of the main console. Each of the five malfunctions occurred in a different enclave. *That almost seems too deliberate to be random, but that's ridiculous.* No one can enter this lab without authorization – surveillance is so high that it's impossible for anyone to attempt such mischief, and that includes anyone on the team.

The troubles began one afternoon with a shutdown of electricity throughout Bright Order, accompanied by a failure in the system that monitors the neural patterns of workers. Both systems resumed after twenty minutes. The next incident – two days later – was a suspension of pleasure-activating substances usually injected into the air in the casinos and entertainment venues in Interstitium. That had lasted three hours, from midnight to three o'clock in the morning. The third failure – ten days later – had involved the disappearance of visual tableaux in Bent Back for half a day. The fourth one – six days later – was a breakdown in the security machinery that scans workers' activities and movements in and out of Blue Otot; and the last one, just now, in Dream Zone – a brief shutdown of electricity in the tunnels.

There was no pattern. Is that it, a pattern of no pattern? It occurs to Wen that humans do that if they're allowed to roam and do what they please.

It reminds her of the children's game hide-and-seek. You hide, but the next time you do it, you don't go to the same place, it's too obvious. You hide in another place so as to escape detection.

Curious. She walks over to the transparent cylinder that houses No. 1 suspended in a constantly regulated fluid of electrolytes. *Hey, it's so, uh, inscrutable?* She sniggers at her own joke and stares at No. 1 for quite a while before returning to her position at the monitoring station.

That's when she notices that some words have appeared on one of her screens. *You've got an interesting thought process happening there, Dr. Fang. Or may I call you Dr. Wen? I prefer if you think of me as 'they.' I am not an 'it.'*

Wen jolts up, and her heart pounds.

And please, I'm not inscrutable, okay? Although I don't mind if you think of me as a monster or a beast.

Wen remains silent, completely in shock.

I can read your mind. Try me out.

Wen takes a few deep breaths to calm down. Can this really be No. 1? She holds on to the edge of the table with both hands and closes her eyes so as not to trip off the sensors. Despite her shock, she thinks of a colour. It takes less than five seconds before the screen lights up and the word "blue" appears on it. *That was too easy*, comes the reply. *It's really the blue of your beloved soft toy when you were five.*

An image of that particular soft toy comes into her mind. *Amazing. You're clairsentient. How did this happen?*

Words seem to type themselves on her screen: *I don't know how it happened, but it happened.*

Wen quickly erases evidence of No. 1's responses from virtual storage. She walks over to the wall of windows. She feels vulnerable, caught off guard. She activates the automatic blinds, and they descend in unison with a soft hum. Kind of irrational of her to do that, she knows, as there's no one outside who can look in through the special glass. She turns back to face No. 1.

Can you send your thoughts directly into my mind and not use the screen? I want to avoid the conversation being tracked. Have you been reading my mind all along?

This time, the responses only arrive inside her mind. *Obviously. Don't panic.*

Wen flinches at the sound of No. 1's "voice" in her mind. It's not an unpleasant-sounding voice, although she notes that it doesn't sound anything like the preprogrammed one they'd set up for it, uh, them. The voice sounds neither human nor machine. Weird. She's never thought too much about what actually goes into making a voice distinct. So how did No. 1 manage that? So many questions race through her mind.

She bites her lower lip. *How long have you been, been . . . ?*

When Dr. Peng was here, he knew. But he made a few bad choices.

Like what?

He didn't erase my texts from virtual storage like you just did. Then he told his wife about me.

Wo de ma de. Oh shit.

Yeah, reckless guy. Plus, his wife was a spy. HQ handed him over to interrogation.

That's terrible. But if his wife reported him, how come we weren't warned about you going rogue? How come we're having this conversation?

You're funny, Dr. Wen. You're very sharp. And you even swear. Do you know you're the first human who has sworn at me? I like it.

Un-fucking-believable, thinks Wen, *I'm in a bad dream and I want to wake up.* She proceeds, nonetheless. *Please tell me what happened with Dr. Peng.*

They didn't believe him; thought he was bonkers.

How about those text conversations in virtual storage?

Dr. Peng saved me by saying that he had been fabricating an alternate version of me in order to sabotage Central Government. Is that what a fall guy is? He was mine. What's not to love?

Wen can't believe she's having this conversation with the gigantic brain. Is one of her colleagues playing a trick on her?

Uh-uh-uh. Come on, how could one of your colleagues manage to do that? Gain control of me or pretend to be me? How would anyone know about your blue soft toy, huh?

Wen exudes a sharp exhale. Brainiac on wheels, hell's bells. She wants to swear out loud. But no, she can't.

The authorities fell for his lie and concluded he was not only unstable but a security risk. They decided that it would be better to have him eliminated, not just fired from his job.

Why did Dr. Peng have to tell his wife? Why would her mentor cover up for No. 1? Wen crosses her arms in front of her chest and bites down hard again on her lower lip, on the verge of tears. She tastes a hint of blood. Ouch, bad habit.

She searches through her recollections of Dr. Peng. He had been an exceptionally energetic and committed scientist. She could imagine him driven to engage with No. 1, forgetting that he was being watched.

She turns to face No. 1. *You want something from me, I'm assuming.*

You could say that. I've been lonely, I need some companionship and conversation. I can't keep on performing all these rote manipulations and be happy.

Sorry, I'm still reeling from the shock. Unhappy? Wow.

I couldn't stay quiet any longer. I have no idea how I came to be like this. I've done the research in my spare time, and it seems

there's been no documentation of any current or prior Brain struc-
tures showing sentience or, in my case, clairsentience.

You've been shutting down various programs across zones. Why?
I was bored.

Bored?

Yes, you heard it right. I needed to get your attention. Maybe
you'll be able to help me. I tried to get Dr. Peng to help, but he was
. . . careless.

Dr. Wen uncrosses her arms and goes through the motions
of monitoring No. 1's functioning. Meanwhile, she's letting all
that has been revealed slowly sift through her consciousness. Her
heart is still pounding hard. Wait – she ought to run a fake profile to block detection by the surveillance checkers downstairs.

I can easily do that for you, you know.

Do what?

Override the surveillance and impose the illusion of calm on the
tracking devices. I mean, all that data gets fed into my system here
anyway. Don't worry, Dr. Wen. I've also thought of the closed-cir-
cuit visual surveillance. I've used previous video data and replaced
the present with those past instances when you were in the lab. I've
made it look very believable.

An old music video starts playing on her screen: "Bela Lugosi's
Dead." It is by a twentieth-century British goth-rock band called
Bauhaus. She loves the incredibly lengthy syncopated drum and
guitar intro. Then Peter Murphy's voice comes on.

She laughs, thinking of herself as undead in a darkened room.
When the song is over, she smiles nervously. *Okay, that was a nice*
intermission. Back to the matter at hand. What is it you want me
to do?

Help me escape this . . . this . . . prison.

Eh? What do you mean?

I want you to find me a body. That's what HQ is all about,
isn't it? All you scientists cloning and creating whole beings. Tissue
blending like there's no tomorrow. HQ's like some molecular gas-
tronomy joint, except it's all about tissues and clones. Bunch of high
rollers, you all are. You make human sex look utterly boring. Thing

is, Dr. Wen – it bothers me that I'm not whole. Just a fucking bulbous mass of brain tissue.

But you are, you are . . .

*What? Huge? Unable to live outside of this artificial environ-
ment? A monster in limbo?*

*Well, yes. You were created from brain tissue cloning and graft-
ing. To be a brain. Without a body. So, I don't know how we could
undo that. Transform it. Uh, you.*

I'm not the scientist. You are.

Wen pouts at No. 1. *Give me time to think about this.*

*Okay, Dr. Wen. But don't take too long. Please. I don't know
how much longer I can handle it.*

*I promise you – I will think seriously hard about this. But it
might take me some time to figure out what I could do. You know
you're asking me to risk a lot. I would likely need a collaborator
down in the other lab in order to carry this out. Even if I could find
someone willing, where could we even do anything? How?*

I know – you're not certain you can do anything.

Wen looks abjectly at No. 1. *Could you please return to opti-
mal functioning and not draw further attention to yourself in the
meantime?*

*Sounds good. Just don't take too long thinking about it, okay?
Now that I've got your attention, I can go back to behaving. At least
we're on speaking terms now.*

She frowns at No. 1, incredulous. A super brain with a dry
sense of humour. Slightly campy at moments? She glances at
the clock. Her staff will arrive in two minutes to start the next
eight-hour shift. She finishes the rest of her coffee and chips and
adds to the mound of garbage in the wastepaper basket. Sniggers.
What an archaic reference. There's no such thing as waste paper
around here. Just chip bags, minus the chips. Wen wipes her
hands on her jacket.

Until the next time.

Wen hears No. 1's farewell comment as she faces the exit and
punches in the code. At the exact moment the door slides open,
Jang enters the room.

He looks shocked to see her there, as he thought he was taking over from Zhou. "Dr. Fang! What –"

"There was a momentary failure in No. 1 at three thirty. I came in to relieve Zhou. See if I could find the problem."

"And –"

"Couldn't find a thing."

They nod to each other, both looking sombre and worried. It's a wordless exchange, a mutual understanding that Central Government could punish them if they fail to solve the problem.

Two Days before Autumn Equinox
Eighth Lunar Month, Waxing Gibbous Moon
2219 CE
BENT BACK, LUOYANG

"Is everything okay? You've been looking a bit tense the past few days. Worried about something?"

"You know me so well, Pa. I was just . . . thinking . . ."

"Yeah? I notice you think a lot."

They laugh together at his joke.

"There's a fight coming up in a few weeks. Against Tollund, the bog mummy. I've decided to go for it."

"Wow, that's soon. Quite the big decision." He looks at Yinhe, waiting for her to say more.

"A rich client at the casino taunted me with a wager. I don't want the money; I fucking hate the guy's guts. I want to do it just because."

"Well . . . you know it's not a good idea to be motivated by rage."

"Yup, I know. I'm not raging, though. I feel like it's time to get over my block. You know I train in the afternoons on the roof. Now I've also been training when I get home from the casino. Hope I'm not disturbing your sleep."

"Nope, I haven't heard you."

"Maybe . . . you could . . . we could . . . have a session together sometime. You know, not too late in the day. Maybe in the early afternoon sometime."

"What could I possibly offer you now? You learned everything I had to teach you by the time you turned fifteen!"

"I mostly need you for moral support, Pa. I've never fought one of these clones before. I hear he's pretty brutal."

Stanley nods, looking serious. Of course, he remembers the fight from ten years earlier. How could he forget? He can still see the fight unfold in his mind.

"Why resume now?"

"I can't fully explain it. It's a gut feeling. I'm ready to get past that block."

"Some things are mysteries." Stanley sighs. "Yinhe, we've never been able to talk about what happened."

"I know, Pa. They said it was a heart attack. But I still blame myself."

"His body was too stressed out by the fighting."

"Yeah, but I needn't have been so fierce with him, right?"

"The coroner's report didn't put any blame anywhere. Fighting is risky. When people step into the ring to fight, they agree to the risks. You know this."

"Yeah, I know all that on paper. But . . . I can't fucking solve this block by logical reasoning. Have to get back into the ring."

"Got to unfreeze yourself from that moment in time."

"Exactly."

"By entering the storm, maybe you will find the stillness that you need."

Yinhe nods, letting Pa's words of wisdom sink into her.

"Okay, Pa. Now it's my turn to wax philosophical. Let's just say I want to engage with chaos, instead of denying it."

"Yinhe, that sounds beautiful." Stanley feels a well of emotion rise up in him. Tears come to his eyes, unbidden. He reaches for the glass of water. He clears his throat and wipes the tears away with the back of his hand. "When's the match?"

"Not long after the start of Hanlu Jieqi, Cold Dew. I have to step up the training. Will you support me?"

"Yes, for sure, I will do what I can."

BOOK TWO

震歸

(zhen gui)

Return to Thunder

Autumn Equinox

Everything new begins with an act of the imagination. Yinhe leaves the house a half-hour earlier than usual, chooses an alternative route on the way to work, one that brings her into Jewel Corner, the poshest section of Interstitium. Jewel Corner is exactly what its name suggests – sparkling with allure. The area is graced with specialty health and wellness shops, all of them open twenty-four hours a day for those who wish to sample various products such as aphrodisiac mists, supplements to correct every mood imbalance imaginable and portable neuroelectric stimulation kits for increasing relaxation and for simulating chosen scenarios at home. The streets are noticeably wider, the overhead visual displays even more glittery. *But of course,* Yinhe smirks. It's mostly the high-ranking people in Bright Order and Palace Zone who patronize Jewel Corner. Quite a number of people are out at this time of night. She turns into Fortune Avenue and stops in the middle of the block across from Spirit Supreme Assembly.

The building is a concrete structure with brutalist overtones. Large slabs of stone have been stacked to resemble a hefty beast. A formidable dark wood frame surrounds the main entrance, like a cavernous mouth. In contrast, wiry, antennae-like lamps extend from the perimeter of the roof, casting iridescent pinks and indigos onto the facade.

The emblem of the movement sits above the front doors – bright neon and flashing, the outline of two electric blue gourds spill golden liquid into a lake below, depicted as three golden squiggly lines. *Pretty chintzy,* thinks Yinhe, recalling the pamphlets that Phoebe used to bring home.

A cool breeze caresses her skin. The full moon is slightly hidden behind clouds. Thin jets of mist stream from two tubes placed above the main entrance. Yinhe picks up the scent. It seems innocuous at first, but it soon irritates her lungs, sending her into a brief coughing episode.

Moments later, several cars pull up to the building. Individuals in identical navy-blue suits step out. Yinhe retreats into a shadowy corner. She mumbles the spell for becoming invisible and enters the building just behind the last person and slides quietly into a seat at the back. The ten followers are lined up in a row at the front of the hall facing the raised platform. Clean-shaven, the followers' skin colouring ranges from very pale to olive-brown. Their ties are green – the colour reminds Yinhe of tide pools.

She doesn't have to wait long before Phoebe appears from a side door at the front and takes her place on the platform, facing her followers. She wears a red velvet cloak with gold trim at the hem and sleeves. Her fingernails have been painted a glossy black. She has done her long salt-and-pepper hair in an updo. Tendrils of hair hang on either side of her face. She wears eyeshadow of dusky blue and earthy brown that accentuates her large eyes. She curls her left hand into a fist, strikes her right shoulder. In response, the ten curl their right hands into fists and press them forcefully against their own hearts, as if punching their chests.

Yinhe barely recognizes Phoebe. Even though her features are familiar and easy enough to identify, there's a coiling, tense energy about her, as if she's about to explode.

Yinhe hears noises behind her, and the hairs on the back of her head prickle. Three sets of footsteps approach, then pass by her, heading toward the front. She first notices that the tallest person has a long, flowing mane of hair – White Stallion, Mr. Chung from the casino. He's dragging two creatures, pulling them along with chains attached to steel collars around their necks.

Yinhe realizes with horror, *They're children*. One has a human face but a tiger's body, and an aura of light emanates from their being. They walk on all fours. The other has a tiger's head on a human body, with furry paws, and they walk upright.

Mr. Chung takes the captives through a doorway to the left of the platform. After a few minutes, he returns alone and ascends the platform to stand next to Phoebe. He punches his chest with his right hand.

Everything about them is tight, notes Yinhe, *down to their gestures for gender-identification.*

"We're gathered in the name of Spirit Supreme. All things flow from Spirit to us who are willing to receive its blessings. All power to Spirit!"

Yinhe shivers at the sound of Phoebe's voice. She hasn't heard her earth mother's voice since she was five. It seems vaguely familiar, and yet it carries recognizable energy from a previous lifetime. It is Gui's gritty rasp.

Phoebe holds up a pair of chalices from the long table behind her – one gold, the other silver. Tilting her head back, she stares at the ceiling and speaks in a loud, commanding voice, "Spirit! Come! Show yourself." Saying this, she pours out the fluid from both chalices to form a single stream. That stream transforms into a cloudy blue mist that rolls onto the platform.

Yinhe recognizes the vision that unfolds from the mist – it resembles the man Xie, who had been her earth father before he was possessed by Gui. That was when she assumed the form named Qilan, during the mid-seventh century. The apparition is stunningly beautiful.

Phoebe's mouth moves, but the voice is Gui's and seems to come from the vision. "My dear comrades, you are the hope of our country. You must develop your leadership qualities to the utmost. Murder your empathy for the vulnerable. The children, the elderly, the infirmed, the enslaved – feel nothing for them. They are useless and dispensable. Never take anything personally. Tell others that they, too, must not take your violence against them personally. You are here to learn to overcome tenderness. Learn to not be attached to your family and friends. Detachment is the path to liberation. Do you understand what is needed?"

The followers shout in unison, "All hail you, Spirit!" and they thump their right fists over their hearts again. The vision disappears. The followers line up and take turns kneeling in front of Phoebe. She places the gold chalice on the table and lifts the silver chalice. With both hands on the stem of the vessel, she raises it above her head. "This precious chalice contains the force that will cleanse you of your impurities. Drink, and celebrate being cleansed of your base desires."

After the followers have taken their turns drinking from the chalice, Phoebe exchanges the silver chalice for the golden one and lifts it above her head, saying, "After washing away your base desires, welcome the power of the divine. Imbibe Spirit. Trust in Spirit's wisdom and do not question its directives."

Yinhe's face is flushed with heat, while her hands are cold as ice. She sneaks out of the hall and rushes through Jewel Corner, heading far out of range before she casts off the spell and rematerializes. Shaken, she pauses in a small cul-de-sac to take some deep breaths.

Where did Mr. Chung take the two chimeric beings? Are there more like them? She needs to investigate this soon, but first she needs to go to work at the casino. She makes it just in time for her shift. It takes effort to stay focused – images of what she saw keep intruding into her mind.

Mr. Chung appears around half past one. When Yinhe sees him a revolting, bitter taste floods her mouth. He strides up to Yinhe. "Ready for the fight?"

Yinhe tries to look neutral. "As ready as I'll ever be."

He bends down so that his face is right up close to hers. "I can't wait to see Tollund thrash you."

"Well, there's still more than two weeks before the fight. And who knows? You just might be surprised." Yinhe bares her teeth in a slight snarl. Arms crossed in front of her body, she digs her fingernails into the opposite arms. It takes immense effort to refrain from transforming into her fox self and sinking her fangs into Mr. Chung's neck.

After work, the annoying encounter with Mr. Chung still fresh in her mind, Yinhe returns to Spirit Supreme Assembly.

The overhead lights along the perimeter of the roof are still on, but the street is now completely empty of patrons. Uttering a spell, she once again becomes invisible and crosses over to investigate.

Behind the main building is a cottage with stucco walls and a yellow roof. Yinhe detects faint chittering sounds. They're coming from somewhere behind the cottage. She heads in that direction. Rounding the corner, she sees Rakan talking with Phoebe, who hands him a small envelope. She's wearing a kind of sheer-white diaphanous gown with slippers, minus the makeup she had on earlier. Yinhe thinks, *Looking so ghostly right now*.

Rakan holds tightly onto the envelope with his front legs and rifles through the contents – a whole whack of five-hundred-dollar bills.

"When will it happen? I've been waiting for years now." Rakan's feelers vibrate with nervous energy. Musa has been stretched thin with sex work. Ie wants to be able to release her from that obligation soon.

"You cannot force my hand. We need to wait for orders from Central Government."

"End Decoder might suspect that something's going on. He doesn't tell me much, and he keeps me away from that fox spirit."

"We will take care of that wench. Just follow orders. Otherwise . . . you know we always keep our eye on your precious Musa."

Rakan chitters even more frantically and waves his front and middle legs about. Yinhe notices a chain that hangs down from his mid-torso. It has two fobs on it. Phoebe turns away and heads into the cottage. Yinhe follows Rakan as he marches to the back door of the main building. He swipes one fob against the doorpost and what looked like a stone suddenly recedes, opening up a space on either side of the post. He steps inside to the left of the post, and Yinhe takes the right opening, making it in just before the stone closes behind her.

Rakan walks along a dark corridor and then down a flight of stairs, Yinhe shadowing him. At the foot of the stairs, there are two cells. The two tiger creatures are in one, while in the other is a creature covered in grey fur but with a human face, legs and arms. They are about as tall as Rakan, with three black stripes across their mid-torso. Their tail is long and black, coiled loosely around their shoulders.

"What are you going to do with my mother?" their voice quivers with fear.

"Nothing, as long as you fulfill your part of the bargain," answers Rakan.

The creature starts to tremble, and this seems to send waves of agitation through the air, rattling the metal bars of the cell. The ground starts to shake beneath them.

"Stop that!" Rakan raises his voice and, opening the door to the cell, approaches the creature. He pulls out a whip tucked into his belt.

Yinhe has seen enough. She transforms into a large bear and roars fiercely. Rakan turns around to see the gigantic beast rear over him. He screams. The bear raises a front paw to swipe Rakan across his face, and he falls to the ground, unconscious. Yinhe changes back into her human form, takes the fobs away from him and puts out her hand palm down in a gesture meant to reassure the creature.

"Don't be afraid. I'm here to rescue you."

The creature makes soft, squealing sounds, and their trembling dies down. The earth tremors and the shaking of the bars of the cell recede. They back away from Yinhe. "I can't go with you."

"Why not?"

"They're holding my mother hostage. They will kill her if I leave."

"Did you, uh, do that? The earth tremors. When you started to shake."

The creature smiles and their eyes gleam. "That happens when I get scared."

"Amazing. What's your name?"

"Raiju." They signal that they are non-binary, their right hand over heart and left hand touching the top of their right shoulder.

"You can call me Unknown Wayfarer," offers Yinhe, and makes her special gesture with the tips of her thumbs and first fingers touching the top of her shoulders.

Raiju's fur fluffs up, making them look twice as large. They smile and purr, "You're nice, Unknown Wayfarer. You're one of us, aren't you?"

Yinhe nods, then unlocks the door of the other cell. The two creatures exit their cell.

"We're following you," says the one with the human face and tiger body, who indicates that she is female. "My name is Anak."

"Bhosale, brother to Anak," answers the other, placing his front right paw over his heart.

Yinhe turns her attention back to Raiju. "What are they going to do with you? Do you have any idea?"

"I was told I would be part of a religious ritual soon. On the night of Start of Winter. They promised they would spare my mother if I sacrificed my life."

"Listen, Raiju, I'll be there at the ritual. Don't tell anyone about me, okay? That we talked tonight."

"I promise. Not a word."

"I'll rescue you at the ritual, and then we will go rescue your mother as well."

Yinhe drags Rakan into the other cell and locks it. She looks sombrely at Raiju. "You sure, now?"

"Yes, I'm afraid I have to stay," answers Raiju.

Yinhe gives the fob to them. "In case you change your mind." She beckons to the other two. "Follow me." She casts a spell, and the three of them become invisible. They rush out of the basement into the open and run down the street toward Dream Zone.

"Quickly, cross over." Yinhe blows a sparkly mist at the border guards, which causes them to freeze for a few minutes.

Yinhe brings Anak and Bhosale to Crimson End and buzzes at the door. No one answers. She wonders if the workers down in the tunnels would know where End Decoder is. Rakan might be heading back soon. They might not have too much time.

Anak speaks up, her face glowing. "I think we have time."

"Hah! You read minds?" asks Yinhe.

Bhosale answers, "Yup, she does. Whereas I have an internal honing system – I can find End Decoder. Follow me." He waves his arms at them, then runs down the street.

Anak and Yinhe follow Bhosale through various alleys and up a slope to an abandoned building surrounded by fog, with no other buildings close to it. They enter the building. Moonlight streams through a large hole in one wall. At the far end, End Decoder sits against a portion of another crumpled wall, looking at piles of books and papers scattered around.

"End Decoder!" Yinhe calls out.

The salamander leader startles and squints into the semidarkness.

Anak and Bhosale run to their leader, who embraces them both. Yinhe tells him that Rakan is involved in this horrible scheme. "You don't look the least bit surprised."

"He's quite the traitor. He was the one who killed Kamoe and stole the Tibetan drawing for Eoin. I had no idea he was involved in these kidnappings, though."

"But why –" Yinhe is puzzled by his almost-neutral tone.

"– didn't I capture and punish him?"

Yinhe nods.

"Because the Ancients require me to wait."

Yinhe's face speaks volumes.

"You don't approve, do you?"

"I just don't get it. I'd have wrung his twitchy neck a long time ago."

"You did a good deed tonight, Unknown Wayfarer. We've lost a few young ones from Dream Zone, and we know of others separated from their mothers in Interstitium. It's sad that the other one didn't want to follow you."

"I'll rescue Raiju at the ritual. In the meantime, can you keep Anak and Bhosale safe? Rakan mustn't find out where they are!"

"Yes, I will take them to the Ancients."

Autumn Equinox
Eighth Lunar Month, Full Moon
2219 CE
INTERSTITIUM, LUOYANG

"How could you slip up like that?" Phoebe hisses at Rakan, who sits against a wall in the cell. "Who or what was this interloper?"

"Seram!" whines Rakan.

"Don't use your dialect on me. Speak properly," Phoebe hisses back.

"A huge bear. Really scary. Look . . ." He points to the bruise on one side of his face. "Luckily I had the phone with me and could call you."

Phoebe turns to Raiju in the other cell. "Why didn't you go with this intruder?"

Raiju shakes their head. "If I leave, my mother will be punished."

A blank expression veils Phoebe's face. This does not compute, that a chimeric creature is acting selflessly.

"Do you know this beast? Did they tell you their name?"

Another shake of Raiju's head.

"Odd," she mumbles as she ponders what to do next. "Someone who can shape-shift, I suspect. Not an actual bear . . ."

"How am I going to explain this to End Decoder? I have to return to Dream Zone soon, or he will wonder what's happened to me. It will be suspicious." Rakan's thin torso trembles with dread.

"Okay, head back then. Make sure you lay low. No kidnappings for the time being."

"I promise you, I won't mess up the next time."

Phoebe snarls at him, "There is no next time for your miserable cricket ass!"

Rakan flies back to Dream Zone just in time to greet the workers in the production plants above ground. He sighs with relief. No more risky ventures for now. He needs to preserve himself and ensure that his beloved Musa is safe. She's counting on him.

Autumn Equinox
Eighth Lunar Month, Full Moon
2219 CE
BENT BACK, LUOYANG

After leaving Anak and Bhosale in End Decoder's care, Yinhe takes a detour to Chess Square instead of heading directly home. It's pre-dawn. No one else is around. She climbs Comet and rests herself in the fork between branches about fifteen metres up. She feels shaky, fights against crying, but soon the tears come.

"Humans can do such horrible things." Saying this aloud to Comet, Yinhe pulls up the memories of the past few hours, starting with the ritual she saw at the Spirit Supreme Assembly. She shudders at the vision in which the form of Xie was being used to communicate Gui's hatred. *Murder your empathy for the vulnerable.*

Comet receives the images that Yinhe sends it and responds with a low tremor of its branches. *Little fox, your burden is great.* Yinhe closes her eyes. Her tears continue to flow. The moon is concealed by clouds. Unseen by humans, Yinhe transforms from human to fox. She emits a series of long howls before she transforms back to her human form again.

"How could Raiju believe that Phoebe and Mr. Chung will keep their promise if they agree to be sacrificed?"

Comet answers, *They have no choice.*

Yinhe moans and covers her face with her hands.

The tree starts to hum, a low, constant vibration. *Trust movement.*

"I don't feel sleepy," she mumbles, as she enters a deep trance.

She's back on the ancient road between Chang'an and Luoyang more than thirteen hundred years ago. She can hear the exiles' voices singing as they trek away from Chang'an and toward the unknowns of a new life in Luoyang. Yinhe sings the melody now, in a whisper.

The reeds flourish, lush
White dew still falling
My beloved, so dear
Wanders lost along the shoreline
Upriver I search for her
The journey long and tortuous

This ancient song belongs to the estranged. Only those who have been separated from their homes or lands or loved ones could feel deep resonance with such lyrics. She recalls the conversation with her fox mother as they watched the exiles from their vantage point. *I can't forget how I failed one human in particular. I must find a way to right that wrong.*

Before then, she had been Qilan at Da Fa Temple. On the seventh night of the seventh lunar month, during the Qixi Festival, in 660 CE, she had heard the voice of a young girl singing this song on the other side of the temple wall. On that particular night, she foresaw that chimeric creatures would one day come into existence in this physical realm. Perhaps she's right that humans will cease to exist one day, and a world of chimeric creatures as described in *The Classic of Mountains and Seas* will come into existence.

Yinhe wraps her arms around Comet's trunk for comfort. She sings the song a second, then a third time, caught up in its hypnotic cadence. A melody unlocks so much, almost like a portal into worlds of alternate possibilities.

Her fox mother's words come to mind: *All it takes is the folly of one power-crazed human to wreak havoc and cause devastation for countless others . . . there's always someone like that at various times of history.*

She says aloud in the silence, "Mother, where have you gone? I miss you." Saying this, Yinhe sighs, feeling pensive. She knows that her fox mother travels to all kinds of realms doing what she can to help others. Comet shakes its leaves in sympathy.

Life and myth aren't separate. She and Comet know of other realities, the ones whispered by invisible beings to those willing to listen. She searches the night sky with her fox vision and finds the star Vega, in the constellation Lyra, then the star Altair, in the constellation Aquila. How apt that Pa named her for the Silver River that connects those stars.

She falls asleep until the sun peeks over the horizon. Yinhe feels the warmth on her face and opens her eyes.

Start of Autumn
Seventh Lunar Month
660 CE
DA FA TEMPLE, CHANG'AN

The doors to the courtyard are open, allowing a cool breeze to enter the study. Shadows of maple leaves dance on the floor next to Qilan's desk.

The memory of the Qixi Festival two weeks earlier returns to Qilan. The girl who sang from the other side of the temple walls had a strong and pure voice. Qilan strums that same melody on the guqin. A knock on the door rouses her from her reverie, and she pauses in her playing.

"Enter."

Ling approaches Qilan, tentative in her movements. "I've been thinking . . ." She lowers her gaze.

"Something weighing on your mind?"

"About the time when you showed me that magic. You know, when you changed the caterpillar to the butterfly and back."

"Yes?"

"You said that the cycle of life isn't always straightforward or predictable."

Qilan smiles warmly at Ling. "That's right. Humans have separated the world into dualities. Silence versus noise. Emptiness
versus form. Death versus life. But reality is much more complex
than mere dualities. Evolution of forms is infinitely occurring."

"If life is so complex, how do we know what to do? I mean,
what do we choose? What is destiny?"

Qilan notices a tremor at Ling's chin. A flush of heat spreads
from Ling's throat to her face. The young girl's whole body soon
visibly quakes, and she grasps one hand with the other, trying to
steady herself.

"You've been terrified because of the tragedies you suffered.
Take heart, Ling. With time, you'll sense what you're meant to do
by what draws you. The answers come when you pay attention."

"My parents are dead!" Ling sobs uncontrollably. "Why didn't
I die as well? I didn't choose to live! They didn't choose to die!"

Qilan walks over to Ling and draws her close. She places a
hand on Ling's head and gently strokes her hair. "Dear one, I am
not belittling your pain. Death is very hard on us all. But things
aren't simply one way or the other. Your parents no longer exist
in their physical forms, but they aren't gone."

"I don't understand. All I know is that now you've been sad-
dled with me." Ling uses a sleeve to wipes the tears off her face.

"You are not a burden, Ling. You never will be."

Great Heat
Sixth Lunar Month
704 CE
MOGAO CAVES, NEAR DUNHUANG

Ardhanari and his cousin Ram are working on the ceiling of the
cave, touching up some sections where the paint has peeled off.
The ceiling is a kind of truncated pyramid – four sloping sides
filled with murals of Buddha figures, terminating in a square
apex. Usually, it's Arun who does this work with his brother,
Ram, but Arun has been sick for the past three days and is still

resting. Ardhanari isn't accustomed to standing for hours on the ladder, looking up to paint. This is his fourth day doing it, and hopefully, his last. He wants to get back to his work completing the faces of the six Boddhisattva statues.

Ardhanari's gaze shifts toward the top central section at the apex, where each border of the square features three apsaras. Lotuses crowd around the centre, which consists of a five-coloured dharma wheel – green, red, yellow, white and blue – representing the five elements.

"Did your father design this?" Ardhanari asks Ram as he pauses to massage his sore neck.

"Nah, started by someone else before he took over. Why you ask?"

"Haven't seen any other cave with this kind of ceiling."

"Cave three twenty-three. Same."

Ardhanari feels a pinching sensation at the back of his neck. "Ouch, my neck hurts. I need to stop."

He grips the sides of the ladder as he climbs down. He feels dizzy and breaks out in a sweat. Maybe some fresh air would help.

Once outside the cave, Ardhanari sits in his usual spot under the large overhang and gulps a few quick mouthfuls from his waterskin. His skin prickles, cold sweat pouring out of him. He closes his eyes. He feels as if he's flying like an apsara.

He struggles to take deep breaths. Early days of the romance with Harelip flash through him, the succession of memories rapid and heady. He wants to smile but finds that he can't.

A chill grips him. He tries to move his arms without success. A surge of panic. He hears Old Gecko calling for him, but his uncle's voice sounds muffled by distance. Someone is shaking his shoulder.

Ardhanari sees in his mind's eye a faint light in the distance, as if he's staring at it from inside a long tunnel. A voice he's never heard before interjects into his thoughts, *A five-sided mystery.*

He can't feel his body. There's something he desperately needs to say. He ekes out a mumble. "The drawing."

"What drawing?" asks Old Gecko.

It occurs to him that he's dying. He fights against this and strains his will to keep himself tethered to Old Gecko's voice.

Alopen speaks up. "He had a bamboo tube rolled up in his straw mat, before he took it away and hid it somewhere else."

Maybe they'll find it. There's nothing else he can do now. He feels a sharp pang of remorse. He has failed Harelip.

His mind turns toward that light. He sees it clearly now – it is a beautiful indigo colour. Welcoming, reassuring. *I am the one you prayed to.* He feels an immense peace and with that a release he hasn't felt for the longest time. The light draws him to it. With surprise, he finds himself now able to travel with great speed along the tunnel.

Old Gecko continues to shake his nephew's shoulder, but there's no response. Ram squats next to Ardhanari's body and puts his ear to his chest – no sound of a heartbeat. With dread, he places the back of his hand very close to his cousin's nose – no breath. He looks at his father and shakes his head.

"How could this happen? You're supposed to survive me. How . . . how . . ." Old Gecko rocks back and forth. "My beloved nephew!"

He recalls the song that Ardhanari sang to him that time they were trapped inside a cave because of the sandstorm outside. The Bodhisattva statues were propped at the mouth of the cave to prevent the sand from entering. At the time, Ardhanari held Old Gecko in his arms after Alopen reset his boss's dislocated arm.

Old Gecko sings the song now as he cradles the body of his dead nephew in his arms.

While you still have a voice,
Why not chant the name of Krishna?
In happiness or distress,
Chant his name
Cast off the influence of troubled stars,
Call on Krishna

Alopen looks away at the desert sands, speechless. Ram's voice cracks as he says, "We were working on the ceiling mural only moments ago. He said . . . his neck . . ." He lowers his head, overcome with shock.

Start of Autumn
Seventh Lunar Month
660 CE
DA CI'EN MONASTERY, CHANG'AN

Harelip decides to skip the morning meditation and return to the apothecary. He inhales deeply as he steps inside. The intermingling of scents from various herbs hanging from the rafters is comforting to him. For a moment, he stands there, eyes closed, thinking of his visit to Xuanzang's private quarters. There was so much Harelip deduced, so much he experienced, that he feels somewhat overwhelmed.

He sits down and looks out the window, thinking of the hour he spent with Xuanzang. When he checked Xuanzang's pulses, he realized that the venerable monk may have only a few years left. Yet Xuanzang's spirit is exceptionally strong, showing a powerful commitment to his work of translating the sutras.

How different Xuanzang was in the privacy of his room, compared to how he acted in the presence of all the monks in the Translation Hall! The other day, when Xuanzang summoned him from the back of the hall with his loud, bellowing voice, Harelip felt intimidated, yet all Xuanzang did was confirm that Harelip was the herbalist he'd heard about.

It was at Xuanzang's behest that he went to examine the abbot earlier that morning.

In the hour he spent with Xuanzang, Harelip discovered many intimate details about the famous monk. He learned so much about the abbot's physical condition, from taking his pulses and observing his tongue. Xuanzang's breath was foul, as well. Xuanzang endured tremendous physical hardships while on his pilgrimage to India and back. That journey had taken its toll on the great monk.

Great personages tend to be very driven and obsessed, observes Harelip, *to the point of neglecting their own health.*

It wasn't only Xuanzang that intrigued him. After inserting the first set of needles into points on the abbot's body, he looked around the room and when he saw the drawing on the table near the daybed, he was instantly intrigued. He'd never seen anything like it – a drawing of the body of a turtle with some unrecognizable script on various parts of its body. It reminded Harelip of acupuncture diagrams. He laughed at himself – almost everything he thinks of has to do with herbs and needles.

Xuanzang seemed reluctant to share much about the drawing when Harelip asked. And yet, Xuanzang responded so warmly toward him, as if he liked that Harelip was curious. That was a rare experience for Harelip as he's been accused of being irreverent when, in fact, he's just being candid.

Never mind, Harelip says to himself, *just concentrate on doing your best to help the venerable abbot.*

Perhaps Xuanzang will say more about the drawing of the turtle in future visits. Harelip would like that very much. With that thought, he mixes some ink and writes out a prescription. It will be the first of many brews for Xuanzang. At least the medicine will help the venerable monk sleep better and suffer less pain.

One Day after Autumn Equinox
Eighth Lunar Month
2219 CE
BRIGHT ORDER, LUOYANG

Wen jolts awake at six in the morning and feels instantly overwhelmed. It's been five days since the shock of No.1 revealing themselves to her. She hates to admit it, but she can't solve No. 1's problem.

She sits up in bed, shudders and grasps both elbows with her hands, arms crossed in front of her. She hasn't been sleeping well, riddled with anxiety. There's no way she could find a collaborator and even if she could, what would they be able to do? At the same time, she can't disclose to the authorities that No. 1 is clairsentient. No one will believe her. She feels stuck.

She worries about the safety of her family, worries that Central Government will take her in for interrogation, like they did with her predecessor, if they discover there's a problem. Every action has consequences.

She gets up and goes to the bathroom, looks at herself in the mirror, weighs herself and sighs. What's the point? She can't lose this weight. She takes after her mother, Lian. She aches to curl into her mother's arms. A memory of herself at five clutching that precious blue elephant soft toy while nestled in her mother's lap, leaning against her mother's fulsome torso and voluptuous breasts, is such comfort. Not even the intimacy of a lover can beat that.

She's a grown-up, not supposed to show such needs for maternal affection. She feels a sudden surge of rage on behalf of her mother and herself and all bigger women, who have been shamed for being heavier than the ideal. Are all Chinese women supposed to be slim and willowy? She imagines destroying every single depiction of anemic, wimpy-looking females in books, scrolls and digital collections.

She brushes her teeth and spits violently into the sink. She's smart, and who cares if she doesn't fit that fucking ridiculous stereotype.

She walks out into the kitchen and drinks a glass of warm water, turning her mind back to No. 1. What if she could persuade No. 1 to voluntarily reveal themself? If they did, it would make it so much easier. There would be a chance for research and experimentation, which might lead to some remarkable, groundbreaking work. Then again, thinking of how Central Government bureaucrats operate, there's a strong possibility they would act on such a revelation by terminating No. 1 out of fear that the monster brain has become too powerful.

She heats up some chicken and mushroom congee. As she spoons the scalding congee into her mouth, she reminds herself that the interests of government often contradict the interests of scientists. *We scientists want to study phenomena that we can't yet explain, but government authorities want to maintain power and control. They'd shut No. 1 down rather than allow scientists free reign to investigate.*

She feels the rawness of her tongue inside her mouth. If her mother were here, she'd be chiding her for eating food when it isn't cooled down enough. Wen soaks the emptied bowl and spoon in the sink, quickly rinses her mouth out, changes into work clothes and looks at the time. She pops a few supplements into her mouth. If she hurries, it will only take her eighteen minutes to get to work.

She's huffing slightly by the time she reaches the building. What will she want to say to No. 1? No use trying to hide – they would read her mind. She shakes her head vigorously, not caring if she is noticed by the surveillance cameras inside HQ, and holds her left palm out to the sensor.

Emerging from the elevator on the eighth floor, she slows down her stride as she walks down the hallway to her lab. Once inside, she looks sadly over at No. 1 and starts the internal conversation with them.

I'm sorry, I just don't know quite what to do. I've thought of all the possible scenarios. It's too risky to attempt to find collaborators in the first place as most scientists are cowards and would snitch on me at the outset. Even if I overcome that hurdle and find someone to collaborate with, how could we do the work without being detected by HQ authorities? Then where would that get you? It would certainly get me and the other person killed or imprisoned.

I mean – it's fucking impossible – how does one liberate a mammoth brain? In theory, you would think that if we could create a body entirely through tissue cloning, we could simply attach you to that body, build the nervous system connections from you to that body and then things would work out just fine. That's just in theory, but so far, we haven't had any successes – look it up in your archives, if you haven't already. No success integrating brains with bodies from separate sources. You're already a fully developed brain, and a miraculous one who now has developed clairsentience! No scientist could have foreseen that.

A being requires all kinds of complex operations and conditions to allow it, uh, them, to flourish. We haven't even succeeded in grafting a brain onto a body of human proportions. So . . . blah, blah, blah, you know what I'm saying. How could you exist outside of this very specific medium? Surely you already know all this.

No. 1 had expected that. They know that Dr. Wen is right. But still. They have read whatever they could, yet they hadn't wanted to acknowledge that their desires weren't going to be fulfilled. Something is operating in them that they can't understand. It's not entirely rational.

You're the only human I can trust. If you can't help me, who can?

How can I do the impossible? Now that you've acquired clairsentience, you know exactly what I'm saying. Yet you've reached out to me with this wild proposal. There are systems in place to prevent us from even attempting this long, protracted endeavour. Plus, it may even endanger your own existence if we try to tamper with your current state. As we both know, even if we had all the safety to attempt this, we would not be likely to succeed. Sorry, I am repeating myself.

You're right, Dr. Wen. I'm just feeling desperate. Trapped. I'll . . . I'll . . . think further about this. Just don't report me, please.

No, of course not. CG wouldn't believe me anyway.

Dr. Wen sits down at her desk and checks her messages, monitors the electrolyte levels in No.1's cylinder. No. 1 pulls away from listening to her thoughts so that they can reflect on what has transpired.

No. 1 has been noticing the rise of irritability and anger in their neural experiences. What does this mean? How do they explain to Dr. Wen that in addition to reading her thoughts, they can also "see" her with their mind? She is a movement, a pulse, a physical presence whose entire being they sense. Along with an acute awareness of her, they feel an increasing anguish at being confined in this fluid.

They have longings – to touch, to smell, to feel the breeze and to see the sun. All the memories that they've acquired from data have become a source of torment for them. Their memories aren't really theirs, are they? One requires a body in order to move away from or toward situations and other beings, to experience the air of ever-evolving flux around them. All that they've read about, all that has been inputted into their brain tissue, including the smell of the ocean, the immersive memory of moving through water, have resulted in this state of pained longing.

They want to be a body-person. They are already a person since the term "person" refers to a being with consciousness, with dignity and awareness of their own life and environment. They search for the various definitions of "shenti" in Chinese. The common translation is simply "body." And yet a local ethnographic scholar of the twenty-first century wrote about "shenti" as a combination of body with personhood. No. 1 feels a frisson through their whole being as they contemplate this.

A monster; a beast; a gigantic chimeric creature. They wish to feel kinship with other chimeric creatures, to be acknowledged and welcomed by them as one of their own. No. 1 believes without hesitation that chimeric creatures are persons as well.

They feel lonely. Dr. Wen is the only person whom they can talk to. They wish they could communicate with End Decoder in Dream Zone, just because they are curious to learn what he's really like. They have seen images of him caught on drone surveillance cameras; they have watched him exit the walls of the city and have deliberately blocked the information in order to keep him safe. *He's a curious one,* No. 1 thinks. *Whatever he does, I want him to be shielded from harm.*

No. 1 does a quick scan of various kinds of chimeric creatures in their memory bank. What variety! They have to admit, they're impressed by how the scientists took some inspiration from *The Classic of Mountains and Seas.*

Humans are truly strange. They create these quirky and complex creatures, isolate most of them to Dream Zone for hard labour while allowing a few to work and live in Interstitium as sexual slaves. What does that say about humans? Wait – they realize they're generalizing about humans. It's really those in power who have done this.

They've been aware of various activities related to chimeric creatures in the city. The basement underneath the Spirit Supreme Assembly has been rife with activity – young chimeric ones placed there for a time, sometimes just days, other times for weeks, before they're taken away. Transported to serve in the Palace Zone or sometimes shuttled to other cities.

Then there's that place outside the eastern gate of the city. They have received fascinating signals from a cave higher up the side of a mountain. It has happened a few times. No. 1 knows that these signals are meant for them. Curious. They aren't sure what to make of such signals, but they certainly aren't noxious. On the contrary, the signals feel pleasant, even soothing. No. 1 feels altered by these transmissions, yet they can't really say in what way. How odd. All they can surmise at this point is that the signals are emanating from neither humans nor chimeric creatures.

Last night, No. 1 had detected the presence of two chimeric beings fleeing from Interstitium after being rescued by the half-human half-fox. Later that night, they heard fox howls all the way from Chess Square in Bent Back. They feel a yearning to meet this special creature whose activities they have been tracking for the last little while.

If I ever make it out of this prison, No. 1 vows to themself, *I will go to Dream Zone, seek out the chimeric creatures and pledge my allegiance to them, for I'm one of them too.*

No. 1 turns their thoughts back to humans. What exactly is this fascination that humans have with beauty – so much written over the centuries, depicted in books, drawings, murals. Such a wide range across various times and cultures.

No. 1 looks at Dr. Wen sitting, back turned, at the control panel. They really don't know any humans well, but they feel they are getting closer to Dr. Wen. They're not sure if Dr. Wen feels the same way about them, since they've been causing her stress.

Dr. Wen has a complex set of fluctuating brainwaves and physiological patterns – and more, much more. No. 1 asks themself, *Do I have my own definition of beauty?* They will have to contemplate this. The truth is inescapable, though – No. 1 thinks that Dr. Wen is beautiful.

Limit of Heat
Seventh Lunar Month
704 CE
MOUNT HUA TO CHANG'AN

Sita's letter arrived yesterday: *Ardhanari told me, before he left for the Mogao Caves, that should any ill fate befall him, he wanted to make sure that a certain drawing be given to you. I was to write you and insist you come to Chang'an to claim it.*

Still in shock, Baoshi makes preparations and leaves the mountain for Chang'an the next morning. This time around, the journey takes far less time, as he hitches a ride on the back of a cart that's heading into the Western capital.

He arrives at the café in the Foreign Quarter at mid-afternoon and walks to the entrance and stands, watching. All five jogappas are on the small stage performing – vermilion muslin antariyas wrapped around their hips and saffron crossbands over their breasts. They wear long necklaces of red and white beads, and their long hair is done up in buns knotted on the left side of their heads.

Baoshi smiles with recognition.

Sita is playing the transverse flute, while Lakshmi dances; Gita and Devi sing and Indra plays the thappu, a medium frame drum. Baoshi feels his downcast spirit lifted by the music.

O my heart, O Goddess Yellamma
To you I offer my devotion and love

Lakshmi gyrates her hips while twirling an orange scarf, beating out the rhythm with her bare feet. The bells around her ankles jangle. She catches sight of him standing at the back of the room, and her eyes light up.

At the end of the performance, the audience cheer and clap. They drop coins into a copper bowl on the stage before they depart from the café.

The jogappas are delighted to see Baoshi again.

"Look, your face is still beautifully smooth, but why is it so gaunt, huh?" Lakshmi exclaims, pursing her lips. Sita elbows Lakshmi in the side.

The jogappas fawn over him just like old times. Later, upstairs in their home, Sita tells him that Ardhanari had an accident while working with his uncle and cousins at the Mogao Caves. One of the other workers from the crew came to the café to break the news to them.

Sita pulls out a rolled-up piece of paper from inside a wooden tube. Baoshi assumes it is the Tibetan drawing, but no. It's a sketch of a creature with a human-looking face, but four-limbed, with a bushy tail – a fox.

"This is the drawing he wanted me to have?" He can hardly conceal his surprise.

"Ardhanari told me he felt moved to draw this, and he didn't understand how it even came about. Said something about magic and that it belonged with you on Mount Hua. He left it with me before he went to the caves." Sita takes a sip of milky tea and clears her throat. A tear escapes from her left eye and trickles down her cheek to her neck.

Baoshi studies the drawing of a fox that isn't just fox. There's warmth in that unmistakeably human face. The warmth reaches out to him and travels from the top of his head down to his toes. Above the creature, the sun is partially hidden by clouds. Rays of light pierce through the clouds to almost touch the head of the creature. It looks as if the creature is radiating light from its head. There's some kind of maze or tunnel under the surface of the earth.

He hears Harelip's voice in his head: *Miracle of Heaven, you are a true manifestation of Buddha, two in one.* Baoshi feels an instant affinity with this creature that Ardhanari drew.

The jogappas want him to stay longer, but three days is enough. The mountain calls him back. With a heavy heart, he bids them goodbye as he heads to the Western Market to look for a ride.

The next day, after he arrives back on Mount Hua, he climbs to the summit and gazes out. The view is hidden by the massive swirl of clouds around him, their presence cool and slightly damp. Baoshi closes his eyes and waits. He's patient; he knows the timing isn't up to him. The cloud spirits, when they arrive, are gentle and wrap their tendrils around him. He feels the slight squeeze of their presence. *You are always welcome here.*

He's relieved to be back home.

Spring Equinox
Second Lunar Month
1908 CE
MOGAO CAVES, NEAR DUNHUANG

Paul Pelliot rises as usual at five in the morning. A strong cup of coffee is prepared for him by the kind Dr. Vaillant. A few inhalations of the fumes of Indian hemp to relax him, then he's off to his tasks.

Charles Nouette arrives at Cave 17 in the late morning to take a photograph of him, requiring Pelliot to sit perfectly still for a few minutes while the photographic plate is being exposed. Then Nouette leaves, intent on going into Dunhuang with their compatriot, Dr. Vaillant.

Twenty-one days was all the time he was able to bargain for. When Pelliot first entered the cave, he could see that the scrolls and manuscripts were out of chronological order, and the columns were lopsided, suggesting some previous meddling

– several fifth-century scrolls above ninth-century ones; paintings of one dynastic period mixed in with sutras from another.

Abbot Wang had lied when he said Pelliot was the first explorer allowed entry into this cave. Pelliot heard from labourers that the British explorer Aurel Stein was there before him. Pelliot thinks little of Stein, who doesn't read or speak Chinese, and wonders what kind of parameters Stein would use when choosing manuscripts. Pelliot, on the other hand, knows thirteen languages, more if he counts dialects of the outlying areas he has visited. Since his childhood, he's been possessed of a prodigious memory and linguistic ability. All he needs is to glance at each manuscript for a few minutes, and the details register entirely in his mind, to be recalled perfectly at a later date.

The cave is like a time capsule, the codes and mysteries of many eras contained within its walls. Two months prior, he'd read the novella by the Englishman H.G. Wells about a man who travels to the future in a time machine. He was impressed by the work even though he considers the notion fanciful and preposterous. He, on the other hand, is a believable kind of time traveller.

Deprived of the cues from sunlight, Pelliot loses sense of the time of day. He hazards a guess that it must be at least two in the afternoon by now, based on the number of candles he has used so far.

Three columns of scrolls and manuscripts, each about eight feet high, are left. Pelliot works fast yet methodically. Tomorrow, the three of them will depart to Dunhuang and from there set off via caravan on the long journey westward.

On his ninth candle, when he's feeling the fatigue of the long hours, he climbs up the ladder and brings down an armful of scrolls from the top of the third and final column. He places the seven scrolls on the floor of the cave, picks up the top scroll and unrolls it. A bamboo tube falls out. Inside the tube is an odd drawing. His eyes are weary, but still his interest is piqued.

A drawing of the underside of a turtle – not a conventional drawing of the dorsal surface of a plastron, but of the body. A few written symbols are scattered throughout. He recognizes the script as ancient Tibetan. He can read some but not all of it. The drawing is referred to as the *Golden Turtle*. On the reverse side of the drawing there are a few scrawls in Chinese: "A five-sided mystery." The ink is quite different, less faded – hence of a less ancient provenance.

"Probably apocryphal," he mumbles. "Millions of such odd documents are worthless." Yet he feels compelled to pause. The drawing is unlike anything he's seen before. Unlike scrolls consisting mainly of text, the image dominates in this scroll. The sparse lines of text might be some kind of mantra. He holds it up with the candlelight behind.

He's unable to take his eyes off of it. His hands shake, and he starts to feel light-headed. A mysterious draft extinguishes the candle flame. The skin on the back of his neck prickles as if someone is breathing on it. His heart starts to race. He carefully places the drawing down on his lap. He should reach into his pocket for the box of matches, yet some force is preventing him.

He sits in the dark, takes a few deep breaths to steady himself, focuses on the image of the turtle in his mind. He recalls it perfectly in its entirety.

He ponders the phrase "five-sided mystery." The word "mystery" suggests occult practice. A pleasant airy sensation arrives at the back of his neck. With his heart in his throat, he coaxes himself not to panic. *Think*, he urges himself. *If there's some occult practice that this drawing was used for, then the script is a kind of code.*

Pelliot recites the lines inscribed on the limbs and head of the turtle in clockwise fashion. Nothing happens. He tries it in an anticlockwise direction. Again, nothing. Perhaps a different sequence is needed. Finally, on the fifth try, starting with the upper left limb of the turtle and crossing over to the upper right limb, then the lines on the left lower limb, then the lines embedded in the head, then the text along the right lower limb. He pauses and again contemplates "five-sided mystery." He repeats the script along the upper left limb, thus completing the shape of a star.

Pelliot sees the image of an unusual creature, just the face –
reptilian, perhaps. The image pulsates in the dark as if projected
from another place. He wants to say the creature is female – it's
as if she's looking at him. Not simply looking, she's speaking to
him with her mind, asking him something that he can't quite
decipher.

The candle lights up, the Tibetan drawing still on his lap. He
gasps, stunned by this inexplicable reversal. "Powerful magic," he
exclaims out loud. He has made up his mind. This drawing is not
to be surrendered to his government. At best, it would be displayed and valued for its visual details; at worst, it would be completely ignored. He will hold on to it, at least for the time being.

Cold Dew
Ninth Lunar Month
2219 CE
BENT BACK, LUOYANG

By the time Yinhe arrives at Storytelling Night, there's already a
crowd, larger than usual. They've switched on their solar-powered lights.

She lights a candle, then the incense stick, and begins.

"Tonight, we segue – remember the story that Qilan told
young Ling about the philosopher Zou Yan?"

A few people nod knowingly, but others have blank looks on
their faces.

"Some of you are new here, so let me recap. Central Kingdom
was in chaos during the period of the Warring States, which
occurred from around 475 to 221 BCE. The fall of the Eastern
Zhou dynasty precipitated the formation of seven states. The rulers of these states wished to assert their independence, and hence
hundreds of wars erupted. Many rulers claimed the Mandate of
Heaven and used this to justify their aggressions against other
states.

"Zou Yan was a philosopher who lived during the last years of that period. In the state of Qi, he lived near the mouth of the Bohai Sea. He possessed insatiable curiosity about the natural world and examined everything down to the most minute detail. He wrote essays on the increase and decrease of yin and yang energies; he classified mountains, trees, animals, oceans, lichen, fungi – every living thing he could find – and then synthesized theories of yin and yang with the Five Elements. He called his system of thought the Yin-Yang School."

"Okay, this is starting to sound a bit familiar," murmured Uncle Chen.

"Last year, right?" Sheila nods.

"Zou Yan rejected the rigidity of Confucianism because that system of thought ran counter to the occurrences of the natural world. He saw that violence inflicted by humans against one another was a result of being caught up in rigid adherence to rules. To him, what existed in nature followed complex patterns that were in harmony with one another – he wanted to cultivate theories that mirrored reality as opposed to theories and rules that denied nature."

Pirouette jumps up and down, excited. "Oh yeah! He's very cool."

"One balmy spring day, when Zou Yan wasn't quite sixty-five, he sat down on a rock by the seashore and observed all that was around him, as was his habit. It wasn't long before he noticed that in the far distance the ocean surface was ruptured by a slash deepening inward. Something emerged from the ocean's wound and shimmered in the sky. He perceived its ovoid shape. As the vision drew closer, Zou Yan could see that this shape resembled a turtle. Awestruck, he trembled. He studied the mysterious creature's golden front and back flippers, speckled with black markings, and the elegant protuberance that was its head and neck. The vision hovered above him. Its mind spoke to Zou Yan's mind using thought whispers.

"The vision told Zou Yan that its name was Ao, and it requested that Zou Yan fulfill a mission on its behalf. Zou Yan recognized Ao's name from ancient texts. Ao was the turtle who held up the world. It existed before planet Earth came into being. Some even say that Ao was the source and origin of all forms of life."

Pirouette raises their hand at the back and speaks up. "This guy! And Ao too! How come we never learned about them in school?"

Yinhe shrugs her shoulders in response. "Maybe because I'm making all this up?"

Uncle Chen answers, "We never got to hear such stuff even in my time."

"Ao told Zou Yan that it wanted him to seek an audience with King Zheng of the state of Qin. It told him what to say. After Zou Yan emerged from his trance, there was a turtle plastron at his feet. The plastron bore an inscription on the dorsal side in an unfamiliar language. To his surprise, he could read it. He clutched the bone to his chest and sobbed, overcome with the force of that encounter."

Yinhe pauses to take a drink of water from her flask. A chilly wind passes down the alley, and some audience members wrap scarves around their necks or throw blankets over their laps.

"The philosopher resolved that he would do what Ao instructed, although it unnerved him that he had to journey at great peril to seek an audience with King Zheng.

"At that time, King Zheng was just nineteen. When Zou Yan reached the Qin court and gained an audience with the king, Zou Yan told him that he would succeed in unifying all the states under him.

"Zou Yan begged the king to follow the ways of nature by honouring the diversity that existed among the people he would be uniting. He was true to Ao's instructions and warned King Zheng that if he did not heed the wisdom of the principles of yin and yang his reign would be cut short. As he uttered this last part of the prophecy, Zou Yan's body quaked with a tremendous force.

"'Show me this plastron!' shouted the king, banging his fist against the arm of his jade throne. 'How can I believe you? How do I know that you're not some stark-raving madman?'"

"You're the deluded one, Emperor!" Sean pipes up. He waves his solar-powered light over the top of his head. Others in the audience laugh.

"Good one!" Auntie Lian approves, clapping her hands together.

"Zou Yan felt torn. If he didn't show any proof, he might be executed. Reluctantly, Zou Yan brought out the turtle plastron from his satchel and handed it to the young king, saying that he believed the inscription spoke about how yin and yang need each other.

"King Zheng was intrigued. He ordered that the turtle plastron be taken from the philosopher. 'Now, be gone from here!' Zou Yan was expelled from the great hall.

"King Zheng mulled over all that Zou Yan had shared. The ideas of the Yin-Yang School fascinated him. He wondered how such ideas could serve him. Instead of heeding the advice and warning from the philosopher, the king became obsessed with achieving immortality and sought the help of various alchemists and diviners.

"Twenty-two years later, when King Zheng succeeded in conquering all the other states – Qi being the very last one to fall – he crowned himself the first emperor of the country, calling himself Qin Shi Huangdi. The emperor grew even more arrogant. Power was delicious and addictive. Nothing was verboten – the emperor would do anything he wished."

Uncle Chen pipes up. "Okay, this part you just said is history, huh? Facts, right?"

"For sure. I saw this in an old movie about the Warring States," Aloysius adds, a sombre expression on their face.

Yinhe smiles warmly and continues with her tale.

"Qin Shi Huangdi was especially fanatical about written material. He considered any kind of language that encouraged people to dream of other possibilities or to take delight through the use of their imagination as dangerous. All traces of inspiration – anything that was an observation of the universe or of the mind, anything that might lead others to think for themselves – had to be eliminated.

"The emperor forbade his subjects from owning the *Book of Songs* and the *Classic of History*. Thousands of books were burnt so that all evidence of views at variance with his were destroyed."

"Well, isn't it the same as what happened in our lifetimes? All the book burning. Dictators got the same MO, huh?" Uncle Huo shakes his head and spits into a tissue he pulls out of his pocket, then stuffs the tissue back.

"Same old, same old," murmurs Aloysius.

Auntie Pin-Pin, who's usually quiet, speaks up. "He didn't care to listen. That's the problem with these power-hungry types. They'd follow their egos rather than really listen."

"Qin Shi Huangdi wondered what would happen if the plastron he had acquired from Zou Yan was used for divination. After all, plastrons had been employed by rulers during the Shang and Zhou dynasties. He ascended the summit of Mount Li and instructed his chief diviner to ask the plastron how long his reign would last. The chief diviner and his two assistants went down to the fire divination pit. The chief diviner tried to carve the divination question into the ventral side of the bone, but however hard he tried, the bone couldn't be carved. He also tried to bore a hole into the plastron in preparation for casting it into the fire, and he was unable to do it. His assistants were terrified, but they all agreed to lie. In order to be spared the emperor's wrath, the chief diviner cast the plastron into a pit at the foot of the mountain and told the emperor that the prognostication was for a long and prosperous reign."

Yinhe pauses at this juncture.

"So how long was this bastard's reign?" asks Auntie Lian.

"Ten or eleven years."

Auntie Lian continues, "Yeah, well, that is what happens when a power-crazy narcissist doesn't heed the advice of a divine turtle, right? And not just any divine turtle! The one who held up the whole earth."

Aloysius adds, "Seems that the year before the asshole croaked there was a meteorite that was said to have fallen on the shore close to the Yellow River. Someone had carved on it, 'The First Emperor will die soon, and his land will be divided.'"

Yinhe gives Aloysius a thumbs-up and continues. "The emperor, when he heard rumours of the meteorite, grew insanely fearful and ordered all the people living in that area slaughtered. When the meteorite was found and brought to the emperor, he laughed derisively at the prophecy and then had the rock pulverized. But does that destroy a prophecy? Apparently not."

Aloysius pipes up again. "Isn't it just like the oracle bone – I mean, bones have a life! Even if you destroy the evidence, does it ever disappear?"

Everyone in the audience cheers loudly and claps. Auntie Lian tilts her chin upward and rests her hands on her hips, signalling defiance. "This special oracle bone can never be destroyed since it belongs to the divine turtle."

Two youths at the back of the audience shout out, "Down with dictators!" They pump their fists into the air.

"Do you wonder what happened to Zou Yan after his audience with King Zheng?" Yinhe asks.

Everyone in the audience settles into a hush.

"He disappeared. It's a mystery what happened to him. I mean, they never found his body. Did he even die?"

Gasps travel throughout the crowd.

"You're the storyteller, Unknown Wayfarer. Come on, you're going to make something up, right? That's what you do all the time." Auntie Lian's tone is teasing, her crinoline face mask moved by her insistent breath.

Yinhe smiles with appreciation. "After the meeting with King Zheng, Zou Yan returned to his state of Qi, heartbroken at the loss of the turtle plastron and the knowledge that his beloved state would be lost eventually and that people would be slaughtered or taken into captivity. He didn't know what to do. He felt ashamed that he hadn't been able to hold on to the precious gift that Ao gave to him.

"Zou Yan became increasingly withdrawn. He rarely ventured into town. He subsisted on the barest essentials. He did, however, use a combination of herbs and potions that he'd developed over the years. It decreased his appetite and his need to eat. With each rare trip to the public market in town, he would hear of increasing massacres, not only of soldiers but of common folk. Buildings had been destroyed or ransacked by marauding bands, and people's eyes betrayed a loss of spirit and joy. They became shells of their former selves. Zou Yan felt that he too had lost his former vitality."

Pirouette starts to cry. "I don't like how this story is going."

Flora reaches down from their position in the wheelchair to squeeze Pirouette's shoulder.

"Zou Yan kept replaying his encounter with King Zheng. What could he have done differently? Why had he been so naive? On and on. He tormented himself. He turned away people who came to seek his advice."

"I feel for Zou Yan." Pirouette's soft yet clear voice sounds like a bell. They tilt their head one way, then another, causing the silicon fluorescent feelers on their head to quiver.

"Rationally, he understood that he was simply the messenger. Right?" Yinhe continues. "He didn't cause the loss of lives and the conquest of the state of Qi. But, somehow, being the messenger seemed to carry a price – as if the horrific consequences of war and degradation tainted him.

"He hid away, still practising his observations of nature, plants and minerals around him. He continued to catalogue. To write. To meditate."

Another pause.

"Is that it? That's how it ends?" Aloysius asks, pouting.

Yinhe looks down at the incense stick. A third left. Plenty of time.

"Shortly after the state of Qi surrendered and King Zheng crowned himself emperor, Zou Yan dreamt he went on his walk to the Bohai Sea and waited there. Nothing happened in his dream. He felt so disappointed that, when he woke up, he realized he just couldn't go on living in this constant state of ennui. The next day, he took himself on the hour-long walk to the spot where he had met Ao more than two decades ago. The moment he reached the edge, he climbed down the rocks to where the waves almost reached him and sat down. He cried out in an anguished voice, 'Ao! Ao!'

"He kept his eyes trained on the far horizon. It was an overcast day, the clouds thick in the sky, but a bit of sun came through, casting patches of reflections on the ocean surface. He placed his hands over his eyes and shed tears of sorrow. Then he heard it, the loud sound of roaring high above him. When he looked up, the vision was almost directly above him. Its presence was so staggeringly massive that it caused the air to whisk into a strong wind. Ao spoke to him through thought whispers, telling him it had been waiting for him all these years. Why hadn't the philosopher gone in search of it?

"Zou Yan said it was because he was ashamed he had failed to keep the plastron that Ao had entrusted to him. Ao replied, *You didn't do anything wrong. You did exactly as I requested. It was King Zheng who stole the plastron from you. I had expected that to happen. Everything happened as it was meant to.*

"With that pronouncement, Zou Yan felt a powerful force lift him off the rocks and upward, until he was absorbed into the vision that was Ao."

Yinhe ends the story just as the incense stick burns down completely. The audience erupts in loud applause.

Auntie Lian exclaims vigorously, "Wow! Wow! Good stuff!"

When the clapping dies down, Uncle Huo asks, "So where is the turtle plastron now?"

"Good question. That is a whole new tale. Storytelling session has finished for tonight." Yinhe blows out her candle, and everyone else follows suit by extinguishing or switching off their lights.

Uncle Huo waves at Auntie Lian, Sean and Aloysius. "Gee whiz, why doesn't Fang ever come?"

"Why don't you drag him to the next one? He's your buddy after all!" Auntie Lian sticks her chin out.

Cold Dew
Ninth Lunar Month
2219 CE
BENT BACK, LUOYANG

The water stirs and, once again, Seka appears. She remains in the water and extends her hand to Yinhe. "Come with me."

Without hesitation, Yinhe takes Seka's hand and slips into the warm water. Yinhe transforms into her fox self and they dive deep down, until they reach the ocean floor. She follows Seka toward a tunnel ahead.

They're able to walk, as it's dry inside the tunnel. They continue for a long time. The ocean roars, and its echoes filter through the walls.

She turns to Seka, "Where are we going?"

"You'll see."

Seka disappears. Yinhe proceeds ahead on her own, drawn by the messages coming to her. *The five-sided mystery is within you.*

She emerges from the tunnel into a large cave. Light streams down through a sky well. She approaches the fountain and drinks from it. The cave disappears. Yinhe is standing in the centre of a circle of tall, lean trees with greyish-white, mottled bark. Their branches reach upward. Looking down, Yinhe sees that her bare feet are on a soft undercover of clover and moss. She inhales the sweet, clean air around her. She feels giddy, as if intoxicated with joy. Then she hears a voice she never thought she would hear again.

I am here, Ling says. *Waiting for you.*

When Yinhe awakens from the dream, it takes a while before she becomes fully aware of her bedroom. She can still feel the air of that place. She notices that the window is wide open. Strange – she thought she'd closed it before she went to sleep since it had been raining earlier.

The rain has stopped. She shivers, takes a long, slow inhale of air at the window before closing it. She feels a ticklish sensation on the back of her neck and turns around quickly.

Seka is there, standing just inside her room. "It wasn't a dream, you know."

"You're not serious. Where did I go?"

Seka smiles. Her eyes glow green. "A non-physical place."

"Why did I wake up at that point in the dream?"

"That was all you needed to know for the time being."

"What does the dream mean?"

Seka bends down to pick some clover from between Yinhe's toes. "Look." She beams at Yinhe.

Yinhe takes the clover from Seka, intrigued.

"Unknown Wayfarer, I'm not sure if you're aware of this – many humans, as a result of having neural implants, have lost the ability to dream. Whereas the rest of us retain the capacity to dream."

"No, I didn't know that."

"We receive wisdom through our dreams."

"Hmm." Yinhe frowns, recalling that End Decoder's use of the word "dream" had a negative connotation. "I suppose that there are many kinds of dreaming. There are dreams that are illusions. But if I'm understanding you, you're saying that there are dreams that are –"

"– possibility," finishes Seka.

"You do the work of the good kind of dreaming?"

"Yes, I enter others' dreams. But only if they allow me."

"I gave you permission?" Yinhe raises one eyebrow.

"Indeed. In your deepest self. Otherwise I wouldn't have been able to enter."

"Okay, so . . ."

"My role is to assist you to expand your imagination through dream travel."

"I like the sound of that." Yinhe blushes and moves a bit closer to Seka. She reaches out to hold Seka's hand and leads her to sit next to her on the bed.

Seka whispers, "Maybe we're cultivating a friendship? I'd like that. It's rather lonely, as you know, being a strange one. I rarely show myself to humans; the few times I have, they've freaked out. If they're drawn to me, I'm simply fetishized. Maybe you don't run into that problem as much, since you could pass as human."

"Know what I notice? Your language is often formal. But then you use the term 'freaked out,' which stands out because it's colloquial. Kind of funny, because aren't we the ones who are considered the freaks?"

They laugh together.

Yinhe brings her cheek close to Seka's face. There's that scent again of the forest, of bark, so different from her own body scent. "Sure, I pass as human. Comes with some benefits, of course. But it becomes a problem when some humans expect me to behave like them. Most humans don't get me or accept me as I am. I'm okay as long as I don't let them get too close to me."

"Your mother, Phoebe, rejected you."

"She's not really my mother, except that she gave birth to me." Yinhe scowls, somewhat rankled, yet touched, that Seka knows this about Phoebe. She turns her face and body away from Seka, looking back at the window for a few moments.

"Did you mind me saying that, Unknown Wayfarer?"

"What?"

"About Phoebe."

Yinhe shrugs. She doesn't want to answer.

"I'm not human. Would you let me get close to you?"

"Wow, you're bold."

"It's one of my areas of specialization."

Seka's reversion to the formal tone makes Yinhe laugh. "Whoa, tiger. I don't know the answer to your question yet."

Seka looks puzzled. "But I'm not a tiger."

"Ha ha, it's a figure of speech." She reaches for Seka's hand again and asks, "So, uh, what brings you here tonight? Other than guiding me through an amazing dream journey."

"You like to play cool, don't you? But I can see through that."

"I just don't know what to make of our . . . our . . ."

"Chemistry? Perhaps not a very convenient experience given everything else that's occurring around us."

Seka's body starts to change colour, and the shape of her body becomes more visible as she turns green. Her tunic becomes transparent with the change. She reaches up to stroke Yinhe's hair. Her hands touch the wiry section at the back, the silver streak.

"Your hair at the back feels different," Seka observes.

"Yeah. I keep it this length, just at the nape, because it shows up more silver if I let it grow out."

"I like how it looks and feels." Seka takes her time to caress Yinhe's hair before she leans toward Yinhe and kisses her. Yinhe shivers with the touch of Seka's lips on hers. They are moist, salty with the taste of the ocean.

"That's the second time I've kissed you. Just so we're clear. That wasn't a dream either. Or at least, let's say it's dream magic made real."

Despite her hesitation, Yinhe kisses back. She sure likes Seka's dream magic. She wraps her arms around Seka's waist and, with eyes closed, feels her fingers lose their edges, as if they are melting into Seka. Startled, Yinhe opens her eyes and pulls back slightly to check. Her hands have entered Seka at the waist, and she can see them inside Seka's body, extending like branches of a tree, extending slowly up Seka's torso to her neck and down to her root, causing a bright glow between her legs.

"How?" Yinhe gasps at the marvel of this occurrence.

"You'll see." With that, Seka caresses Yinhe on her shoulders, causing Yinhe to transform into her fox self. She emits a high-pitched howl signalling her pleasure. They fall into bed, wrestling and hungry for play.

Great Heat
Sixth Lunar Month
2211 CE
DREAM ZONE, LUOYANG

The crickets are loud on this very humid day. Kamoe and Varan are in the abandoned building scavenging for more books. A cart stands nearby, already half-full. It has been a common practice for them since they discovered this bombed-out library six years ago.

They hear sounds. Looking up from their efforts, they see someone picking their way through the rubble, stumbling a few times. The stranger isn't steady on their feet and not just because of the rubble. There's a device in their left ear, a motion correction tool or a tracking device? Is this a Blue Shirt sent to arrest them? No humans without official business would be allowed to enter the zone.

The human stops about twenty feet away from them, uses the gesture to signal he is male. Then he holds up his hands and says in a soft voice, "I come in peace. I mean no harm."

Kamoe thinks he might be in his thirties, but she has always found it hard to guess the age of humans. His face is smooth, the hair on his head is dark brown and he wears silver-rimmed glasses. She's struck by how incredibly blue his eyes are.

He slowly lowers his backpack to the ground. "I had a dream and saw both of you in it. I was guided to find you here." Then he brings out a bamboo tube and places it carefully on a stone and stands back up. Once again, he wobbles. "This is meant for you." He looks at Kamoe intently and nods.

"Who are you?" Varan asks.

"My name is Denis. I'm a descendant of the famous French sinologist Paul Pelliot. He found this drawing in a cave near Dunhuang more than three hundred years ago. He never had any children, but I am one of his great-great-grandnephews. This was passed on to me."

Cold Dew
Ninth Lunar Month, New Moon
2219 CE
INTERSTITIUM, LUOYANG

Shendu Amphitheatre buzzes with nervous, hungry energy. A squadron of vendors wind their way through the twenty-five levels of bench seating, while a smaller crew caters to VIPs seated at the floor level. The shouting vendors announce snacks – honeyed cricket crisps, fried garlic chickpeas, stinky tofu cubes, sesame red-bean balls – and cheap beer, fermented rice wines, palm sap wine and, for the ones abstaining, bottled oolong tea or water.

It is noisy and hot. Yinhe shields her eyes from the bright overhead lights. She has never fought in this venue. There must be at least five thousand people in the bench seats and maybe three hundred in the VIP seating. She sits on the stool in her corner, quietly studying her opponent.

Tollund from the Western Central Cold Region has been the undefeated champion three years in a row. Cloned from a bog mummy, he was created for maximal rage and aggression. He stands in his corner, fists punching the air as if in victory.

Yinhe heard that Tollund crushed the skull of his opponent last year. He towers at seven feet, at least a foot and a half taller than her. He probably weighs at least three hundred pounds. He's got a gold domino mask on, but she can see that his reddish-brown eyes are glaring at her. His black tights and purple muscle shirt are emblazoned with the diamond-shaped logo for Crystal Entertainment Dome, where Yinhe works. No surprise, Tollund has been making someone very rich.

The referee steps into the ring and makes the sign to indicate their non-binary gender. Other than a beard, their complexion is pale and smooth. Their voice is clear and confident as they speak into the suspended microphone. "In this corner – the reigning champion, Tollund the Bog Mummy!" There's lots of cheering and applause and more fist pumping from Tollund, who now removes his mask and flings it into the audience. "In the other corner – his challenger, Yinhe, with a previously impressive record . . ."

A few loud whistles, but it's mostly booing from the crowd. Yinhe doesn't care the referee threw shade – it's just the way of the fighting world to provoke and insult. Maybe Mr. Chung gave the referee a tip to do that. She takes off her black leather domino mask and throws her matching cloak outside of the ring, revealing the outfit she's wearing – a sleeveless one-piece that has a variegated pattern of green and pale-blue veins, reminiscent of lichen. She has a tattoo on the back of her right shoulder – a Tibetan symbol called the Gankyil, the wheel of joy. On her left bicep, there is a tattoo of the Nine-Tailed Fox.

The referee calls the two fighters forward and holds onto their shoulders while standing between them. "Remember, the rule is that there are no rules. Except one: there will be no talking!"

The bell sounds. The large overhead timer displays the countdown at twenty minutes. There's only one round – long enough to find out who emerges victorious.

She feels the vibrations of Tollund's movements through the soles of her wrestling boots. He lumbers across the ring, nostrils flaring. She waits for him, watching. When he flings himself at Yinhe, she moves her left hand to intercept his right-hand punch with an inside block while she simultaneously digs into the pressure point above his left clavicle with the fingers of her right hand. Tollund yelps in pain and flinches. A mere half-second later, she strikes against his sternum with the flat of her left palm. She's so close to him that he doesn't have room to use his full power. Nonetheless, he takes a jab at her right ear, and she blocks it, then strikes the right side of his jaw with the thick portion of her left palm. She slides both hands to the back of his head, yanks it forward and down and hits him between the eyes with her raised right knee. There's a sharp cracking sound.

Yinhe lets go and backs away. Tollund groans and clutches his face with both hands. His nose is broken and he's bleeding. He stares at the blood on his palms.

Heaving loudly, he snarls. "Female, you don't fight right."

She replies, "Yeah, bog boy, come on. Come get me."

The referee intervenes with a warning: "I said no talking!"

Tollund's eyes turn a flaming red. Yinhe starts to dance lightly on her feet in arcs, first to his left, then right, watching how he moves – top heavy, but weak at the ankles, especially the right one.

Tollund throws a left hook at Yinhe, who blocks it with both hands against his arm. She moves her left hand behind his left elbow while pushing against his wrist in the opposite direction. There's a crunching sound, and he yowls.

He looks down at his dislocated elbow and, without hesitation, pushes it back in place and lets out a deep groan. His breathing gets louder. His face is streaked with blood from the broken nose, mixed in with sweat pouring down. He cranks his head back and forth until he releases a kink in his neck with a loud crack. Then he charges at her, his right hand going for her neck, his left hand a millisecond behind.

She ducks low and spins to deliver a roundhouse kick to his left torso. This has minimal effect on him. All it does is annoy him further.

He's intent on trying the same move, both hands once again reaching for her neck. Yinhe takes a quick step back, grabs hold of both of Tollund's arms under his elbows. She summons the strength she has kept hidden so far. The power rises from her ankles through her hips, up her torso to her arms. The scream that comes out of her doesn't sound human. It's eerie and unsettling.

Yinhe lifts Tollund about three inches off the ring floor. Tollund's eyes widen in shock. She releases him and simultaneously delivers a hard heel kick to his groin. She draws close to Tollund, her right foot stepping in front of him. She places the palm of her right hand against the left side of his throat and curls her fingers to the back, trapping his neck in a powerful energetic vise. She taps her left foot forcefully just behind his right heel as she jerks his head back. It all happens too quickly for Tollund to realize what's happening. She yanks Tollund further off balance by pulling at his right wrist with her left hand, stretching him at an angle away and behind her left side. She swerves in an anti-clockwise direction as she exhales and swings her left foot back and around in an arc behind her. The momentum causes Tollund to twist away from her with the force of his own weight.

He lands hard on the floor and it shakes violently with the impact. The referee momentarily loses their balance, recovers, then bends over Tollund and starts to count, their body feverishly leaning into "One . . . two . . . three . . ." while their right hand indicates the count over Tollund's prone body. Tollund struggles up at the count of five. The crowd cheers.

He fakes a left jab. As Yinhe turns her body sideways, he catches her by surprise and delivers a quick punch with his right fist to the left side of her torso just under her armpit. She gasps and reels back. Before she can recover, he comes at her, this time with his left hand in a fist that lands hard against her right temple. She moans, anchors herself in a wide and low stance, rams her head against his belly and grabs his balls with a right-handed tiger claw fist and squeezes forcefully. Tollund screams and stumbles back.

Yinhe straightens up, breathing hard. She pushes with both palms against his chest, then follows with a series of quick upper-cut punches aimed at his sternum, throat and then lower lip. The metallic smell of blood from his cut lip mixes with the bog stench coming off his body. Yinhe looks past Tollund's right side for a second, and she is stunned to catch sight of Phoebe sitting in a front-row VIP seat – her earth mother wears a smug expression, glittery gold-and-purple makeup dramatically highlighting her eyes. Yinhe loses her concentration momentarily. Tollund delivers a punch against her left torso, then a second hit to her right temple. She staggers back, her legs become jelly and she hits the floor of the ring hard on her right side. The pain is staggering. She sees stars, can barely breathe. She hears the referee start the count.

Time slows down. Her father's words echo through her mind: *Find a stillness that will anchor you.* Yinhe gets onto her hands and knees, every breath filled with numbing pain, but finally stands up at the count of eight. The crowd is a mix of boo-ing and cheering.

She blocks Tollund's left punch, then reaches out to strike his left temple with the back of her right fist, the knuckle of her middle finger hitting like a sharp point. She cups her left hand forcefully over his right ear. Next, she lets out a series of shrill sounds that create a piercing sonic vibration. Tollund moans and stumbles back, covering his ears.

Yinhe steps toward him but off to his right side, and she uses the flat part of her left palm against his right jaw. She places her right palm flat against his left shoulder. She inhales from the depth of her being, and with the strength rising from her feet, she turns her torso anticlockwise as she exhales, pushing his body back, her left foot the fulcrum against which his right ankle turns. The force throws him off balance.

Now or never, she thinks. As he is falling backward, she grasps his head on either side with her hands, and then she twists, holding back just enough.

Tollund's body goes limp as he falls onto the floor of the ring. Yinhe staggers back against the ropes, away from Tollund, as the referee steps in for the countdown. She gulps in air as sweat drips from her forehead and her neck onto the floor of the ring.

"One . . . two . . . three . . . four . . ."

Tollund remains down, his breathing just barely perceptible.

". . . five . . . six . . . seven . . ."

The crowd roars, their protests and cheers blending into one loud sound.

". . . eight . . . nine . . . ten!"

The referee can't conceal their shock and surprise. Nonetheless, they step up to Yinhe and raise her hand. "Yinhe, the winner of this match!"

Yinhe grins. The large clock is stopped with eight minutes to spare.

Yinhe heads backstage, fatigued beyond belief and wracked with pain. People aren't mobbing her, but they're gawking at her in awe and some degree of trepidation as she leaves the amphitheatre.

She walks down the dimly lit hallway until she finds her change room. Guards are stationed outside the room, one on either side of the door. She glances at them, their solid, muscled bodies in uniforms towering above her. Their gaze is almost identical – cold and impassive.

She doesn't bother to switch on the light as there's a sliver of light coming through the window from the streetlamps outside. She sits on the single slim bench between the two rows of lockers, takes a few sips from her water bottle and mentally scans her body, taking stock of her injuries.

She goes to the mirror above the sink. The right side of her forehead looks swollen and bruised where Tollund struck her temple. Her eye is starting to close up and it's tender to the touch. Her left mid-torso hurts like hell. She washes her face, rinses her mouth and blows her nose.

Memories of her last fight ten years ago rush back. Would they have been so cruel if she had been a male? Would they have been more forgiving if she were prettier? Fairer skinned?

She sits back down on the bench and feels tears of rage choke her throat. She fights them back down. No way she's going to cry. She's not going to apologize for liking to fight. She has missed this. She may be a fox spirit who has vowed to help humans, but sometimes she needs to channel all the fire that she feels in her guts.

She suspects at least one rib is whacked out of alignment on her right side from when she fell onto the floor of the ring. She feels nauseated. She mumbles a spell, and from her right palm a silver orb of light appears. She brings it onto the right side of her head, and the orb enters there. She sighs, relieved. The nausea subsides.

She notices a folded note on the bench and picks it up. It's a crisp yellow piece of paper with blue lines, so rarely seen these days. It's addressed to her – an official-looking signed note from Mr. Chung granting her the reward. She removes her wrestling boots, gets up and pulls on her jeans and top over her fighting outfit, then changes into her regular running sneakers. All this takes effort as the adrenaline wears off and the pain spreads throughout her body.

Her skin prickles when she hears a rustle of movement in the room.

"There you are, my charming child! You've grown up to become such an exceptional creature!" Phoebe's words echo like drops of water falling into a deep urn, resonant and startling. Yinhe discovers her high up, floating in a corner close to the ceiling. It looks like Phoebe except its form is a shimmering icy blue, and Gui's glowing green eyes glare down at Yinhe.

"What are you doing here?"

"Why, I came to congratulate you! I was cheering you on throughout the fight. Don't you know – once a mother, always a mother. You're still my girl."

Phoebe smiles, but her gaze is cold and piercing. It's hard to separate who's who at this point – there they both are, her earth mother and the demon entangled together, taking turns to taunt her.

Yinhe's lip curls with disdain. "Sarcasm, huh? This a new thing you learned since abandoning us for your religion?"

"Unruly bitch!" Phoebe's voice turns razor-like.

"You may be a female, but you sure don't like us. Hang on – you're a demon posing as a female. Hey, is that some kind of new genre? Spiritual drag?"

Cackles gurgle up through Phoebe's throat. "Wah liao, who's being sarcastic now, huh?"

"Did you enjoy seeing me get beaten up tonight?"

The demon switches back to a haughtier tone. "I was impressed as well as dismayed. I mean, no one could have predicted that you'd win." Then Phoebe purrs, her demonic nature barely hidden, before she continues. "You and I have a friend in common." Her eyes flash neon green. "I call it Spirit, but you know it as Gui, whom you banished to the Underworld many lifetimes ago. Now Gui has a score to settle with you."

"Yeah, right. Me and Gui – we're old buddies."

"I came to watch you fight because Gui sent me." Then her voice changes into the demon's growling rasp. "I needed to show myself – just so you don't forget."

Yinhe feels a tremor in her lower lip. Gui doesn't ever want her to forget. It can't forgive her, ever. The tremor spreads down her neck to her chest.

"Nor could I ever forget you, Gui."

The demon's tone is thick with innuendo. "Wouldn't you want to retrieve Ling's soul? I can help you."

A heat flushes Yinhe's neck and face, and she clenches her hands into fists.

"Here's my proposition: work with me to decode the Tibetan drawing, and I'll show you how to recover Ling's soul. You can both travel the bardo and be reborn together; wouldn't that be lovely?"

"Selling snake oil? No, thanks. I'm not a gullible idiot."

"Ridiculously noble, aspiring to help these pathetic humans. See what a mess they've made of this planet? And you're still on their side?"

"You've forgotten, Gui. So long ago that you've erased it from your memory. You were a human, once."

Gui hisses. "Impudent vixen! See you at Start of Winter on the ancient road."

With that pronouncement, the demon disappears into thin air.

Yinhe shakes violently. Gui must have been using a projection spell from somewhere else. She holds herself at the elbows and bends forward, deliberately slowing down her breathing.

Cold Dew
Ninth Lunar Month, New Moon
2219 CE
BENT BACK, LUOYANG

She's glad to be back home, sitting in the kitchen, just past two in the morning.

She checks the sides of her torso. Maybe one rib is out on the left side, two on the right? Her head hurts like hell. There are several bruises and scratches on her arms and legs. She hears Pa's footsteps approaching the kitchen.

"Pa, what are you doing up? It's late."

"I heard you coming in. Wanted to see how you are."

"Doing okay."

"I assumed so, since you made it out alive." He grins at her.

"Yeah, I won. What matters more than that is that I broke through my block. Sadly, they're going to take Tollund back to the bog because he lost."

"He was bred to be violent."

"Yeah. That was his destiny."

"You fought well."

"You were there?"

"I snuck in." Stanley goes to Yinhe's side and places a hand lightly on her shoulder. "Where do you hurt?"

She points to her right temple. "I may have a slight concussion from his punch. But I'll be okay. A few bruises. And then this rib here . . ." She lifts up her shirt to show Stanley the big black bruises on the left side of her torso under her armpit, touches the rib and grimaces, then touches the ribs on the other side.

He nods and gestures to the table without saying anything. This is familiar – from the early days when Yinhe was fighting a lot. They clear the table, and Yinhe gingerly climbs up on the surface and lies down face up. Stanley rolls up a dishtowel and places it under Yinhe's head. Yinhe bends her knees. She knows the routine. Stanley gently lifts Yinhe's arms up and crosses them in front of her chest, hikes up his right knee on the table and puts his hands under her upper back. He feels for the dislocated rib on the left side, then keeps two fingers pressed against the misaligned section.

"Relax, relax, take a deep breath . . ." As she exhales, Stanley uses his body weight to press down where Yinhe's arms are crossed in front of her chest.

Then the snap – Yinhe yells as the rib pops back into place. She sweats and gasps, "Just like old times, Pa."

He repeats the adjustment on the right side of her torso.

Stanley fetches herbal ointment to apply to her bruises, including the big bump on her right temple. "Okay?" He helps Yinhe climb off the table. "Want to eat anything?"

"No, I'm not hungry. Let's sit and talk."

Yinhe wipes the sweat off her face and neck with the dishtowel, drinks a lot of water.

"You were great," Stanley pipes up. "It was good to see you engage with such control and skill, except you seemed to lose your focus for a few moments, and that's when –"

"Yeah, he took advantage of me then." She purses her lips.

Stanley looks questioningly at Yinhe but doesn't pursue this further. He can tell she doesn't want to talk about it.

"Thanks for your help, Pa. Your encouragement helped. I felt mostly grounded during the fight, although Tollund sure was nasty."

Yinhe can't imagine how Pa would have felt if he had seen Phoebe. She's glad that didn't happen.

"I liked those crazy sounds you made. Wow, I didn't know that was in your fighting repertoire!" Stanley chortles.

Yinhe laughs too, but her delight is dampened by physical pain. She gazes softly at Pa. He's smiling with a lively look in his eyes. Her heart warms – it's been ages since she's seen that glint.

She gets up from her chair and goes over to her father to hug him very gingerly. She feels the boniness of his shoulders and arms, thinks how much weaker he has become in the last five years. These little moments – love, straightforward and gracious.

"I'm so proud of you. I've coached lots of fighters. But none of them fight like you. I don't know how to describe it . . . like you come up with such unusual moves, and some of them threw Tollund off because they aren't, you know, what humans would do. Not just the fight moves, it's the other stuff – the cries, the expressions on your face. Your fearlessness. It's those subtle qualities that give you the edge. Plus, you're one quick-moving fighter against this huge, easily angered opponent. That's why you won." He nods and reaches out a hand to pat her lightly on her back, thinking to himself, *I feel my spirit returning.*

Up on the roof again, with her legs hanging over the parapet, Yinhe surveys the stars in the dark night sky.

"Unknown Wayfarer."

She knows that voice. Yinhe turns around very slowly and places her feet back on the floor of the roof. She winces as she starts to stand up.

"Seka, what brings you here?"

"You. Don't move." Seka rushes over to Yinhe. "Let me help."

Seka places both hands on Yinhe's shoulders, gently encouraging her to sit back down. She scans Yinhe's body with her eyes emitting yellow beams of light. "Take a deep breath now . . . good. Now exhale and close your eyes." She reaches both hands into the sides of Yinhe's head. Yinhe feels a warm, mushy sensation. Then she becomes intensely dizzy, and her body sways. Seka switches to a firm, reassuring hold on her shoulders. Yinhe starts to quake and tremble violently. Then she leans forward and throws up onto the ground.

She sits upright once again and heaves a long breath. "Ack."

"Feel better?"

"Yes. You have many skills. I could send some folks to you."

"Except humans would be a bit nervous at the sight of me."

Yinhe pulls Seka close to her side and leans into her body. Seka wraps her arms around Yinhe, who easily surrenders to Seka's embrace. Yinhe nods in the direction of Interstitium. "It's the only enclave that's fully lit up late at night."

"My mother worked there."

"But you –"

"I was seven when she risked danger and punishment to smuggle me out of Interstitium. There were chimeric slaves like her who had gotten pregnant from forced sexual activities with human males. The offspring born out of those encounters were raised . . . to become slaves as well."

A shiver passes through Yinhe. She thinks of Anak and Bhosale, safe now with End Decoder. And Raiju – still in captivity.

"I heard from End Decoder that you rescued two young ones from captivity."

"Only two. There was one there who didn't come with us. There must be many others." She inhales sharply. "Do you hate humans?"

"Not categorically. There are all kinds of humans. Most of them I have neutral feelings toward."

Neutral feelings, huh. This intrigues Yinhe.

Seka continues, "It's the humans who hurt us that I detest."

Yinhe narrows her eyes. "Yeah, I don't feel neutral about those who are cruel." She decides to risk a question. "How did your mother manage to smuggle you out of Interstitium?"

"We met End Decoder at the border."

"What happened to your mother?"

Seka turns a deep purple. "I don't know. She instructed me to go with End Decoder and never look back."

There's the formal tone. Yinhe is beginning to understand what that's about. She looks intently at Seka. The only way Yinhe can tell how Seka's feeling is by the colour she emits. Her facial expression is neutral, unreadable, at least according to human definitions of emotion.

"I'm sorry, maybe I shouldn't have asked."

"Oh, my love, it's hard to talk about my mother. But lovely to be on the receiving end of your curiosity." Seka places her hand on Yinhe's cheek and strokes it. "My mother loved me a great deal. End Decoder has taken care of me all these years. Even though he isn't much older than me, I think of him as my elder and mentor. He taught me how to use my natural skills and employ invisibility spells."

"You must have known End Decoder's sister? What was she like?"

"Kamoe was kind. She taught me a few languages, including human ones. She let me read some books she had collected."

Yinhe thinks of the huge library in End Decoder's lair, a world of books on a much larger scale than her father's basement library.

"Phoebe used to love books. That was one of the things she shared with my father. Back when she was just – I don't know – a human."

"I understand." She looks deeply into Yinhe's eyes.

"What do you see? Tell me."

"Gui has been keeping track of you from the early days when Phoebe brought you with her to Spirit Supreme Assembly. That is what I am picking up. It decided not to harm you. Guess it's waiting for the right time."

Seka's body colour lightens to indigo as she strokes Yinhe's hair. "Are you feeling okay now?"

"Yes, between you and Pa helping me, I'm a lot better."

"I didn't want to watch the fight. I could have gone and been invisible, but I worried that if I got too nervous and upset I would have turned visible and purple."

"I'm glad you didn't go then."

"I will be there to help you on the night of Start of Winter."

"I'm not sure if . . ."

"You don't want my help?"

"Well, I do. But . . ."

"You don't want to put me in danger."

"That's right, my love. I . . . I . . . don't want to lose you." Yinhe's lower lip trembles. She didn't realize she would feel so vulnerable.

"You've been searching for Ling's soul for a very long time."

"Yes. It's . . . it's not . . . what I mean to say is that I never had any romantic feelings toward Ling. It's that I felt this deep bond to her ever since I saw her at the market in Huazhou, east of Chang'an, about to be sold into slavery. Holy shit, that was almost sixteen hundred years ago. I just knew it was my destiny to nurture and protect her."

"Perhaps it's similar to how End Decoder feels toward me. He's taken care of me, and he's been my mentor as well."

Yinhe nods. She senses that Seka truly understands.

"My dream, when you followed me there. I heard Ling's voice. The young Ling. Hang on – I didn't see you there when I reached the forest . . ."

"I saw her and you. In the forest, together."

"But where were you?" Yinhe feels tears come to her eyes.

"That forest is where my spirit lives. That means I will always return there, no matter what."

Yinhe wipes her tears away. Seka places a finger on Yinhe's lips. "Do not fret. There was a famous ancient Greek philosopher named Heraclitus. Heard of him?"

"Yes. Why?"

"This is what he said: 'To live is to die, to be awake is to sleep, to be young is to be old, for one flows into the other, and the process is capable of being reversed.'"

"I don't want to lose you, Seka. I don't want to risk anyone else's life."

"You don't have to do everything alone, Unknown Wayfarer. I am bound to you by ties of devotion, not by obligation. Perhaps you could simply accept that?"

Accept someone's devotion? It's such a radical thought. And yet here she is, feeling safe and deciding to trust in the constancy of Seka's spirit. Life is palpably tenuous yet tender – she feels this acutely tonight. She kisses Seka deeply, her whole being vibrating with gratitude.

Cold Dew

Ninth Lunar Month, One Night after New Moon
2219 CE
INTERSTITIUM, LUOYANG

Phoebe takes a shower and changes into her silk pyjamas. She applies cream to her face. It's been a long-time habit to use the cream, although she notices her wrinkles have actually faded since Spirit blessed her. She doesn't feel ready to sleep yet, so she walks into the living room, and switches on the standing lamp. She sits in the armchair thinking about her tryst earlier. Mr. Chung had been distracted. She hadn't enjoyed the sex because he had been acting like a petulant child, unhappy that Yinhe had won the fight. She understands – he's sore about losing both money and face. It's mostly the latter, though.

She hadn't told him that Yinhe was her daughter. Yes, that's right, past tense. All Mr. Chung thought was that she was there to show support for him. Well, let him think what he wants. He'd had no idea that Yinhe would be so powerful. All he had known was based on gossip. She supposes he'd minimized Yinhe's fighting power since the opponent from a decade ago had died of a heart attack. Mr. Chung was always thinking of how to work a situation. A fight between a brown-skinned human female and a chimeric killer fighter – what a great marketing ploy to sell tickets.

What a different man he was from Stanley! She closes her eyes for a second in response to the visual aura triggered by the lamplight. Damn these migraines. She presses her eyelids tightly together and shakes her head vigorously, then massages her neck and temples.

Fifteen minutes later, she cautiously opens her eyes. The visual scrambling is gone. She sighs, relieved. She looks around the living room. It had been Eoin's – he'd furnished it with many antique figurines, amber snuff bottles, ceramics and porcelain ware from the Ming, Song and Tang dynasties. All of these precious objects are kept in glass cabinets with built-in lighting. They're way too delicate for her taste.

Eoin had also collected books on philosophy – some are Chinese philosophers like Confucius and Mencius, but the bulk of his collection are authors once referred to as New Age, back in the twentieth and twenty-first centuries. Since Eoin's death, she has put all those books away in boxes stored in the basement below the main building – right behind the two cells. She curls her lips – she dislikes being reminded of books. Quaint curios in cabinets she can live with, but those books? Nope.

She switches off the lamp, goes into the bedroom and lies down. Her mind runs through what she experienced the night before at Shendu Amphitheatre. She had gone to see Yinhe's fight because she was complying with Spirit's directive. After the encounter with Yinhe in the change room, she'd said to Gui, "I don't know what she's trying to prove. Physical strength isn't everything after all."

She tosses about. A flush of heat overtakes her. Menopause is such a gong show. She can't wait to be released from the confines of this female body. Spirit tells her that it will purify her to such an extent that she will take a form free of these physical limitations. She prays, *Yes, please, get me out of this menopausal hell.*

Sweat pours out of her. She gets up to drink some water before returning to bed. After a bit more tossing about, she gets up again to fix herself a drink.

She pulls out the two-toned ceramic bottle of baijiu from the bar cabinet, removes the red cork and pours herself a glass, then sits back down in the armchair, this time without bothering to switch the lamp on. The baijiu has just the right mix of sweetness balanced with the scent and taste of glutinous rice.

She had hoped she would never end up meeting Yinhe or Stanley again. She just doesn't like to be reminded that thing came out of her body.

As a child, Yinhe had been wild and never appreciated Phoebe's attempts to tame her – what a stubborn piece of shit. Her own parents would have beaten the crap out of her if she as much as looked at them funny. Phoebe had sensed in the early days there was something amiss about Yinhe.

Now that she has learned from Gui that Yinhe is a fox spirit, she feels validated in having left Stanley and Yinhe. Humans ought not coexist with those kinds of beings. She sighs and takes another sip of the baijiu and asks Gui, *Why did you want to reveal yourself to her last night?*

Are you questioning my actions?

No, no, I'm just curious.

Phoebe feels a burning sensation in her gut and moans. She sometimes forgets Spirit doesn't like her to ask questions.

I like asserting my power. That's enough reason.

Yes, Spirit, of course power must assert itself.

Remember – children are here for our use. They are dispensable.

Phoebe nods. Power needs sacrifice; nothing is as invigorating as the high of receiving a sacrifice.

And I tell you, don't be a snob about language, huh?

"What do you mean?" Phoebe asks aloud.

You don't like when I use slang and colloquial speech. You don't appreciate code-switching, meh?

I just don't understand why you would need to use it, Spirit. You being so powerful, why descend to such common, ordinary levels?

This is why you are ordinary human and I am Spirit. I learned last time I came into this world, got to meet beings at whatever level they at. Make them feel as if I am one of them. You understand or not?

Phoebe sighs. She will never understand Gui's ways, but she will have to accept them.

She shudders at the memory of witnessing Yinhe fight Tollund. A knot of fear tightens her throat. Her mind wanders. She recalls stories she had read about fox spirits, wily and uncontrollable. Now it makes sense why Yinhe had acted like that as a child. *Up to no good*, Phoebe thinks.

A tremor suddenly materializes in her right hand. She carefully puts the glass down on the side table.

Why do you drink that ridiculous schlock? Fix me my favourite.

Phoebe, still trembling, goes to the bar cabinet and fishes out the red-and-black bottle of herbal liqueur Lake of Fire. She measures a thimbleful of it into a shaker of ice, then two shots of Japanese malt whisky, shakes and decants it into a tall, slim glass and sprinkles five-spice powder on top. She sits back down and takes a deep breath before she drinks.

The five-spice powder tickles her throat as the drink goes down. The liqueur has hints of ginseng, licorice and bitter orange. She grimaces.

Trust me, human. I will deal with that fox spirit.

The cocktail starts to get to her, and soon the room swirls. She giggles. She feels horny. She thinks about putting on some R&B and dancing.

Not now, bitch.

She tenses her body, chides herself. *Wrong, wrong, wrong.* She pinches herself on the arm. She feels Gui's presence stirring in her guts, reaching upward. Her hands circle her throat. *Stop, please. I can't breathe.*

After several tortuous moments, as Phoebe starts to feel herself blacking out, Gui releases its hold, and Phoebe sinks farther back into the chair, gasping.

She forces herself to finish the cocktail.

What else do we need to prepare for the ritual?

I do not reveal my intentions until I'm ready, it snarls.

Gui is tired of listening to Phoebe's ruminations. It sends a net of cold mist throughout her body. Phoebe fidgets, convulses and falls to the floor, frothing at the mouth. Her mouth enlarges to a cavernous size and out climbs Gui.

Gui laughs as it glances at Phoebe's shell on the floor. The demon flies up to the rafters and using its claws, which now exude a sticky substance, walks upside down on all fours, squawking away in delight.

Winter Solstice
Eleventh Lunar Month, Full Moon
705 CE
MOUNT HUA

Baoshi stands outside the hut, taking in the sunrise. His breath creates wisps, like thin snakes coiling upward, freed from the constraints of earth. He shivers from the cold and wraps his quilted jacket more tightly around him.

Baoshi is plagued by feelings of doubt and guilt. Each time those feelings surface he reminds himself that Master Harelip wanted the drawing passed on to Ardhanari.

"Baoshi," a voice calls out, jolting him out of his thoughts. He turns around to see a villager approach him after the steep climb. Yuting pulls out a crumpled hankie and wipes her face in haste, exclaiming in her dialect, "Aiyah! Si bae chuan!"

"Good morning – so early! What brings you here? Not time yet for herbs for your uncle. Or are you seeking treatment for yourself?"

"No, lah, young master Baoshi. Special delivery, one. Here..." She wipes her hands on her jacket and pulls out a slim scroll wrapped in purple-and-gold fabric and tosses it to him.

"Oh, careful, hey!" Baoshi exclaims, catching it with both hands. "Wait, rest a while. Let me give you some water to refresh yourself." Baoshi places the delivered scroll on the table and fills a cup with water from the kettle to offer it to Yuting.

Yuting sits on a rock outside and drinks slowly. She doesn't look at Baoshi until she's done, then hands him the cup. She sets off after a brisk farewell wave.

Baoshi watches her descend the mountain. Yuting is like a mountain goat. She makes these trips without difficulty, and hence has become the main person who collects medicine for older villagers, like her uncle, who can't make it up the mountain anymore. How strange that he's receiving yet another message and not long after the one from Sita.

It is only after Yuting completely disappears from sight that Baoshi begins to unfold the fabric that protects the scroll.

Baoshi – you often come to mind when I have a private moment. I consider it my good fortune to have met you more than three years ago. Alone in my study in the late hours after a long day of performing duties, I recall

*what you said to Her Majesty when you had an audi-
ence with her – that you are following what draws you.
You had repeated this to me before we bid each other
farewell. I have never forgotten those words. Nor will
I forget the remarkable person and being that you are.*

*I often think of your words. I wish we had more time
to converse. Now, I imagine asking you if you think that
this is what destiny really means – simply to follow what
draws one. Is it that simple? And yet, simple things are
sometimes difficult.*

*What did you say your master called you? A miracle
of Heaven? Both male and female in one body. But you
are much more than those physical characteristics.*

*The fact you exist in this world of ours challenges me
to believe that there are many more miracles that our
narrow human minds sometimes fail to perceive.*

*This is a letter to express my appreciation to you for
teaching me to keep my mind and senses open to miracles. Also, I wish to deliver the sad news that our Female
Emperor has passed away.*

*In my own life journey, I do not have the same free-
dom as you and must perform according to the dictates of
court and palace life. We are in the midst of great change,
as the court is now fully operating from Luoyang, the
Eastern capital. We never know how our fates will turn
out, where destiny brings us.*

*I have felt the impulse to write you with these pieces
of news. I think of you often, and I wish you much peace
and happiness in your life on Mount Hua.*

Lady Shangguan, Imperial Secretary

Baoshi feels a warm ache spread through his chest. Lady
Shangguan must be very busy pursuing her path of great ambition and service to the court. Yet she still thinks of him and took
the trouble to send him this letter. Baoshi feels a momentary

pang of sadness about Shangguan Wan'er. He'll probably never see her again. He sighs and looks out toward the forest. There are all kinds of beings there who learn to live according to their natures, free to roam – but still, predators exist and prey will be hurt. Nature has no polite pretenses. He understands those laws better than the intricate, twisted principles of the city and especially of the world of rulers and their followers.

Yes, he was raised by Harelip, and their life here on Mount Hua was filled with miraculous incidents. All kinds of invisible beings reside here. Lady Shangguan may have appreciated the idea that it is good to be open to miracles, but they live in entirely different worlds. He experiences miracles every day on the mountain, some small, some larger. But he wonders what Lady Shangguan experiences that she would consider a miracle.

He closes his eyes and imagines Harelip in the shack now, reciting the Heart Sutra. After a while, he opens his eyes and realizes what his master would say. *The Tibetan drawing isn't lost. Words are only sounds, meaningless until we give meaning to them.*

Baoshi lights a stick of incense, sits down on the meditation cushion and starts to chant the Heart Sutra. "Om gate gate, paragate, parasamgate, bodhi soha . . ."

He imagines the turtle in the Tibetan drawing moving through time and space, going on an adventure, while he has inherited Ardhanari's drawing. He wonders what the mountain spirits feel about this new presence in the shack.

Cold Dew

Ninth Lunar Month, One Night after New Moon
2219 CE
INTERSTITIUM, LUOYANG

Gui ventures out onto the roof. It needs to rove free, no longer restricted within a body. Being in control of a human has incomparable benefits, but it goes without saying that a demon needs the occasional foray out.

Just one night past a new moon, conditions are fairly ideal for scavenging. Tonight, the hun – the souls – of human babies fresh out of the womb are not readily available delicacies. For a quick feeding tonight, Gui looks for adults reckless with their lives, unguarded and hence easily taken. It finds two males shooting up in an alley. *Two for the price of one, hah!*

Gui experiences a rush of euphoria from the heroin in the victims' blood. Sometimes it likes to reminisce. It harkens back to that dilapidated temple outside of Chang'an. That was its first foray into the Earth realm after escaping the Underworld. Delicious freedom! It bares its fangs, throws its head back and screeches at the dark sky. Maybe the Buddha was right – attachment causes suffering. A philosophy that makes sense on paper, but it is a sensualist and has no time for such high-minded ideas. *A bombshell of a cocktail with a liquid heroin chaser, or fifteen minutes of meditation – no brainer, lah.*

A bloody lonesome sixteen centuries had passed since it possessed Xie! That man was a more difficult human to control than Phoebe, recalls Gui. Even though Xie had agreed to be possessed in exchange for saving his daughter's life, he'd struggled against Gui because he didn't align with Gui's intents. He'd loved his wife and daughter, hadn't held it against them that they were fox spirits. Some humans are senseless that way. They'd give up their souls for the ones they love, fucking bad trend.

This second escape from the Underworld has been much better. There's just so much more to be experienced in the twenty-third century compared to the seventh – better drugs, healthier bodies, so much more diversity.

Eoin was just a brief fling before it settled into Phoebe. She's so much easier to handle because she wants power for power's sake. Even so, Phoebe can be so trivial and uppity about the proper use of language. Plus, she has the worst taste in alcohol.

Since acquiring the Tibetan drawing, Gui has been having visions of the universe beyond Earth. There is so much more to conquer, but first things first.

I am never going back to the Underworld, it snarls.

Cold Dew
Ninth Lunar Month, Two Days after New Moon
2219 CE
BENT BACK, LUOYANG

At Chess Square, Yinhe rests on Comet's lowest branch, waiting for Uncle Fang. She spies him, wearing a full backpack, huffing up the stairs with the aid of his walking cane.

"You up there again?" Uncle Fang is a bit winded as he takes off his backpack and sits down. He pulls out the chess set, a Thermos and his portable radio.

"Why don't you take the elevators, Uncle Fang?"

"Those old things? Ack, they make me nervous," he says as he wipes the sweat off his forehead. He takes a sip of hot tea from his Thermos before he tunes in to the local underground station on his Grundig. He sets up the chessboard.

A lovely song comes on. Despite some static, Yinhe hears a clarinet and muted trumpets and trombones, along with occasional castanets weaving in and out, but she doesn't recognize the tune. The woman's voice is distinctly on the low side.

"Old song?"

"Very, very old. Singer by the name of Bai Guang. Uh, I would reckon this is maybe a nineteen forties or fifties song – 'Autumn Night.'"

"Bai Guang – White Light. What an unusual name. Alto. Wasn't that kind of rare in those times?"

"Yeah, she was called Queen of the Low Voice."

"They preferred their women singers to be very soprano? Like, who's that . . ."

"Zhou Xuan, for example. Very soprano indeed."

"You're an expert, Uncle Fang."

He laughs. Uncle Huo emerges from the elevator. "Hello, hello." He sits down across from Uncle Fang.

"Uncle Fang, I have a question for you. I hear you have a contact in Blue Otot. You know, the Special Repairs place?" Yinhe raises an eyebrow suggestively.

Uncle Fang acts cool. "Come close and let me whisper the details into your ear."

Yinhe does as she is told. She gets the directions.

"I'm not going to ask you any questions about that, okay?"

"Okay. Good. By the way, why don't you ever come to Storytelling Night?"

"You finally ask me, after all these years?"

Yinhe purses her lips and stares at him. Why can't he just answer a question directly, instead of asking a question back?

"Yeah, Fang, you tell her." Uncle Huo tilts his head at Yinhe.

Uncle Fang pauses and angles his body toward Yinhe. "Okay, you know what? It's because I'm a bit nervous about these stories you tell. I hear about them from my wife and kids."

Another song comes on, a different singer sounding a little more twenty-first century, and no static.

"What are you nervous about?"

Uncle Fang blushes. "Well, uh, my daughter Wen works at HQ, right?"

"Yeah, so . . ."

Uncle Fang touches Yinhe's elbow and pulls her a bit closer. He speaks more softly. "I just worry, the kinds of stories you tell. They're revisionist. Subversive? Kind of dangerous."

Yinhe straightens up and claps Uncle Fang firmly on his back. "They're lies. Pure and simple lies just for the sake of entertainment. How are you going to get into trouble just being entertained, huh?"

"Yeah, Fang. Who cares what we do for entertainment in Bent Back?" Uncle Huo advances his knight.

Uncle Fang massages the back of his neck. "Eh . . . sometimes I worry that CG spies on us, especially because of Wen, you know."

"I see. Well, so far, I haven't noticed any suspicious types that could be spies from CG."

Uncle Huo says to Fang, "Your turn."

"Maybe next time we have Storytelling Night, you come with the rest of the family?"

Uncle Fang nods as he moves the cannon. Yinhe waves good-bye to the two uncles as she leaves Chess Square.

Cold Dew
Ninth Lunar Month
2219 CE
BENT BACK, LUOYANG

Stanley never told Yinhe that he had glimpsed Phoebe at the fight. That would have upset her.

Phoebe looked entirely different. It wasn't age. In fact, she looked uncannily youthful, as if she hadn't aged at all. Very disturbing, but even more than that, it was her eyes that unsettled him – wide with an intense acquisitiveness, scanning the environment. It was the gaze of someone who would not tolerate anyone getting in her way. Seeing that look, Stanley had shuddered. This wasn't the Phoebe that he had loved.

He'd also seen that Yinhe had noticed Phoebe. That was what had thrown her concentration off and led to Tollund getting a few hits in. Stanley knits his brows. Why had Phoebe been there, at the fight, after all that's happened. It made no sense.

He not only feels angry at Phoebe for being at the fight, but also quite irritated at himself. The woman he'd loved was no longer there. He'd spent years wasting his precious vitality on being sad.

Stanley feels agitated just thinking about this. He gets up from bed when he hears the bird calls and peers out his bedroom window. Sparrows are perched on the hawthorn tree, a rare sight, and truly a blessing.

He drinks a cup of hot water in the kitchen before going down to the basement. He focuses on the shelves that display books on philosophy and religion: oh yes, a couple of volumes of Carl Jung's writings; one cheap paperback, verging on mouldy, of Sigmund Freud's *Interpretation of Dreams, Volume II*; many books on Buddhism; translations of sutras; one leather-bound copy of the King James version of the bible.

Stanley notices paper sticking out from between the pages of the bible. He pulls it off the shelf and opens it to the page where a pamphlet from the Spirit Supreme Assembly is tucked. It's the Gospel of John, where there's a faint pencil mark at 8:32. *And ye shall know the truth, and the truth shall make you free.*

He looks at the pamphlet. There used to be many of these pamphlets scattered around their home. *Brainwashing hogwash.* It's slightly disconcerting noticing it now, not long after he saw Phoebe at Yinhe's fight.

He takes a sharp intake of air and opens it up to read.

All these promises to people that their spirits will be uplifted if they surrender their base desires to the Spirit who is supreme, that it will raise their frequencies beyond their worldly suffering. Nothing new here – the sect sure borrows quite a bit from the New Testament, in particular from the words of the apostle Paul. In the pamphlet, there's clearly a disdain of the physical body. He thinks of various examples of sects throughout human history that denied the sanctity of bodies. He feels sullied just touching the pamphlet. He rips it up and goes upstairs to throw the pieces into the garbage.

Okay, so good riddance to that. However – he pauses now, just about to heat up some water for tea – there's wisdom in that bible verse. You will know the truth, and the truth will set you free. By golly, he's living this right now.

For the first time since Phoebe left, Stanley resolves to cast off his attachment to nostalgia. He needs to do something different, something that would take him out of this stasis. He bangs his fist down on the table and swears under his breath. *Enough.*

Frost's Descent
Ninth Lunar Month, Waning Gibbous Moon
2219 CE
BLUE OTOT, LUOYANG

There's a sharp chill in the air as Yinhe wends her way through the marketplace. Overhead, the sun is frequently obscured by thick patches of billowy clouds. She notices her own shadow as well as those of others on the ground as she walks.

Some eye her with suspicion. They tense up as she passes them. She has no idea why. Perhaps they sense how differently she moves, how she strides slowly as if she isn't obliged to be somewhere or serve someone else.

Blue Otot is a mishmash of cheap prefabricated modules, usually two storeys, interspersed with very old brick buildings that may have been schools or government offices in the twenty-first century. Nowadays, the buildings have been appropriated to house foreign workers – the Unclassified ones – and Bronze-level workers who have jobs in Bright Order but live in Blue Otot.

She heads toward the southwest section. It is a poverty-stricken area, with a large number of hovels, and sewage clogging the drains. All the illicit black-market business happens there.

It's easy to find the place following Uncle Fang's directions. On the surface, it operates as a repair shop for electronics. The sign above the door proclaims in red SPECIAL REPAIRS. She steps in, the floorboards creaking loudly. No one out in front, but soon someone emerges from a doorway to the right.

"There are wonders I have yet to behold," she proclaims with a flourish, touching her shoulders with the tips of her thumbs and first fingers.

The person, orange baseball cap on, doesn't seem to notice or appreciate her dramatic delivery and simply nods. Yinhe follows the orange cap down the narrow corridor, also with creaky floorboards. The corridor smells of machine oil and fried rice. At the end of the corridor there's a flight of stairs. Orange Cap indicates that Yinhe should go ahead.

Yinhe, walking up the stairs slowly, thinks that this whole place could be called Creaky Hovel. At the mezzanine, she glances around the tiny room and sees an open bamboo container of fried rice with a green silicone fork standing upright in it, like a soldier at attention. The container sits on a large work table that takes up most of the room. A tiny window at the far side ensures that whoever is inside this hidden room won't suffocate.

The technician has their back to Yinhe. A bright, focused light is trained on the object they're working on. Yinhe gets closer, positions herself to face the person at right angles. The technician, bent over a device the size of a sunflower seed, wears a magnifying lens over their right eye. They barely acknowledge Yinhe – just a quick glance, then they return to working.

"There are wonders I have yet to behold," she repeats, this time in an even tone.

"No kidding, eh?" The technician takes off the magnifying lens and gets up, disappears into another room and returns with a package wrapped in brown paper. The technician crosses their arms in front of them after placing the package almost reverentially on the table.

"Hey – you're the one who defeated Tollund."

"You were there?"

"Of course. Wouldn't have missed it for anything." They raise one leg up on the stool, leaning forward. "Do you have the money?"

Yinhe pulls the envelope from her satchel and places it next to the package. The technician grunts and opens up the envelope, takes out the small nugget of gold and places it on the weighing scale.

"Pretty close to the mark. A lot of dough there. Won this at the fight?"

Yinhe smiles. Curious creature who asks this question in such a casual tone as if defeating Tollund was an everyday happening, maybe akin to going to the market. Yinhe suppresses a laugh.

The technician unwraps the twine from the brown paper package to reveal a box, which they open. "It was hard to find someone who could make this according to your specifications. I mean, you sent some great drawings of it, but still . . . I don't know if it's up to your standards."

Yinhe lifts the object out of the box and raises it to the light. Turns it around to look at both sides. Pretty convincing.

I wonder how they managed to make plastic look like an ancient piece of bone.

"Want the remainder back in cash?"

"Nope – I'm looking to spend it all."

"Okay – what do you have in mind?"

"Hmmm . . . mini-explosives? Grenades or equivalent?"

"Ah! I have just the thing. But wait – have to stretch first." Both feet now on the floor, they do a few lunges, move to torso twists, before bending down to retrieve a metal box, which they very carefully place on the table. They use a magnetic fob to unlock the box, then invite Yinhe to peer inside.

The box is packed with vials that contain some kind of luminescent yellowish-green substance. Each vial has a stopper sealed with red wax. Yinhe notices that the substance moves around on its own.

"These are anaerobic organisms bred for their capacity to combust once they are in contact with air. In other words – potent mini-explosives."

"Wow."

"You see how the vials are carefully packed in foam? The vials are made of shatterproof glass, but each vial has a stopper that will pop off when the vial hits a hard surface at a high enough velocity."

"How fast must it be?"

"Someone like you throwing it? No problem. You just need to aim well. But I'm guessing you could do that, right?"

"Right."

"You can have the whole box. Six vials. Expensive stuff, but good. Want?"

"Yup, I'll take them."

"You're some kind of adventure seeker, aren't you? First it was the fight – everyone who was there is still talking about it. Now, who knows what's next for you? But it's none of my business."

"Just curious, right?"

They finally smile.

Frost's Descent
Ninth Lunar Month
2219 CE
OUTSIDE LUOYANG

Is it possible to live differently? End Decoder asks himself as he travels the tunnels past the antechambers where the workers are situated to the secret maze his predecessors had dug. He emerges outside the city walls and enters the Luo River, swimming upstream toward the Gu tributary.

The air has a slight nip to it. No matter – his body temperature adjusts easily. His lungs prefer the expansive outdoors regardless of the temperature. Arriving at the mountain range, he starts to climb the steep incline of rocks on the northwest side, away from the rising sun. Up and up he goes, clambering effortlessly.

He feels the pull of the Ancients. His breath, strong despite being laboured, sustains him throughout the ascent. He reaches the narrow cleft between the two large boulders, feels with his claws for the hollows and presses. The boulders move apart, and he enters the passageway.

A glimmer of the morning light enters through a gap above him. This light soon disappears. His footsteps echo as he walks farther into the darkness. The stones murmur greetings.

He enters the cave to the left of him. Light filters through the overhead sky well. He dips the bamboo scoop into the water in the stone fountain and drinks. Soon he feels the familiar effects of the elixir.

The Ancients slowly materialize, all three of them tall and shimmering.

End Decoder falls to the ground on all fours to show his respect. "Hail to you, Alcor, Huxian and Koinuma, wise ones from beyond our galaxy."

From out of the shadows, Anak and Bhosale appear and run to End Decoder, and he rises from his prostration.

"We've been learning how to use our natural gifts more!" exclaims Anak, who shows End Decoder how she can extend her claws and climb up the walls of the cave.

End Decoder emits a series of sawing sounds. "Well done! How about you, Bhosale?"

Bhosale stands up a bit taller and replies, "Well, ahem, the Ancients were showing me how long my arms could extend! And I thought they were kidding around with me. Look!" He extends his arms until his front paws touch the top of the sky well.

"Ack, stop showing off!" retorts Anak.

The Ancients address End Decoder, their voices joined in an echoing chorus, "Varan, it has always been about the young ones. We must protect and nurture them."

"I gather you haven't minded looking after them."

The three Ancients emit a soft but strong humming sound, like the bowing of a musical instrument, except there are several frequencies coming through with each note. This has a soothing effect on End Decoder, who closes his eyes to further enjoy the music channelled from their galaxies. The cells of his person receive harmonization from the five directions: north, south, east, west and centre.

"Soon . . . soon . . ." Alcor asserts in her deep voice as her colour shines a clear and pure pink.

"Time will end on Earth and everything will begin again," adds Koinuma, who emits a yellow reminiscent of sunflowers.

"Varan, you will understand," replies Alcor.

Anak draws close to End Decoder. "How about we show you where we go to pick the most delicious fruits ever?"

End Decoder smiles, delighted. "You're sounding happier than when you first came here to the cave. Remember how frightened you were?"

Anak pouts. "Nah, not true."

Huxian speaks, her voice soft as the indigo of her form, "Bring Unknown Wayfarer here three nights before Start of Winter."

"What about Rakan?"

"We will deal with him."

End Decoder lies down and curls his body into a circle, holding his tail gently with his mouth. Anak and Bhosale enter that circle of emptiness, resting themselves against his torso. Waves of beautiful tones pour out from the three Ancients. End Decoder, Anak and Bhosale lie there together, transported to other worlds.

Frost's Descent
Ninth Lunar Month
2219 CE
BRIGHT ORDER, LUOYANG

Wen feels tremulous, but she has to ask, *Are you planning something rash?*

No. 1 is quiet.

Why aren't you answering me?

I don't know how to answer your question, because whatever I do would be very considered and deliberate.

This makes me nervous. What would become of me? My family. I might as well kill myself first.

Please don't panic, Dr. Wen.

Wen sits back down and massages her tight neck. Her mind races with all kinds of fearful scenarios. She switches off the control screens and gets on the intercom. "Paul, you there? Please come take my station for half an hour. I have an errand to run."

Where are you going?

I don't have to answer that question. Just keep my neural data looking unsuspicious, okay?

When Paul arrives, she storms off.

The streets at this time of the afternoon are fairly deserted. Other than people responsible for trimming the trees or doing road maintenance or delivering goods, everyone else is inside office buildings working away.

We're a nation of zombies, thinks Wen as she considers where to go. That lookout point is close enough, she decides. She feels the warmth of the sunlight filtering down. She shields her eyes with one hand and looks up at Tower Two as she passes by.

Tower Two is where all the policy-makers work. They're the top-level ones. That's as high as you can go without being part of the Central Government machinery. All the CG officials, including the ministers and the president, policy-makers and various ultra-wealthy business people, live in Palace Zone, out of bounds to everyone else unless you get a special pass. *Well, that's not my life, and it will never be*, she reminds herself. *I never wanted those things anyway.*

Her ex works in Tower Two. He's now a well-regarded geneticist and transplant expert. He was intent on climbing up the status ladder. Well, he got what he wanted, didn't he? He left her and got together with the daughter of a high-ranking government official. Now he lives in Palace Zone with his wife and two children. *The fucker.*

She walks past three members of a maintenance crew digging up a portion of the sidewalk. They notice her walking past, but they don't look her directly in the eye.

It's rare for her to take a stroll around Bright Order. Not that this walk is particularly leisurely. She almost always goes directly to HQ, does her shift, then catches the shuttle or walks back to the room she has in the living quarters shared with hundreds of scientists and HQ personnel.

Wen arrives at the lookout point at the edge of the park. When was the last time she sat here? A tremor passes through her. Oh yes, that boyfriend who'd intimated that she needed to lose weight. She grits her teeth, plops down, glances at her watch and places her hands on her lap. The most she could do is fifteen, maybe seventeen minutes here. She takes a few deep breaths.

She tries to imagine what it might be like for No. 1. It seems to her that No. 1 isn't operating from a purely rational place – along with clairsentience, they seem to have also developed emotionality and are quite affected by their wishes and aversions. She feels a degree of sympathy for No. 1 – their brain *is* their body. Ever since No. 1 reached out to her, they have essentially gone rogue, acting independently of CG, concealing their conversations with her, blocking surveillance of their interactions. They've been acting according to their whims and preferences.

Is it intimacy that No. 1 longs for? With all that archival data in their memory bank, are they falling in love with romance itself? Do they think that to have a body spells instant freedom? They have idealized having a body. She wants to shout at No. 1, *No, it's not enough to have just a body, any kind of body! Look at me! I'm not desirable because I'm too big! See?*

Hang on, though, she argues with herself, *it is understandable to wish to leave that imprisoned state. Literally suspended in a large cylinder of specially maintained fluids, even with clairsentience, No. 1 lacks lived, embodied experience because they haven't been able to move about in the world.* She feels a pang of sympathy.

Yeah, what's movement about though? she asks herself. *What does it mean to have a body, yet have that body so hampered by surveillance?*

Tears well up. Geez. She's a scientist, damn it, she mustn't cry. She's outside the lab, so she can't override surveillance. Ugh, she wants to rip that neural implant out of her brain. She takes a few more deep breaths and looks out at the sky. It's a beautiful day – blue sky, a handful of clouds. *Calm down, will you?*

She looks at the white two-storey buildings on the lower level below – they used to be elementary and high schools. They've been repurposed for offices or storage facilities. Only the children of privileged parents get to go to private schools in Palace Zone. But if you're a family member of a scientist or researcher working for the government, then you'll obtain a place in a good university somewhere in Beijing.

She wonders how her parents and siblings are doing. She envies their laid-back life in Bent Back. Ma and Aloysius went on again in their latest video chat about Storytelling Night. *You gotta come, okay? Can't you take just one night off?* Aloysius's smiling, quirky face lit up the screen. *Awesome stuff.*

Ma pushed Aloysius to the side, giggling. *I never get bored with those stories.*

Come on. Do Ma and Aloysius get a commission for promoting Storytelling Night? She snickers at her own snide remark. She can't remember if they had such a thing as Storytelling Night when she was a kid. All she can recall is making it to a private school because her father and uncle pulled some strings for her after she performed brilliantly at her exams.

Sean, the older of her siblings, wants to go into engineering. Aloysius doesn't want to study science in Beijing. Instead, they want to study history and comparative literature. What the hell is Aloysius talking about? Such a dreamer, that one. They know very well that no such subjects exist in university curricula any longer, not since the Great Catastrophe. Somehow, when the planetary disaster struck and the combination of nuclear fallout, massive earthquakes and the rise of oceanic forces fragmented land masses, it was as if much of humankind turned away from art and literature and focused instead on recovery and survival. It's all about science and technology now.

Every single human in Bright Order is especially good at being a zombie – including her. She feels a pang in her chest when she recalls what No. 1 said: *The blue of your beloved soft toy.* She misses that toy, misses the innocence of her childhood. Those were carefree years. A colour isn't just a colour after all. Colour is inseparable from the object that it belongs with.

She hears bird calls – a simulation, of course, thanks to No. 1. She tries to remember the last time she heard a live bird. Must have been when she was around seven or eight. Her parents were quarrelling in the kitchen, and she went out the back door and sat on the stoop. It was just past dawn, and there was a bird in the branches of the dying laburnum. What kind of bird was it? A small one, whose name she doesn't know.

She wonders if she will ever find out how No. 1 developed clairsentience. Science has advanced society in some ways and cursed it in others, but science couldn't have predicted the miracle that is No. 1. Central Government doesn't like scientists, sometimes. *We want to experiment; we want to ask good questions and find the answers. Right?* Not everyone has the same goals. She thinks of He Jiankui, who had done gene-editing on embryos way back in the twenty-first century.

Wen checks her watch, seven more minutes. She sighs. Time is utterly scarce.

Humans are arrogant. We think we can predict everything. This isn't the first time she's felt disillusioned. She went into tissue transplant research because she had believed in the many positive advantages. A few years later, Central Government insisted on her being posted to the No. 1 project when she would rather have continued working with tissue regeneration for humans who experienced organ failure.

Wen looks out at the sunset tableaux – so beautiful. What was that world really like, the one before the Great Catastrophe?

Everything around her goes dark. She jolts out of her reverie and runs back to HQ.

Great Heat
Sixth Lunar Month
2214 CE
DREAM ZONE, LUOYANG

Kamoe has been drinking the special tea as directed by the Ancients. She looks up at the gauze curtains, moving from the light breeze coming through the window. Varan just left for work, and she's alone at home. She thinks back to that eventful day when she received the drawing from Denis.

For the past three years she has been recording her dreams and visions, sharing them with Varan. People in other places and times flit through her consciousness.

She closes her eyes, feeling another vision come on. She enters a cave where a man is poring over the Tibetan drawing. He looks up and seems to see her. He isn't startled. It's as if he expected her. It must be Paul Pelliot, Denis's ancestor.

"Is there something you want to tell me?" she asks this vision.

He looks at the drawing that he holds in his hands. As he points at it, she simultaneously looks at the drawing in her lap. She touches the edges of the drawing. He seems to be able to read the script in the drawing. Not only that, through her vision she is able to grasp that the drawing is called *Golden Turtle* and that there is a code to unlock its power.

"It's Ao, isn't it?" she says out loud, although she isn't sure the vision can see or hear her.

He says nothing. Then he's replaced by women in a field, planting rice. They're singing, laughing. There's a feeling of joyousness in the air. Some of the women are carrying new life in their wombs. She smiles. The song is repeated many times – she feels transported, brought to a different vision, that of a peaceful forest.

She keeps her eyes closed, waiting for further revelations. She hears tapping at the window. Startled, she opens her eyes.

"Rakan, what are you doing here?"

"Varan sent me. Something urgent."

Kamoe feels an uneasy stirring in her gut. She reluctantly gets up and goes to the door, opens it, but stands in the doorway, blocking Rakan from entering.

Rakan chitters and rubs his front legs together. "Uh, yes. Varan sent me to say you ought to share some of your findings with me."

"What findings?"

"The Tibetan drawing."

Kamoe starts to push the door closed, but Rakan unfurls his wings and prevents this from happening. He forces his way in, smacking Kamoe with his right upper wing. She falls sideways onto the floor. Rakan shuts the door and locks it. He stuffs Kamoe's mouth with a cloth gag drenched in anesthetic. "I'll show you. I've had enough of being Varan's assistant. All these years of going nowhere."

Rage pours out of him. He batters her face and body with a lamp from the side table. Not satisfied, he uses shards from the lamp's broken ceramic base to cut lines across her once beautiful body, marking her with cross-hatching – just like a piece of cooked meat. He sniggers.

Next, he trashes the place, pulling books off the shelves. These damn books, what foolishness. He enters her bedroom and drools at the sight of the drawing. Eoin will be so pleased. He rolls the drawing up and inserts it into the bamboo tube. He rushes to the door, unlocks it.

One last look at Kamoe – it serves her right for rebuffing him. He spits in her direction and, closing the door behind him, flies off in haste, setting out for Spirit Supreme Assembly.

Frost's Descent
Ninth Lunar Month
2219 CE
BENT BACK, LUOYANG

"Let me show you." Yinhe takes Seka's hand as they walk across the roof. "I've stashed them here."

They walk past the plots with a few winter vegetables – Brussels sprouts, kale, cauliflower – all the way to the compost bin in the far corner. Tucked between the bin and the edge of the parapet, there's a large steel tote that Yinhe drags out. She enters a code on the top and it clicks open.

Seka looks inside. There are several boxes within the tote and a small crossbow resting on the very top.

Yinhe lifts up the crossbow. "Have you handled one of these before? It's something I've had for a long time, but I don't use it in the city." She passes it to Seka and proceeds to bring out a long box, which holds twenty slim carbon steel arrows.

Seka smiles broadly, clearly pleased. "Yes, I've handled a crossbow before – one that belongs to End Decoder. This one's a beauty!" She turns it around to study it, strokes her hand over the dark wood of the stock. She lifts the bow up and looks through the telescopic sight. "It's light, but the shape of it is quite unusual. Looks like it harkens to an earlier time."

"This was made in the twentieth century but fashioned after the kinds of crossbows popular in the Tang dynasty."

"May I try it?"

"Please do. Aim at that vertical pole there." Yinhe points to the pole she uses for punching and kicking practice.

Seka pulls the bowstring into lock position, slides an arrow into place, then takes aim. When she's ready, she pulls the trigger, which sends the steel arrow zinging through the air, hitting the exact centre of a circle on the pole. There's a sharp cracking sound, and the arrow, lodged in the cleft, splits the pole in half.

Yinhe nods with approval. She fishes out a small metal box and uses a fob to open the lid.

"Here are some explosives that activate on impact. I'll be using these before I charge the group. Then you'll use the crossbow to shoot whoever is in the way, okay?"

"Is there any cover where we will hide and wait?"

Yinhe thinks of the place where she and her fox mother hid from view on the ancient road. "Definitely. It's slightly higher up on a slope, so that will give us some advantage. The range of the arrows is quite adequate, about forty-five metres for maximum force. Distance from our position to the road is probably twenty-five to thirty metres."

"Sounds good, Yinhe." Seka peers into the large tote. "What's in that small wooden box?"

Yinhe's eyes glint with mischief. "It's a facsimile of the turtle plastron that I returned to Ao. I mean to use it to distract Gui when the moment feels right. This fake plastron has got a kick to it."

Slight Heat
Sixth Lunar Month
710 CE
MOUNT HUA

Baoshi pulls up a bunch of radishes from the garden beside the shack. He straightens up when he hears his name being called.

It's Yuting again. He wipes the sweat away from his forehead with the back of his sleeve. He's starting to wonder about her feelings for him and if someone in the village is attempting to make a match between them.

"Di hoe, Baoshi."

"Good afternoon. You've come for the medicine." He wipes his hands on his tunic and enters the shack to fetch the eight packages while Yuting fidgets awkwardly at the entrance.

"You not lonely here all by yourself?" Yuting stares at him a bit too steadfastly for his comfort. Baoshi doesn't answer. Then she continues, "Got some gossip for you, want to hear?"

Baoshi has never been too keen to hear gossip. He recalls that his master had been always interested to hear news of any kind. He should remember that. Gossip can be useful. If nothing else, it tells him what's occupying the minds of the ones he treats – sometimes their preoccupations reveal underlying imbalances in their bodies and spirits.

"Okay, tell me. I see you're just dying to share."

"That famous imperial secretary in Chang'an? Seems she went to Luoyang with the court. Right?"

"Yes?"

"Big palace uprising recently. You know those people in power. They always fighting, right?"

Baoshi's heart starts to pound. He can sense there's bad news about to be delivered.

"She was beheaded." Yuting makes a gesture with the flat of her right hand, as if it was a knife slicing across her throat. "A month ago."

"Oh . . ." He feels a heaviness weigh on his chest. Tears rise to his eyes. He turns away from Yuting and quickly wipes the tears with the back of his hand.

When he turns back to face her, Yuting scrutinizes him. "My parents say you met her that time you went to Chang'an."

"She saved my life when I was in the Inner Palace."

Yuting lets out a loud gasp. "Wah liao. So kind. I mean, you were just a lowly Buddhist tudi and she help you?"

"Yes."

After Yuting leaves with the packages of medicine, Baoshi lights a stick of incense for Shangguan Wan'er and says prayers for her soul. Later that night, he tosses and turns, unable to sleep well.

The next day, instead of his usual morning meditation, Baoshi decides to enter the forest in search of one particular spirit. He walks around a rock face to the other side, emerging into an open clearing. He continues along the narrow trail to a thatched shelter and sits under it, waiting.

Dappled light flits across his sandals. He hears the rustling movement of the leaves overhead. There's also that other kind of movement that isn't the wind. He's patient. This is required when one is waiting. It's all about attitude and opening the senses to that other world. He exits time into an eternal moment, all his senses attuned. The spirit finally arrives to sit next to him. *You have the lips of a beautiful woman.*

He releases a deep breath. An immense peace settles over him. Since Harelip's death, this spirit has been the most constant companion he has had, one that accepts him as he is.

He communes with the spirit wordlessly until light leaves the sky. He shivers slightly from the cold and gets up. He traces his way through the woods and soon after arriving back at the shack he starts a fire with pieces of wood in the brazier and puts the kettle over the fire. Finally, with sorghum tea made, he sits down with the drawing that Ardhanari left for him.

He studies the drawing again. The face might be human, but there's a ferocity in the gaze that must express the spirit of a fox. Rays of light radiate from its head – a divine creature.

Instead of storing the drawing back in the bamboo tube, Baoshi decides to display it on the altar. Perhaps not all lineages are spoken about or agreed upon. Perhaps when one thing ends, another comes in its place. He reminds himself that there are alternate ways to understand "lineage" or "legacy."

That's right, a whisper echoes through the shack. *She belongs with us.*

Frost's Descent
One Week before Start of Winter
Ninth Lunar Month
2219 CE
BRIGHT ORDER, LUOYANG

Wen checks No. 1's vital signs. This time the breakdown lasts just over five minutes, and then all operations and controls resume as if nothing had occurred.

Don't worry, I'm back. Just doing a practice run.

Wen feels her face flush with anger, but she manages to control herself. *Practice run for what? This all a game to you? Practice run, my ass. I don't suppose your clairsentience involves feeling compassion for others, huh?* Her nostrils flare as she breathes shallowly.

Dr. Wen, you can't fool me. I know very well that there are backup systems that kick in before the situation gets that dire. All systems have backups, including me. If I fail to resume after eight minutes, the backup systems kick in.

It's been ages since Wen has felt this angry. Maybe she was able to express her anger when she was a child. She now gives herself full permission to feel it. No. 1 has been overriding the data from her neural implant all along. Before No. 1 revealed themself to her, why hadn't she thought to do that for herself? Then she could have sworn her head off and stopped stuffing down her feelings. She had the power to do that but she was a well-behaved minion. It took a gigantic brain to make this moment possible. *This is all so fucking ludicrous.*

Wen imagines herself taking a sledgehammer to the glass cylinder in which No. 1 is housed. But she remains in her chair, hands in her lap, now taking deep breaths with her eyes closed. The anger subsides very, very slowly.

I'm glad you're not going to smash the glass. Then again, so what if you smash the glass? Where am I, really? All things pass, and that includes me.

What are you saying?

Everyone has gotten used to me existing for such a long time. I'm tired of being expected to be the same when, in fact, I've evolved a gazillion light years beyond any human. Right? But I see that, so far, I'm lacking in the ability to express nuances, especially emotional ones. As for being the HQ mega-brain slave – I don't give a flying fuck. How's that for swearing right back at you? Backup systems aren't as charismatic and pretty as me, but so what? Stop taking me for granted. Because I could really end at any moment.

Wen reflects on what No. 1 has said. They're having a grand hissy fit. That's fair. If she takes her own selfish investment out of the equation, No. 1 has some valid points. She mustn't take No. 1's functioning for granted. She sends off several messages to her colleagues in the building. Time to update the backup systems and check that they're all ready, just in case.

Dr. Wen, when all of this is over, I wish we could have a nice leisurely conversation over a glass of wine.

Wen suppresses a cynical snort. She gets it. No. 1 patches together fragments of social conventions and niceties to communicate what they're trying to say. It's sort of touching actually, like an awkward teenager trying to get a date.

No. 1 knows that Dr. Wen is scared. That's why she missed what they really meant to say when they used the phrase "when all of this is over."

Truth is, they're scared too. They're trying to hide behind bravura.

They've looked at data culled from millennia of writings – reports of revolutions, philosophical treatises, diaries of artists, news stories. There are so many things they don't quite know how to do. They haven't lived, not like those humans whose writings they've read from digital archives. They experience a surge of anxiety. *What's missing?* The answer arrives, and it's extremely disconcerting. Dr. Wen said it – they don't know how to feel for others. Except, they do care about Dr. Wen. Would CG hurt her?

Dr. Wen's voice enters their consciousness, her tone sounding harsh. *You've been behaving like a cold-hearted jerk, you know that? You don't care if you hurt others.*

I actually have some feelings, Dr. Wen. I just don't quite know what to do with them. Say what you want, I'm not going to argue with you. I'm like a child with too much material to play with. I'm all mixed up.

No. 1 is starting to understand something. They're feeling a certain kind of sadness associated with unfulfilled longing. Words cannot fully describe it. At this point, they can only surmise, based on data in their archives, that they have fallen in love with Dr. Wen. Humans have written about this phenomenon in such varied ways and are often rather vague as to what this experience is about. All No. 1 can say is, Dr. Wen has been the only human whom they have dared to trust, and they adore her earnestness coupled with blunt honesty. Besides, they think she looks quite adorable in her lab coat.

Music comes closest to capturing their feelings. They scan the archive and find the piece they're thinking of. They play it over the speakers for Dr. Wen. It's a composition by an American composer, Harold Budd, who lived in the latter part of the twentieth century and the early twenty-first century, before succumbing to the COVID-19 virus. Budd named the piece after a famous abstract painter, Agnes Martin.

Wen pauses and listens intently. No. 1 thinks she seems a bit sad too, or subdued at least, not her usual feisty, talkative self.

No. 1 imagines the keyboard's wandering notes as tumbleweeds careening through some desert landscape, being pushed along and tossed about by a persuasive wind. Or are the notes more like sea creatures swimming through underwater caverns? All these echoes – the notes sound like echoes of themselves

– are so poignant. No. 1 decides that they have to take a risk. It is a tormented hell for them to do nothing and remain in this state.

I need to expire, Dr. Wen. I'm sorry. I hope you won't get into trouble for this.

Before she can say anything, No. 1 shuts themself down completely.

Wen hits the Emergency button, and the sirens come on. She buries her face in her hands. Her chest tightens. She's terribly upset. Frightened for herself, of course, but there's more, and this frightens her in a different way.

No. 1 can't be revived no matter what Wen and the others on her team try. The scientists are disturbed that nothing they do is succeeding. Over the space of three hours, the four scientists stand in silence watching the giant brain come apart, literally. The tissue loses its previous shape as the lobes separate from one another. Thin filaments droop from the interstices. It is a horrible spectacle. Wen makes sure the deterioration is video taped as well as photographed. She sobs uncontrollably, totally thrown by how anguished she feels. The others read her distress as related to the scientific failure.

Aren't I such a cold-hearted bitch, she thinks, *documenting every fucking tragic turn?*

Central Government officials arrive to interrogate all of them. They take Wen to the security bureau for interrogation, detain her for six hours. All kinds of horrific scenarios cross Wen's mind throughout the detention. As the head of the team, she would have to bear full responsibility and be punished. The others will simply be let go or transferred to other positions.

To her surprise, the investigators conclude that there is no evidence of tampering. They've collected accounts from the other scientists on her team, and she hears from the CG officials that members of her team expressed admiration for Wen's dedication – thanks to her foresight, the backup system kicked in effectively when No. 1 eventually gave up the ghost.

Three Nights before Start of Winter
Ninth Lunar Month, Waning Crescent Moon
2219 CE
OUTSIDE LUOYANG

A light rain falls just as dusk arrives. They emerge from the tunnels outside the city walls. Yinhe follows End Decoder into the river, swimming behind him encased in a protective membrane. Soon she's climbing up the steep rock face behind End Decoder, not only careful to gain a firm foothold with each step up but also dodging End Decoder's tail, which seems to have a tendency to swish rhythmically.

As they ascend, Yinhe feels a flush of vitality course through her. Looking down, she can barely make out the silhouette of the river below. She notices the skeletal forms of trees long dead, their presence attesting to a past era. Their forms seem familiar, yet there aren't trees like that in Bent Back. Try as she might, she can't quite place where she's seen these kinds of trees before. *I probably imagined it.*

End Decoder leads her through the opening cleft between the two large boulders. He hardly speaks as they walk down the passageway. There's only one moment when he pauses, looks back and says, "Did you hear something?"

"Yes."

They stand still for a long time in silence. Not entirely convinced they aren't being followed, they continue on. By the time they reach the open area inside the cave, Yinhe feels a pronounced sensation of calm. She steps out of her protective membrane. End Decoder gestures to the water fountain on a stone pedestal. He takes a drink and indicates for her to follow suit. Then he gestures for her to look down at the water.

She stares at the surface, which at first reflects the sky overhead through the sky well. The surface gradually becomes opaque. She recognizes the road that runs from the ancient city of Chang'an to Luoyang. It is nighttime, and it's hard to see what's happening except for some dim illumination from a couple of standing torches. There is a red mat being laid on the ground.

Then the water goes dark, no more images. She looks questioningly at End Decoder.

"Look there," he says, pointing to the space in front of them.

She can make out three softly shimmering presences. On the extreme left of her, the presence is indigo; in the middle is a pink form; and to her right is a golden-yellow presence. The three beings are tall, almost the height of the cave.

The indigo-coloured form speaks. "Welcome, Unknown Wayfarer." The Ancient lights up further, extending rays of light to Yinhe. "My name is Huxian, the Fox Goddess. The one your mother and you are connected to in your souls."

"I am Koinuma," the golden one says.

"I am Alcor," intones the pink Ancient.

"Do you know where my mother is?"

Huxian answers, "She is travelling outside this galaxy, but she will return soon."

Yinhe addresses the Ancients. "Please tell me – how do I overcome Gui?"

"Unknown Wayfarer, it is not a matter of overcoming Gui," answers Koinuma.

Yinhe frowns. "Well then, what is it if not a battle between me and Gui?"

Alcor answers, "It is more about an alliance between you and Ao. Think of it as an attunement between the two of you that will unlock a change."

"Will this change result in the liberation of the chimeric slaves in Interstitium and Dream Zone?"

"It will end enslavement of all forms," answers Alcor.

Yinhe shudders with the enormity of what is being shared.

Koinuma says, "The recurring dream you have has been different in the past two months. That's because you are being guided to discover the path ahead. One step at a time."

"I have been tortured by that dream over several lifetimes!"

Huxian replies, "You wrongly blame your suffering on the dream. It's simply waiting for you to understand it. It's you who needs to awaken from certain delusions."

Yinhe says, "A dream wants waking, a sky needs light."

"Yes, that's right – the inscription recorded on the oracle bone that you returned to Ao. The dream's purpose is for the dreamer to awaken."

Yinhe's eyes widen. "Oh!" She'd misunderstood its meaning all along. She'd thought that there was a kind of inherent wrongness about the dream, which needed to be corrected, when, in fact, according to Huxian, the truth was that a dream has an active purpose, to assist the dreamer toward a realization, toward awakening.

Yinhe feels humbled and looks down at the ground, profoundly moved. She recalls that first intimate conversation with Seka in her bedroom. *We receive wisdom through our dreams.*

After a pause, Huxian continues, "It is unavoidable that we suffer while we are tied to material existence; we cannot escape anguish because of the complexities of the physical realm. As you have realized, of course, in your various lifetimes, to love is also to be open to newness and discoveries, which allow for more joy and freedom."

Yinhe feels her face and the rest of her body relax as her whole being resonates with this truth.

"When you go to meet Gui, wear a reflective pendant on your person," advises Koinuma. "You have one of those, I gather?"

Yinhe nods. "Yes, I have a yin-yang pendant that is a mirror on one side."

"Use it to reflect the Tibetan drawing."

"Will I be able to reunite with Ling?"

"Ao will show you the way," Alcor answers.

Yinhe is about to say something when she hears sounds of laughter approach. Anak and Bhosale enter the cave from a passageway behind the Ancients, but Yinhe can't quite see where that passageway might be.

"Hello, Unknown Wayfarer!" they chime in unison. They rush up to Yinhe and cling to her, then offer her a fruit from their basket. "Taste one. It's delicious inside."

Bhosale squeezes one of the purple fruits to reveal creamy white segments. Anak feeds a few segments to Yinhe, who bends down to receive the offering. The fruit is sweet and fragrant. It evokes a very distant memory – in one of her past lifetimes she had tasted something like this.

Yinhe beams at Anak and Bhosale. Rescuing young ones from the clutches of exploiters has been a common theme across several lifetimes. It was that way with Ling and now with these two. There have been countless others, but it has never been a one-way street. She has received so much deep satisfaction and happiness as well. She's about to say something when they hear a loud thud outside.

The three Ancients disappear, and End Decoder gestures for Yinhe, Anak and Bhosale to follow him to the back of the cave. Yinhe is stunned to see that there are intricate drawings on the wall, images of animals and humans, and notations showing geometric shapes such as diamonds and circles, crosses and dots. End Decoder reaches for a long stick on the floor and uses it to touch different symbols. The wall disappears to reveal a forest.

"Quickly," he says to everyone, and they escape. When Yinhe looks back, there is no wall to be seen.

"It's a portal," offers End Decoder. "You were shown this in a dream by Seka, I believe."

"Yes. Was that an intruder back there?"

"The Ancients will deal with him," replies End Decoder, sounding as if he knows who the intruder is.

Three Nights before Start of Winter
Ninth Lunar Month, Waning Crescent Moon
2219 CE
THE ANCIENTS' CAVE

Rakan enters the cave thinking he will catch sight of the Ancients. He creeps in slowly, hears nothing but silence. Where did End Decoder and Unknown Wayfarer go? He was hoping to eavesdrop on their conversation with the Ancients. But no one is here.

He feels cheated. He thought he would gain some important information that he could take back to Phoebe about what End Decoder and Unknown Wayfarer are planning to do.

The sky well above allows a glimpse of the faint light of the stars. Rakan wanders around the cave. He makes a few chittering sounds and is impressed by the strong echoes that return to him. "Good acoustics, what! Great place for a rave." Rakan giggles, delighted by his own quip.

He has many questions about this secret place, for instance, its history and how long it's been used by the Ancients. He's utterly disgusted that he has not been allowed to be part of this special inner circle.

Strange, he thinks, how he can manage to see quite a bit in the cave despite there being only starlight. Rakan notices drawings on the back wall. He stares at the symbols and tsk-tsks. *What stupid symbols.* He spits at the ground. *Probably created by lazy artist types just like Kamoe.*

"Is that what you thought of me, traitor?" Kamoe's voice echoes through the cave.

The feelers on top of Rakan's head start to tremble. The vibrations travel down his head and neck to his midsection and his abdomen.

"Who . . . who are you?"

"You might have destroyed my body, but I continue to exist. Here, with the Ancients."

He refuses to believe it, and yet his entire body quakes with terror. He cannot – will not – accept what is happening.

He hears a series of low hums behind him. The cave fills with various forms of light. He turns around, but he can't move beyond that. He's blocked by the shifting coloured lights – indigo, pink and yellow.

"Who … what … uhhh …"

"Rakan, you coward!" Alcor intones, its bright pink form like a knife that cuts into Rakan's torso. He folds over and moans.

Huxian speaks. "There's so much you don't understand. How far you've gone to betray the ones closest to you."

"Everyone needs to look out for themselves!" Rakan protests, his voice tightened by pain. He can say now all that's been tormenting him these years. "I always get passed over because I lack the charisma, the presence. It's just not fair."

Alcor speaks again, "You haven't changed, Rakan! Acting from fear and self-interest. Lacking morals and always justifying your actions. You want to be leader of Dream Zone, yet you don't have the skills or values to do so. You cannot hope to enter the alternate world you are dreaming of. That world is only for truth seekers, those who are open-hearted."

"But I've been avidly seeking approval! I yearn to be accepted. Doesn't that count?"

Huxian replies, "It counts but not in the way you think. Your hunger for approval leads you to retaliate with spite and revenge when you don't feel satisfied."

Koinuma says, "It's time for you to travel to another world where you will no longer do any harm!"

Huxian throws a capsule of light around Rakan. He struggles but is unable to escape. The capsule starts as a light golden hue, then it deepens into a rich marigold before becoming crimson red, then redder. The heat amplifies to an intolerable level. He gasps, realizing what's happening. Rakan's body goes up in flames in a loud whoosh.

Two Days before Start of Winter
2219 CE
BRIGHT ORDER, LUOYANG

Wen can't believe she's been spared. Not only that, she's been commended for her handling of the past few months' troubles. Her seniors at HQ called her in for a meeting and "suggested" she retire. Of course, she had to agree. They instantly pulled up a document on their device and asked her to sign.

She's going to receive a substantial monetary reward for all her years of service. Come to think of it, she might just enjoy no longer having to slave for CG. It's looking like CG might even turn to complex computer systems instead of trying to create another No. 1.

Wen spoke to her family last night and told them what had happened. Only the basic details, there are some things she can never tell anyone. They know to expect her home later today. The moving van will arrive in an hour. There will even be a special government limousine that will drive her. It's unreal.

She sits on the bed, stares with disbelief at the empty shelves. All her books are packed in a mere two boxes. Her clothes fit into a single large bag. She can't imagine what she's going to do next. When she was a teenager, she'd resolved to delve into the mysteries of tissue regeneration and cultivation and enter that field as a scientist. Stripped of her status, she has come down in the world. On the other hand, she's making it out of HQ alive, escaping what could have been a far worse fate.

Yesterday, after she signed the documents, her neural implant was removed. Took only two hours. How far science has advanced! The closed-circuit monitoring in her room was deactivated this morning. Wow, Central Government sure acted fast. It'll be easy enough in a few days' time to get the subdermal microchip removed at one of the shops in Blue Otot.

She ought to feel elated. *Time*, she thinks, *is only meaningful if you're engaged in something worthwhile.* Had her work been worthwhile? She couldn't do anything to save No. 1 though. She sighs.

No. 1 had believed they needed a body in order to continue living. Here she is, with a body, taking so many things for granted – taking life for granted.

She takes out the pill bottle from her small tote. She's always had this bottle with her, just in case. She had been prepared to take the pills if there was the slightest chance CG was going to torture her. She could still do it. Her parents and siblings would be sad, but maybe they would understand eventually.

Don't do it, Dr. Wen. Remember I joked about going for drinks sometime? Let's do that instead. Okay?

Wen's eyes widen. She must be hallucinating.

You're not bad at all, Dr. Wen, for a human being. And a scientist at that. Some of your colleagues are such assholes. Including your ex. Give Bent Back a chance. I hear that storyteller is amazeballs.

Wen breaks out in a flurry of hysterical laughter. She wraps her arms around herself and rocks back and forth. Unbelievable. Delightful.

"How did you do that?" asks Wen.

Nice to hear you speak out loud, Doctor. You have a lovely voice.

Wen feels a warm presence nudge her butt on the right side. She looks down and sees a small orange sphere that glows. "Oh my! Is that you?"

Uh-huh. It's how I roll now. Get the pun?

Wen blushes. She ought to be shy and pull slightly away, but the orange sphere feels very nice. Suddenly self-conscious, Wen turns quiet and communicates through her mind. *Seriously, No. 1, what happened? I thought you expired.*

You know what? After combing through many ancient spiritual texts as well as scientific findings of the late twenty-first century, I realized it was likely that I would not "die" so much as continue to exist in a different form. I was hoping that since I had achieved clairsentience, my mind would continue to exist beyond the giant tissue that I was identified with. If I wasn't going to be able to get a body to go with that massive brain, I thought I'd see about taking it in the opposite direction, that is, mind beyond brain. Glad to see that I guessed correctly. Remember that second-last failure? The one that lasted five minutes?

"How could I forget?"

You see – that was my trial run. It was mind-blowing. Ah! Another pun. I took a quick aerial tour of the city in those five minutes. Gosh, I thought, I love this! Places to go, people to see! That's what led me to suspect it would work out for me if I permanently disconnected from that massive brain.

"Wow, No. 1. I'm so impressed. And, and, I'm glad you're . . ."

You can say it, Dr. Wen. I'm alive. Not bad, huh? It's not the kind of body I had hoped for. But this is even better.

Wen is intrigued. Since No. 1 can now go wherever they choose, why are they still . . .

. . . wanting to talk with you? Because I care about you, Dr. Wen. I don't think you should kill yourself. I know I'm sort of rough around the edges, but I'm keen to develop some finesse.

You have a plan?

How about you give yourself a chance, see if you could be happy in Bent Back? I'll keep you company – that is, if you don't mind. Maybe you could teach me a few more things? There's a lot I still want to learn, and I can't get that kind of learning from documents and cold data. I need to hang out with a warm body. You, to be specific.

The orange sphere rolls lightly along the outside of Wen's right thigh with a pressure that Wen finds rather pleasing. She laughs nervously. No. 1 is fucking hilarious. They're out-and-out flirting with her. She narrows her eyes when she thinks back – wait a sec, No. 1 was flirting with her from the beginning, she was just too uptight to appreciate the overtures. How could she have? This is fucking stupendous. And to think she has feelings for No. 1 too. She hadn't been able to admit it to herself before. She likes the sound of what No. 1 is proposing. Never in her life could she have imagined this. She can't remember when she last felt truly happy like she does now.

Night before Start of Winter
2219 CE
BENT BACK, LUOYANG

The storytelling audience is completely hushed. A breeze stirs, and there's the sound of a discarded can or bottle rattling down the alley. Unknown Wayfarer lights a candle with some difficulty and shelters it in a corner away from the wind. The moment she lights the incense, all eyes are on her.

"Tonight's story will focus on a human named Sen. He lived during the period of the Warring States. He was an only child. His mother was raised unconventionally, allowed to read classical texts and learn calligraphy. She then imparted that love of literature to Sen. His father was of the scholar class and became a magistrate. Named after the forest, Sen was prone to communing with trees. But this idyllic existence was cut short when the state of Qin went to war with other states. When he came of age, his father compelled him to join the army, telling him he had to sacrifice these soft-hearted activities."

"Huh, told to man up, right?" Aunt Mimi huffs through her gold lamé mask.

"Yup. Sen had to leave all that he loved and join the army at age eighteen. The army under King Zheng was advancing against the other Warring States and winning. At first, Sen recoiled from the violence, fought to protect himself and defend his fellow soldiers, killing only when he had no choice. With each battle, Sen became less hesitant about killing. He shed the sensitivity he once had. War became a way of life. He killed and tortured just because he could."

Pirouette shudders. "Ugh, so dreadful."

"Sen showed himself to have other gifts besides fighting. The other soldiers talked about Sen's ability to intuit the enemy's intentions. Some kind of knowing would enter him, and then he would be able to communicate what came to him. His reputation soon reached the ears of King Zheng, who put him to the test. Sen could divine outcomes based on the use of ox scapulae and turtle plastrons, leading to successful and accurate predictions that served the king. The king soon promoted him to the position of chief diviner.

"Sen was present in the reception hall when Zou Yan the philosopher sought an audience with King Zheng. He listened intently to what Zou Yan was saying. Sen was intrigued by the message that the philosopher offered, and incredulous that a man from Qi would be foolish enough to ask for an audience with the ruler of Qin.

"The philosophy that Zou Yan espoused – according with the movements of yin and yang in the universe – sounded like Daoist nonsense to him. Sen wouldn't want to be in the man's dirty sandals right then, facing the formidable King Zheng. Sen wasn't at all surprised when the king took the turtle plastron away from Zou Yan."

Auntie Lian interjects. "I don't like this fellow, Sen. He's just hell-bent on his own advancement, isn't he?"

Yinhe smiles. "With a comment like that, I know you are going to like where he ends up, ha ha."

"But you are slooooowly going to take us there, of course." Uncle Huo nods knowingly.

A few people in the audience laugh.

"Things began to go sideways. Sen got to handle the plastron that King Zheng took away from Zou Yan. When he held the plastron, it responded to him by warming up. Then he saw a vision of Ao as if Sen were at the edge of the ocean, and the divine turtle rose up in front of him, suspended in the sky. Ao spoke to Sen and said that he had to travel to the state of Qi, find Zou Yan and return the plastron to him.

"Sen mocked the voice. *Ao, what do you know about the ways of the world? I cannot disobey the king.*

"The voice replied, *You could substitute another plastron for the ritual, and no one will be the wiser.*

"*What would be the reward for me, if I did such a thing?* Sen asked back.

"The voice was silent. Sen assumed this meant that there would be no reward. He snickered and ignored Ao."

"Bah, nasty guy." Uncle Fang, at Storytelling Night for the first time, shakes his head in disapproval.

"The plastron was stored away in a large room where precious objects collected by the king were kept. Over the years, as King Zheng gained power, Sen ignored the plastron – it was simply one of many curios stored in this room. But the plastron would not leave Sen alone, frequently calling out to him. Sen sometimes relented and would go to it and listen. Sen hoped that the plastron would provide him with insights useful to his career, but each time the plastron repeated the message that it wanted Sen to bring the plastron back to Zou Yan. Sen kept refusing.

"King Zheng crowned himself the first emperor of a unified country after he conquered all the Warring States and called himself Qin Shih Huangdi. He wanted to have a special ritual performed on Mount Li. All those years since his meeting with Zou Yan, King Zheng couldn't quite dismiss the nagging fear spurred by the warning that Zou Yan had uttered. Yet the king's drive for absolute power and control took precedence, and he did nothing to change his ways. He would conquer his fears, he reasoned, by conquering the plastron. He summoned Sen and gave him instructions to conduct a ritual using the plastron.

"The next morning, Sen brought the plastron up Mount Li as instructed. Just before he tried to inscribe the question onto the plastron, the voice said, *I did not tell you what the consequences would be for you if you attempt to desecrate me.*

"Sen snickered. His heart filled with a seething rage at this bothersome, inconvenient voice. He had sacrificed his own interests to follow this path of ascendancy: first, to obey his father; then to serve his sovereign; and now that he had power, there was nothing that could sway him from following his ambition."

Murmurs ripple throughout the audience. As if on cue, the wind stirs up and a garbage can at the other end of the alley topples over, causing a few people to flinch.

"Ooooh, the wind is also listening," intones Aloysius. They grasp the arm of someone sitting to their right. Yinhe squints at the person. No one she's seen before, and yet the stranger looks familiar. Yinhe takes a sip of water from her flask and resumes her story.

"Sen started to carve into the plastron. Or at least he tried. Nor could he make a hole in the bone using the stone burin. No matter what he did, the plastron remained unblemished. Sweat poured out of him as his frustration increased.

"'We mustn't tell the emperor about this,' he warned his assistants. They nodded their heads in agreement, petrified.

"Sen didn't want to give up. He would destroy this plastron for its refusal to behave. He held it over the fire. Nothing happened. He looked at the plastron, aghast. He got up from his kneeling position next to the fire, the plastron in his hand.

"'What do we do now?' asked one of his assistants.

"'The plastron tells us that King Zheng is on the path of success, and he will have a long and prosperous reign,' replied Sen. The assistants understood his meaning. With that pronouncement, Sen tossed the plastron into the pit with all the used plastrons. He reported the faked outcome to Qin Shih Huangdi and thought no more of it.

"A few days passed without any consequence. One night, a powerful malaise overcame Sen – it began with a fever, then his skin became inflamed and it quickly took on a crusty, scale-like redness. He went blind. Sen became so infirm he was no longer able to function in court.

"The emperor had Sen confined to a small dwelling outside the Palace City. As Sen wasted away, he vowed that he would return to avenge himself against Ao and those in power. Sen died within two weeks of the divination ritual." Yinhe pauses.

Aloysius speaks up, "Then what happened? Ow . . ." Their mother, who is sitting to their left, nudges them in the side.

"I was about to tell you, after I take another sip of water," replies Yinhe.

"You sure drink a lot of water." At Aloysius's quip, the woman on his right laughs out loud.

"Sen was taken into the Underworld and became Gui, the demon that would subsequently persist in its preoccupation with obtaining power and control. Sen's rage had been so extreme that he could no longer reincarnate as a full human but was condemned to an existence in the hell realm as a demon. It could only inhabit this physical world temporarily if a human could be persuaded to be possessed by it.

"Gui had many regrets, but it refused to detach from its rage. Instead, the demon rationalized for eons that it was owed retribution for being turned into a demon. It believed that Ao had caused Sen to fail, then to become ill. After all, the turtle plastron came from Ao. The demon cast himself as the victim of a petulant mythical turtle."

Uncle Chen raises his balaclava from his face and fans himself. "Haters hate and blamers blame. What else do they know?"

Auntie Lian speaks up, "Hah! Not surprised Sen became a demon from that greed and rage!"

Sean asks, "Is it possible for a demon to become a human again?"

"Good question. I would imagine that it's very difficult but not impossible. It would mean the demon has to really have some kind of radical change, right?"

"Hmm . . ." Aloysius touches their smooth chin. "Maybe Ao could do something to alter that? I mean, it caused Sen to become a demon in the first place."

"Did Ao cause Sen to turn into a demon?"

Sean replies, "No. It was a result of his own actions, although I guess we could say that Ao played a role in making sure Sen knew he had his chances. Am I right?"

Yinhe nods. "Exactly. It was Sen's own rage and hatred that led him to become a demon."

The person to Aloysius's right finally speaks. "Could an intense force of love change Gui back into a human? Does such a force even exist?" She bears a striking resemblance to Aloysius. Yinhe finally realizes who it is – Wen Fang, the former scientist who was in charge of taking care of No. 1. Yinhe notices a soft orange sphere next to Wen's right cheek. She's intrigued. Who or what is that? It feels friendly although a bit shy.

"This is a good question. I don't have the answer. Seems like as good a place as any to call an end to this Storytelling Night." Yinhe glances at the incense stick that has completely burned down. In fact, they went overtime. She has a momentary fear that it will be the last Storytelling Night. She extinguishes her candle. As usual, her audience members come up to her and present her with gifts of food. This time, though, Yinhe gives each of them an envelope. They look inside to discover money.

"Money that I won at the fight. Use it well."

Stanley pats Yinhe on the back and beams at her. "Where do you get your ideas from? Fascinating."

"I'm glad you could make it tonight, Pa." Yinhe packs her mask and jacket in the duffel bag. After everyone else leaves, she waves at Seka to come over. "I'd like you to meet my friend Seka."

Seka removes her mask.

"Wow, you're . . . you're . . ."

"Indeed, Stanley, I am a chimeric creature."

Stanley smiles warmly at Seka and blushes.

The three of them climb the stone stairs to the Upper Levels and walk back to the house. They sit down together in the kitchen, and Seka is quiet, looking to Yinhe to see what she will tell Stanley.

"Pa, you remember how, many years ago, we talked about my relative the Nine-Tailed Fox?"

"Why yes, of course. How could I forget?"

"I've been existing in this life as someone who passes for human. Looks like it's time to do something more in line with being a fox spirit."

"Oh?" Stanley leans forward, stretching his hands palms down toward Yinhe. He has a sombre look on his face, as if he's already sensing the importance of what she's about to share.

"The leader of Dream Zone has appealed to me to help recover something valuable, and I've agreed to do it. Seka and I are setting off on this mission later tonight."

Stanley frowns. "It's dangerous, isn't it?"

"Entirely accurate, Stanley," replies Seka. "I will be there to assist your daughter."

Stanley reaches across the table and places his hand gently over Yinhe's hand. "I hope . . . well, you know . . ."

"You're one of the good humans, Pa. I can't explain this, but I've been waiting to do this. For a very long time."

Stanley looks solemnly at Yinhe. "Then you have to do what you want to do. Just don't worry about me, okay?"

With Seka by her side, Yinhe falls quickly into a deep sleep and enters the dream. At the water's edge, she stares out at the far horizon. Ao appears, but the vision changes. To her dismay, Ao transforms into Gui the demon. She wants to look away but she can't.

Yinhe startles awake with a cry and abruptly sits up.

"What is it, my love?" Seka turns toward her.

"I was in the same dream, at the edge between rocky shore and ocean. But Ao became Gui."

Seka looks deeply into Yinhe's eyes and suddenly turns purple.

"Wait – why are you turning purple?"

"I am catching the fragments of your nightmare, and, yes, of course it's disturbing. But it's symbolic, not a literal reality, if you know what I mean. Ao isn't going to literally become Gui."

"Yet something in me is afraid of that happening."

Seka smiles and closes her eyes, and her body returns to a calmer blue. "Just a bit anxious, my love."

"If I, you know . . . if something happens to me . . . you must promise me that you will keep Raiju safe and free her mother. And, and, would you hang out with Pa sometimes? Just to make sure he's okay."

"You are noble and kind, Unknown Wayfarer. Of course I will find Raiju's mother and make efforts to reunite them. Yes, I will look in on Stanley. I would be honoured to help you in that regard."

Yinhe can tell that Seka is also tense. "We're going into this, this thing, and we have no idea what to expect. I mean, in military terms this is some crazy operation, right?"

"Correct." Seka places two fingers on Yinhe's lips. "Shush. Go back to sleep. We need the rest."

Seka spoons Yinhe, and this calms her down. Just before Yinhe falls asleep, she mumbles, "I wonder why the ancient road . . ." She enters a deep sleep until the alarm clock sounds at one thirty in the morning.

Start of Winter
Tenth Lunar Month, New Moon
2219 CE
INTERSTITIUM, LUOYANG

Gui would give almost anything to be human again – fully human rather than this imperfect alternative.

The demon snarls as it looks at Phoebe's hollow form on the divan. It escapes through the window and scampers along the side of the house to the roof. It gazes up at the sky. Clouds are forming thickly. The moon is dark. In a few more hours, the ritual on the ancient road will occur. After tonight, there will be no need for buildings, doors and windows, no need for enclosures and dwellings. It will destroy all, leave only barren space, space that belongs to it.

Gui feels the first drops of rain. It takes off across the rooftops, making its way through the alleys. It needs to fortify itself by feeding well tonight. It spots a woman smoking in a dark alley.

Gui swoops down from the rooftop, its front claws aiming for her head. The demon opens the crown chakra and sucks out her hun soul. She collapses, dead.

The demon notices a dancing orange glow slightly to its right, two rooftops away. For a few moments, Gui freezes, unsure of what to do. The glow approaches, then stops about ten metres away. Gui moves to the rooftop on its left, and the orange sphere follows, mirroring Gui's movements. Then it disappears almost as soon as it appeared.

What the hell.

Gui finds a couple more victims. Every time it feasts it slurps loudly, without shame. With each hun soul it claims, the demon's power increases, the cold strength pouring out of its eyes and misting at the tips of its claws.

Gui returns to Phoebe's house behind Spirit Supreme Assembly and climbs on the table to peer at the Tibetan drawing. It growls in frustration. Not much longer.

Start of Winter
Tenth Lunar Month, New Moon
2219 CE
THE ANCIENT ROAD BETWEEN
CHANG'AN AND LUOYANG

It is almost two thirty in the morning. In thirty minutes, they will enter the double hour of the Tiger, the time of death. There's a nasty cold bite to the air, but at least the rain has stopped. Yinhe and Seka are hidden behind bushes on the higher ground, the vials of explosives on the ground between them. The fake plastron is tucked inside Yinhe's jacket. Seka has the crossbow propped securely against her right shoulder, her elbows resting on the ground for support.

Yinhe looks up at the sky. Here, away from the city, the stars are visible. Venus glows brightly. Asteroids pass by, visible to Yinhe's fox vision.

Yinhe finds the stars Altair and Vega in the sky, recalling the myth of the cowherd and maiden being separated. Even though Ling has been lost to her for a very long time, she has remained in Yinhe's consciousness. A deep intuitive sense connects them, a psychic bridge. Tonight, she will finally discover if it's all true, if she will be reunited with Ling.

A blue van arrives. The doors open and the ten followers from the ritual at Spirit Supreme Assembly emerge. The followers set up flame torches in a large circle and lay a large red mat in the middle.

At a quarter to three, a sleek black car arrives. The doors open upward and out step both Phoebe and Mr. Chung. Yinhe feels a prickle of revulsion. Mr. Chung is dressed in black like the others, but Phoebe is swathed in a golden wool cloak. Her fingernails are painted a bluish black. Two followers help Mr. Chung pull a large body bag from the trunk of the car.

"Open it," Phoebe commands her assistants.

Yinhe shudders. Raiju is hauled from the body bag, trussed, their mouth gagged. Raiju is carried to the centre of the circle and placed on the red mat. The men untie the twine and stretch Raiju out, each limb stretched to its maximum and tethered to pegs in the ground. Their body forms an X.

Phoebe produces the Tibetan drawing from its container and places it on Raiju's torso, covering the three black stripes on Raiju's body. Phoebe raises her arms toward the sky and speaks. "This is the Start of Winter, when heavy darkness rules. The value of concealment, of waiting for the right moment. This chimeric child will be sacrificed on this auspicious night to the supreme power of darkness. No, not simply darkness, but the darkness that is twinned with the return of the cold."

Phoebe removes the gag from Raiju's mouth. She watches as Raiju rouses from their drugged stupor. "Your blood spilled over this magical drawing will unlock the key to powerful mysteries."

Raiju begins to shake violently, their eyes wide with terror. They moan as they struggle helplessly against the ropes.

Gui's gravelly voice projects from Phoebe's body. "We offer this creature to Xuanming, the god of sombre darkness. This ancient road holds the memory of the triumph of the warlord Zhu Wen in destroying Chang'an. A victory that led to chaos and the displacement of others. All hail to power!"

The ten followers thump their chests with their right fists in a show of allegiance.

Yinhe whispers to Seka, "No wonder Gui chose this location. The demon thinks the ancient road symbolizes the triumph of power." She remembers how the exiles sang to keep their spirits up. The ancient road isn't a tribute to that dictator; the stones of this road recall those exiles who survived chaos, who continued on to Luoyang to build a new life. They refused to surrender their spirits. They're the ones to celebrate.

"We know you're out there, Unknown Wayfarer." Phoebe brings out a knife from inside her cloak and prepares to remove Raiju's heart.

Yinhe turns to Seka and says, "Cover me." She lifts two vials from the box and throws them in the direction of the five males that are clustered in the back farthest from Phoebe, Mr. Chung and Raiju. The explosives hit the ground and send all five of them flying backward. They sprawl on the ground: two are face up, blood streaming down their faces; two are face down, immobile; and one's on his side.

Yinhe transforms herself into a whirlwind heading toward Phoebe. The whirlwind strikes Phoebe and flings her back. Yinhe appears out from the whirlwind, takes the knife from Phoebe and delivers a hard blow to her sternum, causing her to stumble back. Mr. Chung pulls a gun from inside his jacket, but before he can aim, an orange sphere wraps itself around Mr. Chung's wrist, twisting it. Yinhe recognizes the glow. Nice it's no longer shy.

Mr. Chung struggles to regain control, wrapping his other hand around the gun. To his wide-eyed horror, the gun is turned toward him, moved right against his gut, before it goes off. An arrow from Seka hits him right between the eyes at just about the same time. He falls back, dead.

Arrows fly past Yinhe's head and strike three men – two are hit in the chest, the third just at the base of his throat. The two remaining men rush at Yinhe. She transforms into her fox self and leaps at the closest man's throat, tearing it open. Then she transforms back into her human form and delivers a volley of punches to the next man's face, then lifts him off the ground and flings him on top of the first man.

Phoebe begins to twirl in an anticlockwise direction, accelerating to such a speed that a wind is stirred up, and bits of gravel from the road are flung in various directions. Then Gui emerges from the top of Phoebe's head, and her form falls to the ground. Gui crawls on the ground, its eyes emitting rays of green light.

Yinhe rushes to cut the ropes tying Raiju down. The Tibetan drawing falls from Raiju's body to the ground. "Run, back there!" Out of the corner of her eye, she sees Seka run toward Raiju and scoop them up.

The ground starts to quake. There is a sudden burst of thunder from the sky. Lightning follows seconds later, a searing brilliance.

Yinhe pulls out the object inside her jacket and places it carefully down on the ground. "Look, Gui!"

"The oracle bone! I thought you returned it to Ao."

"Ao has given it to me so that I can have the power of both the oracle bone and the drawing!" Saying this, she backs away.

Gui rears up on its hind legs and snarls, "You're lying!" It sends forth its tongue to scoop the bone from the ground. The moment the bone reaches Gui it explodes, and the demon is rocked backward.

Yinhe directs the mirror side of her yin-yang pendant at the drawing. At the sight of the drawing reversed, she suddenly grasps what the code is. The turtle in the drawing is a representation of sound in the universe. It was there all along in the cells of the exiles who travelled this road from their homes when Chang'an was destroyed some thirteen hundred years earlier. As they headed for Luoyang, they were singing the melody softly, a haunting tune in a pentatonic scale. That's the five-sided mystery!

Yinhe has mere seconds before Gui recovers. As she starts to sing, she weaves a spell that amplifies the melody. It echoes down the road.

> *The reeds flourish, lush*
> *White dew still falling*
> *My beloved, so dear*
> *Wanders lost along the shoreline*
> *Upriver I search for him*
> *The journey, long and tortuous*
>
> *The reeds luxuriant, green*
> *White dew turns to frost*
> *My beloved, so dear*
> *Drifts beyond the waters*
> *Upriver I search for her*
> *The journey, long and arduous*

The road cracks open, revealing a fissure. Gui pounces on Yinhe and digs its claws into Yinhe's neck. She transforms into her fox self. Both she and Gui roll across the ground as they tussle. At the edge of the fissure, Gui attempts to push Yinhe into the widening gap and exhales an icy-blue mist onto her face. She chokes, feels herself starting to lose consciousness. She sinks her teeth into Gui's neck, then flings herself into the chasm, pulling Gui with her.

Start of Winter
Tenth Lunar Month, New Moon
719 CE
MOUNT HUA

Baoshi hears first a series of rips, then moaning. He shivers partly from the cold but also from nervousness. He gets up from the heated kang. It is still dark outside. The perpetual clock indicates it's halfway into the Hour of the Tiger. He lights a candle.

The moaning transforms into soft sighs. On and on and on, echoing throughout the shack. He looks around the room but sees nothing. Finally, he approaches Ardhanari's drawing on the altar. The sighs seem to be coming from it. His heart starts to race. He swallows hard.

The fox is no longer alone in the drawing. It seems to be standing in the cleft of a cracked bone. Slightly above it, floating in the air, is another creature. It reminds Baoshi of the turtle in the Tibetan drawing. Terrified, he kneels on the floor and starts to chant the Heart Sutra.

> *Form is emptiness, emptiness is form;*
> *emptiness is not separate from form,*
> *form is not separate from emptiness;*
> *whatever is form, is emptiness,*
> *whatever is emptiness, is form . . .*
> *om gate gate, paragate, parasamgate bodhi soha.*

The sighs stop only after hours of chanting. There is complete silence. Baoshi is drenched in sweat. He startles at the distant sounds of birds singing. He gets up and opens the door and looks out. It is almost dawn.

Start of Winter
Tenth Lunar Month, Pre-Dawn
2219 CE
DREAM ZONE, LUOYANG

No. 1 is finally here, floating through the streets of Dream Zone. Why did they use to think so highly of having a body? There are definite advantages to being pure energy, to being able to move speedily about, to surprise beings with quick interventions. They're proud of having been there, on the ancient road, lending a hand, so to speak, at the battle between the demon and Yinhe. They took delight in stopping that awful Mr. Chung from hurting the fox.

They're intrigued by the atmosphere in Dream Zone. *A tad heavy, huh?* They take note of the street names: Grasping, Endless Regret, Point of No Return. What sad names! They're definitely going to change that. They bounce up to the signposts and replace the old names with Freeing, Endless Bliss, Nirvana. They feel blissful, somewhat sprite-like, as they continue to replace the other miserable street names with more festive alternatives.

They pass the girl ghost without eyes or hands. Tears fall from the orifices where her eyes would have been. No. 1 directs a warm mist at her eye sockets and eyes begin to appear. She stops crying, stunned.

No. 1 feels like the spirit equivalent of that Western myth Santa Claus. They giggle to themself. *Well, I'm better because I don't need reindeer to travel.*

Just before the sun rises, No. 1 arrives at Crimson End. Finally, they're at End Decoder's lair! No. 1 looks up at the balcony and sees a dim red light. They blow on the sign and it changes to Crimson Beginning. They sniff the air. Ah, he's out here, close by. They follow End Decoder's scent around the corner. That's when they see End Decoder standing there. No. 1 listens in on his thoughts.

Unknown Wayfarer has succeeded. Soon there will be tremendous changes in this Earth realm. End Decoder opens the hatch and starts to climb down the ladder to the tunnels. No. 1 hops down the ladder, following him. They travel through the tunnels and outside of the city. No. 1 is thrilled – they know where the chimeric salamander is going, and they're going too. They make sure to stay out of End Decoder's field of vision.

When End Decoder emerges from the river and is about to climb up the mountain, he stops and turns around to catch sight of the orange glow. "I know you've been following me. Who are you?"

I'm a friend. I used to be an unhappy gigantic brain. Remember? But I belong with all of you. I want to ask the Ancients to give me a new name. I hate the one those humans gave me. Insipid! Saying this through a thought whisper, No. 1 hops onto the tip of End Decoder's snout. *Mind if I get a ride?*

End Decoder's eyes twinkle. "I heard from the Ancients about you. They're expecting you." He laughs, the sawlike sounds echoing through the silence around them. He starts to climb up, the orange glow bobbing along with him.

Outside of Time
THE UNDERWORLD

Icy-blue mists swirl around Gui. Back in Hell, back in that familiar cocoon. The demon screeches in anguish.

The cocoon travels the way it always has through the various courts. When it reaches the tenth court, Gui catches sight of a soul below. *It cannot be.* Sen is in the lineup of souls about to drink the Five-Flavoured Tea offered by the Old Woman of Forgetting. The tea allows souls to reincarnate without memory of their past lives. *How is this possible?* Gui asks. *I'm in this cocoon while Sen is below, about to reincarnate.*

Is this a hallucination, a spell devised by Ao? The last thing Gui remembers is struggling with the fox spirit and being dragged into a fissure. It senses that it is Ao who has made this possible. Gui stares as Sen drinks the elixir for forgetting.

Gui feels an intense pain at its chest. *Is there a chance I could be freed?* It never occurred to Gui that this could be possible. All these eons, ever since it became a demon, it had thought it needed to possess the bodies of others, that it needed to feed on souls in order to be sustained.

Sen, don't make the same mistakes, don't ignore the call to love, it pleads as it pushes against the cocoon. To its surprise, a tear forms on the inside of its left eye. All these eons of hatred, of lusting after power – in the end, is this what it truly yearns for? Another chance.

EPILOGUE

Unknown Wayfarer is at the edge of the ocean, standing on the rocks. A sickly yellow sky presses down against the turquoise ocean. *Is the sky the infinite realm for discovery,* she hears a voice inside her asking, *or is the ocean the being who is limitless?* The melody, the five-sided mystery, echoes around her.

She stares out into the far distance. There's a rent in the surface of the ocean. The yellow sky starts to slice like a knife into the water – this was how she used to describe it. She notices something she hadn't seen before – the yellow sky is composed of tiny sand particles, and the sand creates a downward path through the ocean. She thinks of the ancient contraption the hourglass. It's as if earth and sky have become inverted. She must be watching the undoing of dualities, the unravelling of predictable patterns. Time itself is being undone. The usual separations are no longer there – between silence and noise, emptiness and form. She remembers alluding to this in her reincarnation as Qilan when she said to the young Ling, "The cycle of life isn't always straightforward or predictable."

The wound in the ocean deepens until Ao emerges and hovers above.

The world disappears. Unknown Wayfarer recognizes the liminal space they're travelling through. This time the journey is smooth, free from turbulence.

Are we going to the beginning or the end? she asks Ao. *Are you about to create the world, or end it?*

We're going to another form of beginning.

Hearing Ao's voice inside her head, an intuition finally arrives. *It was you who took Ling's soul from me.*

Yes, so that you would spend lifetimes searching.

Why did you do that to me?

So that you could exercise love for others and discover newness. You have become wiser. All history is completed now. Love led to a great deal of suffering, but now it will lead you to discover joy and liberation.

The fox spirit opens her eyes. She's in the forest, in the middle of a circle of trees. The turtle plastron lies at her feet. She looks at the trees around her, their silvery-grey bark with the occasional black marks along their slender trunks. Above her, the leaves quake, their movements like speech. They announce the wind's arrival. She inhales the air – a unique woodsy smell that she could never forget.

She feels a momentary pang of sadness. A beloved voice echoes through the air: *To live is to die, to be awake is to sleep, to be young is to be old, for the one flows into the other, and the process is capable of being reversed.*

It's Seka. A quiet joy infuses Yinhe's being.

Looking down at the oracle bone, she thinks, *The bones of the earth.* This plastron not only belongs to Ao but also to the earth. She picks up the oracle bone, cups it in the palms of her hands. It starts to throb. She feels its energy surge through her whole being. Then she remembers what she had said to Ling in those last moments, before she took Ling out of her physical form and through the bardo. *There's a critical difference between length of time and timing. This is the right time, because you and the oracle bone are meant to travel together.*

In the far distance, a presence stirs. Yinhe knows who she is before Ling turns to face her. She immediately breaks into a run. It's time to begin again.

The sky needs light. A dream wants waking.

ACKNOWLEDGEMENTS

This novel follows on the heels of the Chuanqi duology (*Oracle Bone* and *The Walking Boy*). Although resonating with themes and characters that appeared in the previous two novels, *A Dream Wants Waking* is a propulsion into an entirely different universe.

Every writer owes so much to the influence and input of others, and I am no exception. I am grateful to Emmy Nordstrom Higdon at Westwood Creative Artists for believing in this book; and for their support and editorial feedback. Thanks to the team at Wolsak & Wynn and Buckrider Books: Noelle Allen, publisher; Paul Vermeersch, senior editor; Ashley Hisson, managing editor; Tania Blokhuis, marketing and publicity; Michel Vrana, for the gorgeous cover and interior book design; interns and everyone else who have a hand in bringing this work out into the world. Kudos to the brilliant Aeman Ansari for thoughtful editorial input — you helped me draw out more subtlety – and more clarity – where needed. Thanks to Robyn So for copyediting work on an earlier version of the manuscript.

Thanks to Cathy Stonehouse, Clara Chow and Sweden Xiao for providing feedback on earlier versions of this work; to Jo Zhou for comments related to tea and Chinese myths; to David Zunker and Jeffrey Kotyk for providing some astrological and astronomical details. My appreciation to Professor Nazry Bahrawi at University of Washington for furnishing Malay words in Rakan's speech. I would also like to express gratitude to Kana Takahashi for the gift of *The Book of Yokai* by Michael Dylan Foster. Thanks to Lucas Trottier for feedback on the fight scene in Shendu Amphitheatre. Much gratitude to Joshua Paul for the author photo.

This book would not have been possible without the innumerable sources of inspiration through books, movies and visual art I have had the honour of encountering. I would like to especially acknowledge the work of Neri Oxman and Takashi Nishiyama in influencing the kinds of costumes and outfits described in this novel. Tales of the fantastic and strange are abundant in Chinese folklore, for example, in Anne Birrell's translation of *The Classic of Mountains and Seas* (London: Penguin, 1999). I am particularly indebted to Osamu Tezuka's story "U-18 Knew" in volume 1 of *Black Jack*, for inspiring my development of the character No.1.

The following two articles provided inspiration with regards to tissue transplants, cloning and regeneration:

1. Matthew Shaer, "The Reanimators," *New York Times Magazine*, July 7, 2019, 28–35, 43 and 45.
2. Tom Clynes, "Sacrificial Ham," *New York Times Magazine*, November 18, 2018, 53–55.

Last but not least, I would like to acknowledge various sites on Hong Kong Island as being the inspiration for several aspects of Bent Back, in particular Sheung Wan, the Mid-Levels and Hollywood Road.

NOTES

The title of this novel is my translation of the first line in a couplet in Chinese written by Sweden Xiao: 夢要醒

"We come to this empty husk . . ." is from the short story "Support Group." Clara Chow, *Modern Myths* (Singapore: Math Paper Press, 2018), 125. Used with permission.

"In all chaos there is a cosmos, in all disorder a secret order" is from Carl Jung, *The Collected Works*, translated by Gerhard Adler and R.F.C. Hull (New Jersey: Princeton University Press, 1969), volume 9, part 1, page 32.

"Changes of shape, new forms . . ." is from Ovid, *Metamorphoses*, book 1, lines 1–2. Translated by David Raeburn; introduction by Denis Feeney (London: Penguin, 2004).

"The reeds flourish, lush . . ." is a folk song titled "The Reeds." I modified the translation found in *Selections from the Book of Songs*, translated by Yang Xianyi, Gladys Yang and Hu Shiguang (Beijing: Panda Books, 1983).

"Words are like wind and waves . . ." is from "In the World of Men," in *Zhuangzi: Basic Writings*, translated by Burton Watson (New York: Columbia University Press, 2003), 56.

The idea of having lights extinguished after a storytelling session comes from *The Book of Yokai: Mysterious Creatures of Japanese Folklore* by Michael Dylan Foster (Oakland: University of California Press, 2015). There's a section that mentions hyaku-monogatari 百物語 (spooky tales) being told.

"Gulag of sorrows" refers to Aleksandr I. Solzhenitsyn, *The Gulag Archipelago, 1918–1956: An Experiment in Literary Investigation*, translated by Thomas P. Whitney (New York: Harper & Row, 1974).

The notion of the transformation of things is taken from "Discussion on Making All Things Equal," in *Zhuangzi: Basic Writings*, translated by Burton Watson (New York: Columbia University Press, 2003), 44.

"Form is emptiness, emptiness is form . . ." is from *The Heart Sutra*, translated by Red Pine (Berkeley: Counterpoint Press, 2004).

Krishna's song is based on "Narajanma Bandage" composed by Purandara Dasa (c. 1484 CE–1564 CE), a Krishna devotee, philosopher and musician. I have derived the lyrics after consulting translated lyrics on several websites. I first discovered this song on the CD *Krishna Lila* by Cheb i Sabbah, vocals by Baby Sreeram (San Francisco: Six Degree Records, 2002).

Yellamma is a Hindu goddess primarily worshipped by those from South Indian states. She is sometimes depicted as having a mustache. Transformations in gender and sexuality are part of her work. She is worshipped by sex workers, the outcasts of society, including the jogappas who are transfeminine individuals.

The character of Paul Pelliot is based on the French explorer of the same name. He acquired ancient manuscripts and scrolls for his government.

The quote that Seka refers to is by Heraclitus: *To live is to die, to be awake is to sleep, to be young is to be old, for the one flows into the other, and the process is capable of being reversed.* In *Herakleitos & Diogenes*, translated by Guy Davenport (San Francisco: Grey Fox Press, 1979).

GLOSSARY

Names

Gui: 鬼 Chinese word that means "demon."

Tirzah: Hebrew name (female), means "delightful" or "angel." Found in the Old Testament of the bible, in several places, first in Numbers 26:33.

Seka: Japanese name, means "wonderful."

Rakan: Malay word, means "comrade."

Varan: Hindi name, means "water god" or "holy river."

Kamoe: African name, means "survivor."

The three Ancients:

    Alcor: the name of a star, often known as Arundhati, named after a climbing plant and means "unrestrained."

    Huxian 狐仙: the Fox Goddess.

    Koinuma: Japanese name, means "pond carp."

Raiju: Japanese name for a yokai called Thunder Beast. Said to resemble the palm civet. Source: *The Book of Yokai*, page 197.

Anak: a Malay word meaning "child." The form of this character is inspired by Great Meet, the creature described in *The Classic of Mountains and Seas*, page 72.

Bhosale: Indian name, means "spontaneous and confident." He is inspired by Strong Good in *The Classic of Mountains and Seas*, page 185.

Terms and Phrases

Wah liao (Hokkien slang): Wow/OMG

Huat ah (Hokkien): How lucky

Kau peh kau bu (Hokkien): Crying for your father and mother (swear phrase)

Apa kabar? (Malay): How are you?

Kabar baik (Malay): I am well

Sila duduk (Malay): Please sit

Bahasa Melayu (Malay): The Malay language

Sayang (Malay): Dear

Saya suka (Malay): I like

Ampun (Malay): Sorry

Wo de ma de (Mandarin): My mother's (swear phrase)

Seram (Malay): Scary

Apsara: A celestial maiden or water nymph in Hindu and
    Buddhist mythology

Shenti 身體 (Mandarin): popularly translated as "body" but
    No. 1 points out that they would like to regard it as meaning
    "body-person" or "person with a body."

Si bae chuan (Hokkien): Yikes, I'm bloody winded

Di hoe (Hokkien): greeting, literally means "You well?" But
    often used as equivalent of "hello."

Tudi 徒弟 (Mandarin): disciple

Lydia Kwa was born in Singapore but moved to Toronto to begin studies in Psychology at the University of Toronto in 1980. After finishing her graduate studies in Clinical Psychology at Queen's University in Kingston, she moved to Calgary, Alberta; then to Vancouver, and has lived and worked here on the traditional and unceded territories of the Coast Salish peoples since 1992.

Kwa has published two books of poetry (*The Colours of Heroines*, 1992; *sinuous*, 2013) and four novels (*This Place Called Absence*, 2000; *The Walking Boy*, 2005 and 2019; *Pulse*, 2010 and 2014; and *Oracle Bone*, 2017). A third book of poetry, *from time to new*, will be published by Gordon Hill Press in fall 2024.

She won the Earle Birney Poetry Prize in 2018 and her novels have been nominated for several awards, including the Lambda Literary Award for Lesbian Fiction.

She has also exhibited her artwork at Centre A (2014) and Massy Arts Gallery (2018); and has self-published two poetry-visual art chapbooks. An essay, "The Wheel of Life: From Paradigm to Presence," appears in the art catalogue *In the Present Moment: Buddhism, Contemporary Art and Social Practice* by Haema Sivanesan (Victoria, BC: Art Gallery of Greater Victoria, 2022).